Lenny's yell split the [ ] slope, yanking Gracie forward on her [ ] on the litter with her shoulder in the basket. Ribs knocked against the raised metal railing. Pain snatched the breath from her lungs.

The litter pendulumed below Lenny, dragging Gracie along with it. She dug her knees and feet into the rocky soil. "Stop!" she bellowed into the radio.

A long whistle blast sounded faintly from above.

The litter stopped moving. A scrabble of pebbles rolled down the hill. No sound, but two rescuers breathing heavily.

"Litter, sitrep," Ralph said over the radio.

Grunting against the pain, Gracie pushed herself up off the litter and crouched on the steep hillside, propping herself in place by planting a hiking boot against the side of a boulder. "What the *hell*, Lenny?"

His breath coming in quick huffs, Lenny pointed down the hill and off to the left. "There."

"Litter, sitrep," came Ralph's voice again, more sharply.

"Stand by one," Gracie said, in as normal a voice as she could muster. She slid around so she was facing downhill and swept the hillside below with the light of her headlamp, straining to see what Lenny had seen.

Then she saw it . . .

A few feet below them on the slope lay a human arm.

Berkley Prime Crime titles by M. L. Rowland

ZERO-DEGREE MURDER
MURDER OFF THE BEATEN PATH

MURDER OFF THE
BEATEN PATH

M. L. ROWLAND

BERKLEY PRIME CRIME, NEW YORK

THE BERKLEY PUBLISHING GROUP
Published by the Penguin Group
Penguin Group (USA) LLC
375 Hudson Street, New York, New York 10014

USA • Canada • UK • Ireland • Australia • New Zealand • India • South Africa • China

penguin.com

A Penguin Random House Company

MURDER OFF THE BEATEN PATH

A Berkley Prime Crime Book / published by arrangement with the author

Berkley Prime Crime Books are published by The Berkley Publishing Group.
BERKLEY® PRIME CRIME and the PRIME CRIME logo are trademarks of
Penguin Group (USA) LLC.

For information, address: The Berkley Publishing Group,
a division of Penguin Group (USA) LLC,
375 Hudson Street, New York, New York 10014.

ISBN: 978-0-425-26367-9

PUBLISHING HISTORY
Berkley Prime Crime mass-market edition / October 2014

PRINTED IN THE UNITED STATES OF AMERICA

10 9 8 7 6 5 4 3 2 1

Cover design by Diana Kolsky.
Interior text design by Kristin del Rosario.

For Mark

ACKNOWLEDGMENTS

A heartfelt thank-you to:

Nancy Chichester, Trace Hall, Diane and Terry Hiebert, L. Lee and Norman Lapidus, Jeff Norwitz, Officer Michael Travis.

My editor, Faith Black.

Anne McDermott.

The awesome men and women of Bear Valley Search and Rescue with whom I served for a dozen years.

And to all the Search and Rescue volunteers who routinely risk their lives "So That Others May Live."

PROLOGUE

THE station wagon shot over the edge of the cliff, head-lights parallel beacons slicing the night. It smashed against the mountainside. Glass shattering, steel shriek-ing, the car cartwheeled, plunging down and down and down, smacking into trees and boulders, crashing through bushes, until finally, at the bottom of the canyon, it slowed. Rocked once. And stopped.

The groaning of settling metal drifted away with the dust.

The cooling engine ticked to a stop.

Dead silence.

CHAPTER

1

GINA Ramirez was missing, and Gracie's little toe hurt. Her sock, crusty from the previous day's wear and pulled on in the dark that morning, had bunched up inside her hiking boot. Even with a liner sock, the fabric rubbing against a blister on the outside of her toe had begun to burn only a quarter mile out on the high-mountain trail along which she now hiked. Exhaustion from searching for the missing fifteen-year-old girl for five out of the last seven days manifested itself in stubbornness, an unwillingness to stop to remove her knee-high gaiter and her boot and place a square of moleskin over the raw spot.

As Gracie limped down the trail, she swiped away sweat burning the outer corner of her eye with the back of her wrist. Sweat stained the armpits of her orange uniform shirt and saturated the rim of her floppy hat, plastering ropy strands of damp hair to her forehead and the back of her neck. The waistband of her desert camo army pants was wet where the strap of her heavy pack was cinched atop bruised hips.

Behind Gracie hiked Lenny Olsen. A burly six-foot-five with a wild thatch of straw-colored hair, he was one of the newest members on Timber Creek Search and Rescue. Normally the young man's ready grin and effusive banter never failed to make Gracie smile. But that morning, Lenny was so glum, so grimly silent, it took a mumbled curse or size 12EEE hiking boot kicking a stone to remind her he was there.

The fawn-colored National Forest Service trail along which the two searchers hiked meandered just below the mountain ridgeline at over nine thousand feet. Rounded clumps of manzanita crowded in on both sides, shiny leaves against smooth, dark red bark. On the right, white fir and ponderosa pine reared up against the clear cerulean sky. On the left, intermittent openings in the trees below offered Sierra Club–calendar glimpses of the Bavarian-style resort town of Timber Creek. And beyond, Timber Lake glittered, diamonds on cobalt satin, beneath the afternoon sun.

Gracie breathed in the cool, sweet high-altitude air. Any other day, hiking in heaven on earth would have sent her spirits soaring with the ravens. But that day, hoofing it down the trail, she barely noticed the natural world, brilliant and perfect, brought low by a cruel world where a teenager could vanish without a trace.

Media alerts and flyers papering the entire valley and surrounding communities displayed a picture of the missing girl: bright dark brown eyes, a wide smile revealing tiny pearl teeth, shoulder-length black hair held back from her face by a pink headband. Gina Ramirez. Age fifteen. Five foot one inch tall. Eighty pounds. Last seen wearing a dark pink T-shirt with a light blue hoodie, blue jeans, white sneakers, diamond-chip earrings, and a thin gold bracelet with a pink enamel heart.

According to the briefing search teams received upon their arrival at the Incident Command Post, the girl had last been seen around ten o'clock the previous Monday night. Bouncing up the stairs to her bedroom, she had called a cheerful good-night to her parents sitting in the living room watching Animal Planet on the flat screen with their two young sons. The following morning, Gina was gone. Her bed hadn't been slept in.

Seven grueling days of searching followed. More than one hundred searchers representing fourteen teams from five southern California counties. Ground pounders. Trackers. ATVs. Aviation. Dog teams. Horse teams. Vehicle and boat patrols. Street by street, knocking on doors, passing out flyers, talking to locals, questioning tourists, dredging the lake. Neighborhoods. Businesses. Marinas. Every building, vehicle, and boat within a two-mile radius of the girl's house had been searched. And searched again. Every trail in the surrounding mountains had been hiked. And hiked again.

Not a single piece of evidence had been found. Not a single clue. Every possible scenario had been examined. Every tactic exhausted. With each passing day, hope for finding Gina Ramirez alive faded like the last glimmer of afternoon sunshine on lake water.

By the end of her fourth day of searching, Gracie was on autopilot, her mind numb, shutting out everything but the present and the bulldog obsession to keep searching, to find little Gina Ramirez alive and bring her home to her family. She squinted behind her Ray-Bans, head swiveling from side to side, eyes skimming the steep incline thrusting up on her right, plunging down on her left, trying to pick out anything resembling a clue, any unnatural color standing out against the surrounding gray rock and the green tapestry of bushes and trees. A flash of gold. An ordered pattern.

"All teams stand by for announcement." Ralph Hunter's voice over the radio microphone clipped to Gracie's chest pack made her jump. She slid to a stop on the trail, pulled off her gloves, and tucked them into a pant-leg pocket.

Lenny stopped so close behind Gracie his breath tickled the back of her neck. "What's happening?" he asked. "Did somebody find her?"

"Nope." Gracie withdrew her GPS from its own little pocket on her chest pack and held it aloft to acquire satellite signals. "They would have announced it."

"Then what are—?"

Ralph's voice over the radio cut Lenny off. "Per IC, all teams return to base. Repeat. Return to base. All teams acknowledge."

"Shit," Gracie whispered.

"What's happening?" Lenny asked again.

"Ground Forty-six. Acknowledged," a man's voice said over the mike, then a woman's: "Dog Eight copies." Another man's: "ATV Seventeen. Ten-four."

Gracie waited, poised to call in, hand on the radio microphone. "They've called the search."

"They called it?"

She cleared her throat and thumbed the mike button. "Ground Forty-three. Copy." She jerked her gloves back on. "We're done."

Lenny bent to peer into her face. "That's it?"

Gracie looked into his wide eyes, a startling cornflower blue. "That's it."

"It's *over*?"

Knowing she was lecturing, she said, "Technically,

they're probably only suspending it, not calling it off, so they can resume later if they find any clues or evidence." She concentrated on wrapping the straps of her trekking poles around her hands. "For us, for now, it's over."

"Fuck!" Lenny stomped twenty feet back up the hard-packed trail, stopped, and bent over, elbows on knees, head hanging, taking in deep breaths.

Exhaustion anesthetized most of the pain, but tears burned Gracie's eyes.

They had done everything they could.

But it hadn't been enough.

Little Gina Ramirez had officially become a statistic.

CHAPTER

2

GRACIE pressed the accelerator all the way to the floor and guided her Ford Ranger pickup, a rust-spotted maroon, around the steep curves of Cedar Mill Road on the five-mile climb from the valley floor up to Camp Ponderosa high in the mountains. The air, warm and soft, tickled her arm hanging out the open window. Ponderosa and Jeffrey pine towered overhead. A lone raven wind-surfed the canyon updrafts. Massive cotton ball clouds hovered in a robin's-egg blue sky. "Just another day in paradise," Gracie said with a sigh.

Even though her arms and legs felt as if they were weighted down with sacks of wet cement, she noticed a perceptible lightening of the gloom that had persisted since the search was suspended the day before.

After the long debrief at the Sheriff's Office, she had headed home, afterward remembering nothing of the ten-minute drive. She stumbled into her cabin, stepping out of dirty, smelly search clothes directly into the shower in the downstairs bathroom. With the sun still four fingers above the horizon and filling the bedroom upstairs with an amber glow, Gracie flopped down onto the camp mattress that served as her bed and was asleep in less than a minute.

Eleven hours later, the alarm jarred her awake.

Gracie lay motionless in the tangle of bedsheets and contemplated calling in sick to work. Because of the search, she had already missed three days in the past week. Her pseudo-boss, Jay, the manager of Camp Ponderosa, the year-round residential camp where she worked seemed to be understanding, even supportive. But she couldn't risk any complaints about her performance. She couldn't afford to lose the job practically before she had started.

So she dragged herself out of bed and pulled on a pair of khaki shorts and a forest-green Camp Ponderosa T-shirt. Her toilette lasted all of sixty seconds—throwing cold water on her face, scrubbing her teeth with a dry toothbrush, and catching her unruly auburn hair up in a clip on top of her head. Breakfast was two cups of double-strength Folgers Instant gulped down during the ten-mile drive across town.

The twisting stretch of Cedar Mill Road unwound before the Ranger like a serpent. Gracie lifted her foot off the accelerator in anticipation of an upcoming turn.

A silver Dodge Ram hurtled around the curve up ahead, taking it too wide and fast and sending the box trailer it was pulling swinging wide into Gracie's lane.

"Shit!" She cut the steering wheel hard to the right and slammed on the brakes. Tires slid on asphalt, then gripped the gravel on the shoulder. The Ranger stopped with four inches of its front right tire hanging over the edge of the road, which dropped sharply away in a twenty-foot tumble of rocks and scrub juniper.

The Dodge Ram roared past.

Over her shoulder, Gracie glimpsed a lifted hand, a flash of pearly whites. "Eddie," she muttered.

Eddie Wilson. Jay's younger brother. Camp Ponderosa's live-in head of maintenance and security.

Gracie had met the man only once, on her first day of work. He seemed nice, certainly friendly enough. She'd seen him several times since but only from a distance and knew practically nothing about him except he drove through camp—and apparently everywhere else—like a bat out of hell.

She flexed her hands still fizzing with adrenaline, backed the Ranger onto the pavement and continued the drive up the hill.

The truck bumped off the asphalt and onto dirt. Another half mile up, it crested a rise and swept beneath the hewn-log entryway into camp.

Owned by a megachurch in Orange County, Camp Ponderosa rested on the largest privately owned parcel of land in Timber Valley—real estate literally worth millions. Ten acres of lodges and cabins with the pristine spring-fed five-acre Lake Ponderosa, surrounded by nearly two hundred more unblemished acres of pine—cinnamon-barked ponderosa, sugar with cones a foot long, Jeffrey with bark smelling of vanilla; white fir and California black oak, interspersed throughout with boulders of California granite, some the size and shape of elephants. Mountain chickadees, acorn woodpeckers, pygmy nuthatches. Chipmunks, ground and gray squirrels, and a coyote or two.

It had taken Gracie a single day to realize the little piece of Eden was beyond price—an unparalleled treasure to be nurtured and protected.

The Ranger rolled past the Gatehouse, the cottage

housing the camp offices, down a short hill and over a narrow creek lined with cottonwoods and rushing with snowmelt. A large grassy recreation field opened up on the left,
a paved parking lot on the right. The road angled left, continuing on into the rest of camp. Straight ahead, in front of
a tumble of boulders, rustic signs announced LOADING/
UNLOADING ONLY BEYOND THIS POINT and the ten-mile-per-
hour speed limit. Weeds crowded the feet of an eight-foot-
high carved bear holding another sign, DINNING HALL, with
an arrow pointing to the right.

Annoyed at the misspelled sign and vowing that someday, when she had been at camp long enough, she would get
them to fix it, Gracie swung the truck in the direction of the
arrow and parked in one the spaces in front of Serrano
Lodge. Painted a grayish brown, the two-story cinder-block
building blended in neatly with the surrounding rock.

Stepping down from the truck, Gracie was engulfed in a
chirping, twittering symphony of birds. Ten feet away, a
chipmunk no larger than a teacup sat flicking its tiny tail
atop a boulder. A red-shafted flicker sailed overhead to land
on the branch of a nearby oak tree. For a moment, Gracie
stood still, pulling the fresh, dry scent of pine on high-
mountain air into her lungs and savoring the peace.

Then she stooped to catch a foam coffee cup skittering
across the pavement, tossed it into the garbage can next to
the front door, and walked into the lodge.

A Lysol-over-mildew smell from a long-neglected water
leak pervaded the entire first floor of Serrano Lodge. Gracie
walked along the narrow hallway, lined with dark green
industrial carpet and walls painted celery, past door after
door of lodge rooms.

She was reaching out to push through the two-way swinging door into the dining hall when the door burst open from

the other side. A girl of sixteen, possibly seventeen, stalked by without a word or glance. A camp T-shirt ripped off short showed eight inches of creamy midriff. Low-slung denim shorts revealed coltish legs. A pink ponytail swung beneath an A's baseball cap worn backward. A blue backpack was slung over one shoulder.

With her back pressed against the wall, Gracie stared after the young woman. She couldn't remember her name, but she had seen her several times before. Always the same revealing clothing. Always enough eye makeup to supply an entire cheerleading squad. Always the same expression that screamed, *Don't fucking talk to me or I'll rip your fucking head off.*

Talk about Trouble with a capital T, Gracie thought.

She pushed off the wall and through the swinging door into the dining room where she was bombarded with the boisterous chatter of forty-three middle-schoolers and eleven adult chaperones overlaid with the heady aroma of French toast, syrup, oatmeal, and coffee.

On the left was a serving window and another swinging door leading into the kitchen. On the right, at the far end of the room, a stone fireplace rose up to the ceiling. Across the room, tall windows offered a panoramic view of oak and pine and granite.

Gracie edged past a table of giggling preteen girls. "You ladies ready for high ropes this afternoon?"

Six voices answered in unison, "Yes!"

"Don't forget. Sneakers and long pants." Gracie returned gleeful shouts of "Hey, Miss Kinkaid!" with waves and smiles and negotiated her way through the tables to the far corner of the room where she wrestled a pink plastic cup from a pile of green stackable dish racks, filled it with coffee

and a splash of hot chocolate, and elbowed through the
swinging door into the kitchen.

". . . slut!" hissed a female voice.

Gracie stopped dead in the doorway. The door swung
closed behind her.

The windowless kitchen was lined with stainless steel
counters, dishwasher, stove, and walk-in refrigerators with
a large, rectangular butcher block prep table in the middle.

Jay Wilson, the camp's manager, stood next to the dishwasher on her left. Serene Bishop, the head cook, scowled
at her from the far end of the prep table, chest heaving,
breath coming out in quick whispers through flared nostrils.
One hand held a large chef's knife in a death grip.

For several seconds, the three stared at one another in a
culinary *tableau vivant*. Serene brought the scene back to
life by banging the knife down on the table. She stalked out
of the room and down the back hallway, lime green flip-flops
slapping on faded linoleum.

"Good morning, Gracie," Jay said, turning away to load
a dish rack with dirty plates and glasses. "Welcome back,"
he said with a flip of his hand. "Welcome back."

"Thanks." Gracie sidled over to lean up against the stainless steel counter. "Sorry if I interrupted."

Jay shrugged off the apology with another flip of his
hand. "Serene's a little upset because Jett called in sick again
this morning."

Calling in sick makes her a slut? Gracie blew little ripples
into her coffee and studied her boss over the rim of the cup.

Jay Wilson wore his XXXL madras plaid cotton shirt
tucked into khaki pants belted high up on a fifty-two-inch
waist. With a wealth of carefully coiffed silver hair, a tuft
of whiskers beneath his lower lip, and large central incisors,

he reminded Gracie of Peter Pettigrew, the rodentlike character from the Harry Potter movies.

But his voice was pleasing, as fluid and smooth as warm honey, which Jay used to maximum effect in his role not only as manager of a church-owned camp but also as a lay preacher.

Today the man's fleshy cheeks were flushed an unhealthy crimson. His forehead glistened with sweat.

Maybe it's his heart, Gracie speculated. She guessed his weight topped three hundred pounds. Carrying all that weight around was hard work. Especially at altitude.

The reason for Jay's bulk was no mystery. He vocally scorned physical activity of any sort, routinely driving the eighth of a mile from the office down to the kitchen. His preferred diet was mashed potatoes, gravy, and fried chicken, and he bought and consumed mini–candy bars by the case. What was a mystery was why he chose to work at a camp high in the mountains surrounded by the nature he so loathed.

Gracie took a sip of coffee, considering that maybe Jay's color was attributable to the tête-à-tête she had interrupted mid-tête, which brought her around to wondering if it was indeed Jett who Serene had called a slut and, if so, why.

Jett McKenna, kitchen manager and Serene's boss, was the object of the woman's almost pathological loathing.

Gracie, however, found Jett's lack of pretense refreshing, respecting, even envying, her fearlessness in dealing with people and life in general. But Jett had a hair-trigger temper that flared unpredictably like a desert cloudburst at Serene for putting too little salt in the oatmeal or Emilio, the young man who helped in the kitchen, for a speck of dried food on a serving spoon. The anger quickly dissipated, sun shining again on mesquite and barrel cactus, all forgiven, all forgotten—at least on Jett's part. But those who bore the emotional cuts and bruises of her mercurial behavior—Serene in particular—didn't seem to forgive or forget quite as easily.

At first, it puzzled Gracie how Jett was able to keep her job at a church-owned camp. A high-school dropout and ex-hooker with a police record, the self-proclaimed born-again Christian had a mouth even more foul than some of the men on Search and Rescue. She wore her dyed blue-black hair razored short on the sides and back with soft wisps up top combed forward and waving around like a peacock feather. Faux jewel-studded rings—one an elaborate dragon with ruby eyes—adorned her fingers. For work she toned down her preference for strategically ripped animal prints and black leather to black T-shirts and jeans.

But it quickly became apparent to Gracie that Jett was stiletto sharp and quick, an organizational wizard. In five years, she had clawed her way up through the camp ranks from dishwasher to kitchen manager, no mean feat at an institution where, as a rule, employees were hired in at one position, remaining there forever and ever, amen. Under the woman's supervision, the camp kitchen served upward of forty thousand on-time, underbudget meals every year. Jett made the camp money and thus made Jay look good. So Jett stayed.

Still, Gracie mused, if Jett didn't try harder to control her temper, the cauldron of rancor that churned and bubbled just beneath the surface in the camp kitchen would boil over and she might find herself out of a job.

Gracie took a sip of coffee and reflected that normally Jett's presence in the kitchen precipitated Serene's foul moods. Her absence should have been cause for great rejoicing.

Jay sprayed scalding water over a rack of dishes, sending a plume of steam billowing around him. "Anything more on the missing girl?" he asked over his shoulder.

A lump formed in Gracie's throat. She recognized the signs of post-traumatic stress from a prolonged unsuccessful search—the feeling as if she were walking around on egg-shells, frustration and grief held in check by a spider's web. It might be weeks before she could talk about the search without tearing up, months before she wasn't constantly thinking about it. She cleared her throat and said, "They suspended the search yesterday."

Jay pushed the dish tray along the rollers into the auto-matic dishwasher, slid the door closed, and flipped the On switch. "Tragic," he said, grabbing a towel from a nearby hook. As he dried his hands, he turned around to face Gra-cie. "Just tragic. Only the good Lord knows why He chose to punish that family that way."

Gracie opened her mouth to respond, thought better of it, and shut it again. In the month she had worked with Jay, she learned he wasn't interested in hearing anyone else's opinions on anything, especially theology. Gracie wasn't exactly sure what she believed, but she was pretty sure life's cruel twists and turns weren't the result of a vindictive Supreme Being yanking the puppet strings of the minions on earth. Sometimes life just sucked.

Serene reappeared behind the prep table, picked up the knife and began whacking with practiced precision at a head of red cabbage.

The head cook stood at least six inches shorter than Gra-cie's five-foot-eight. Her russet hair was blunt cut to chin length and parted in the middle, accentuating large brown eyes. She wore a camp T-shirt, a dingy yellow that washed out her already pale face. A perpetual frown puckered her mouth and creased three vertical furrows between heavy eyebrows.

Serene, honey, you need to get laid, Gracie thought. She stopped, her coffee cup halfway to her mouth. *What the hell am I talking about? I need to get laid.*

It occurred to her suddenly that the teenager wearing the short shorts and "fuck you" expression was Serene's daughter, Jasmine, whom she had never met but whom Jett had referred to more than once as "the Demon Spawn." A daughter like that could certainly render a single mother permanently surly.

"Morning, Serene." Gracie ventured, then took another sip of coffee.

The reply was a tightening of pale lips.

More to bridge the awkward silence than anything, Gracie asked the room, "So Jett called in sick this morning? What's wrong with her? Cold or something?"

Jay turned away to wipe down the already spot-free counters. "Flu. I hope I don't get it."

Serene chopped away with renewed vehemence at the poor cabbage, no doubt a stand-in for Jett's head.

The silence stretched until it hit Gracie that Jay and Serene were waiting for her to leave. "Well, guess I'll head on up to the Gatehouse," she said, pushing away from the counter. "I have a bunch of paperwork to do, then I'm on the high course all afternoon."

"Bible study this afternoon," Jay said. "Three o'clock. Why don't you try to make it?"

Gracie blinked. "Uh, thanks. I have to be on the high course this afternoon." *Didn't I just say that?* As she placed her cup in the dirty dish rack, a gnawing in her stomach reminded her that she still hadn't eaten breakfast.

One of the perks of her job was all the camp-prepared

meals she could eat while she was at work. But she wasn't going to hang around the kitchen eating her French toast, and the prospect of breakfast with the teeming masses out in the dining hall was daunting enough to prompt her to look for something more portable. She hauled open the massive stainless-steel door of the walk-in refrigerator, leaned inside, and grabbed up the first thing she saw—a plastic container hand-labeled *cold slaw*.

"Have a good one, Serene."

The knife stopped, poised in midair.

"See you later, Jay." Gracie pushed out through the kitchen door.

As it swung closed behind her, she thought she heard Serene's soft voice above the tumult of the dining room: "You, too, Gracie."

THE ground floor of the Gatehouse served as the camp
offices with the walk-out basement-garage around back
functioning as the maintenance shop. At one time the building might have resembled Snow White's quaint little cottage
in the forest. But dingy, peeling yellow paint; missing roof
shingles; and shaggy yews overwhelming the front windows
lent it the general air of not having been tended by seven
hardworking dwarves for years.

Gracie backed in the Ranger and parked in front of one
of the shop garage doors. With her pack over a shoulder and
the container of coleslaw in hand, she wove her way through
the shop, past sawhorses and band and chop saws and signs
in various stages of routing, staining, and drying, through
a door at the back and up a flight of wooden steps, taking
them two at a time.

On the main floor, to the right past a small bathroom, an
arched doorway led out to what once was a living room,

now the front office and reception area. Another archway straight ahead led into a full kitchen, which in turn opened out into the front office.

The furnishings of the front office were latter-day Elks Club. Wooden end tables and mismatched lamps flanked two sagging brown plaid couches. A portrait of a blue-eyed, blond-haired Jesus hung above a stone fireplace skunk-striped black from years of smoky fires. Casement windows off to the right offered a world-class view of the valley's evergreen-clad mountains.

To the left of the stairs, a hallway led to two former bedrooms. One was now Jay's office. The other was used for his daily Bible study which, for reasons inexplicable to Gracie, was attended solely by the women who lived in camp during the summer, whom Jett dubbed the Camp Women.

Gracie crossed the hall into the kitchen, poured herself a cup of coffee from the previous day's pot, and stuck it in the microwave, drumming her fingertips on the counter as she waited for it to heat.

Out in the front office, the door opened, jingling a little bell hanging down in front. A tiny Asian woman stepped into the room.

Gracie walked out of the kitchen to greet her. "Good morning."

The woman, a full foot shorter than Gracie, bowed and held out a red plastic shopping satchel. "I come to pay," she said. "Korean Methodist."

Gracie took the bag. A quick peek inside revealed multiple packets of bills rubber-banded together. Gesturing to one of the couches, she said, "Have a seat. I'll be right back," and cut back through the kitchen and down the hallway to Jay's office.

Sitting down at the desk, she meticulously counted out

the money. Six one-hundred-dollar bills, eight fifties, 104 twenties, 50 tens, 61 fives, 160 ones, two quarters, and one nickel. A total of $4,045.55.

When a cursory search of the area turned up three bags of mini–candy bars but no receipt book, she scribbled one out on a sheet of computer paper, jogged back up the hallway, and handed it to the woman with a smile and a thank-you.

The woman, who hadn't moved from her place just inside the door, bowed again, responded "Thank you," and left, closing the door quietly behind her.

Back in Jay's office, Gracie stuffed the packets of cash into a large manila envelope along with a dated note explaining who the money was from and taped it closed. She laid it on top of the metal safe on the floor of the large closet, thinking that more than four thousand dollars was a lot of cash to have lying around. She slid the closet door closed and made a quick call down to the kitchen to let Jay know the money was there.

As Gracie walked back up the hallway, she checked her watch. Plenty of time for paperwork before she needed to be down on the high course for that afternoon's program.

But first, breakfast, such as it was. Back in the kitchen, she grabbed a fork out of a drawer and pulled the lid from the container of coleslaw.

"Gack!"

The container flew across the room and smacked against the refrigerator. Night crawlers in black soil splatted on the yellowed linoleum floor.

Gracie crouched down and studied the glossy pink worms. "Sorry about that, guys," she said with a full-body shiver. "I hate worms." With the fork handle, she scooped them up one by one and dropped them back into the container, resealed it, and placed it back in the refrigerator. She wiped up the remaining dirt with a paper towel and washed her hands.

Granola bars from her pack would have to last her until lunch. She picked up her coffee and walked down the stairs to the basement level.

At the bottom of the steps, opposite the shop, was Gracie's office—an eight-by-ten-foot windowless room with unpainted cinder-block walls, lit by a bare hundred-watt lightbulb in the middle of the ceiling. Floor-to-ceiling wooden shelves running the length of the room held spools of parachute and accessory cord, a rope cutter, and plastic bins of climbing helmets and harnesses, stuff sacks of climbing rope, and steel hardware.

To the right of the door was a metal folding chair and an old wooden desk with a single center drawer, a gooseneck lamp, and a forest green princess telephone on top. A narrow three-shelf bookcase wedged against the far wall held mountaineering and Search and Rescue books and manuals.

At the desk—so short she couldn't cross her long legs, Gracie spent the next hour opening mail, answering and making phone calls, working on ropes course scheduling and paperwork, and other mundane but necessary tasks that made it possible for her to do what she considered to be the best part of her job—working outdoors.

British megastar Rob Christian—whose life Gracie had saved on a search six months before—had created a foundation for the development of The Sky's the Limit, a summer adventure program for low-income, at-risk kids, with the stipulation that Gracie be hired as its director. The church that owned the camp had also offered Gracie additional hours and the accompanying income to manage the camp's two ropes courses—one a high ropes course with elements thirty feet off the ground, designed specifically for individual challenges, the other with elements much lower to the ground and designed specifically for teams. Previously Eddie had been overseeing the ropes courses. How the man felt about Gracie taking over that portion of his responsibilities, she hadn't a clue.

Gracie's initial delight at the job offer, her excitement to be doing something other than serving up macaroni salad from behind the Safeway deli counter, evolved into anxiety that she wasn't up to the task, that Rob's faith in her was misplaced. Ten years was a long time between jobs paying more than minimum wage. But once she was immersed in the work, she was relieved to find it fulfilling and its challenges satisfying but, most of all, to be putting money into her depleted checking account.

And here we are already, she thought, standing up from the little desk. The first session of camp was almost over. High ropes course that afternoon. Closing campfire that evening. And the next morning after breakfast, the forty-three middle-schoolers would be loaded on school buses for the trip back down the hill to Compton.

Fifteen minutes later, all but the last, and heaviest, bin of high-course equipment for the afternoon program had been carried out and loaded in the bed of the Ranger. Gracie squatted to lift the forty-pound bin of steel hardware, then groaned as the movement strained leg muscles still stiff from the search.

"Hullo, Gracie," came a deep male voice behind her.

Gracie dropped the bin with a squawk and spun around.

Eddie Wilson leaned against the doorjamb.

He wore faded Levi's and an emerald green T-shirt with the sleeves cut off. Arms tanned and folded across a broad chest displayed well-muscled biceps to maximum effect. A toothpick moved at the corner of his mouth.

Jay and Eddie Wilson shared the same long eyelashes and

thick, curling hair, but otherwise they couldn't have been more physically different. Jay was Gracie's height and Pillsbury-doughboy soft and round, preferring plaid shirts, khakis, and loafers. Eddie was three inches taller, lean and fit, favoring blue jeans and T-shirts. Jay resembled an amiable hippopotamus when he walked—ponderous and deliberate. Eddie moved like a mountain lion, every movement fluid and calculated.

Where the hell did you come from? Gracie wondered. Annoyed at being surprised with her rear end up in the air, she only barely managed to keep the edge out of her voice. "Eddie. I didn't hear you come in."

"How's it goin'?" Eddie drawled in a voice as smooth and rich as melted caramel.

"Going well. Thanks." She stepped to the other side of the bin so she faced Eddie and bent again to lift it from the floor.

"Here, let me get that for ya." Before Gracie could react, Eddie stepped forward, lifted the bin out of her hands, and carried it out of the room as easily as if it were filled with balloons.

"You forgot the 'little missy,'" Gracie grumbled to herself. Jay had told her that he and his brother had been born and raised in New Jersey. So Eddie's good-ol'-boy drawl was pure affectation. But she knew what was really irking her was how hard she had to work to maintain a physical strength level most men came by naturally and took for granted.

She heaved her pack over one shoulder, yanked on the string to turn off the light, and followed Eddie outside.

Out in the shop yard, Eddie lifted the bin into the bed of the Ranger. "That it?"

"That's it."

He slammed the tailgate shut and dropped the back window of the shell, then turned around and smiled down at Gracie.

"Thanks," she said, unable to keep from smiling back.

Gracie was sure that if the man had been wearing his cowboy hat, he would have tipped it. "My pleasure," he said, dimples appearing on both cheeks. Shining chestnut hair curled over his forehead. His eyes were an exquisite green.

Damn, he's a good-looking cuss, she thought. Aware of the stirrings of physical attraction, she looked Eddie full in the face and said, "There was a plastic container in the walk-in fridge with night crawlers in it."

Eddie hooked his thumbs into the front pockets of his jeans, opened his mouth to answer, then closed it again. He looked like a ten-year-old caught with his hand in the cookie jar. He moved the toothpick to the other side of his mouth. "Them are mine," he said. "Use 'em to fish."

"It was labeled 'cold slaw.' "

He cocked his head at her, an inscrutable twinkle in his eyes. "I knew what was in it."

"They're in the refrigerator upstairs." Gracie lifted the back window of the truck, dropped her pack into the bed, and closed the window again.

"You're on that Search and Rescue, ain't ya?"

"Yup," Gracie said. Dammit if the man's drawl wasn't contagious. She looked at her watch again. She needed to be down at the high-course meeting the staff, not standing around chatting up a good-looking married man. "Whoops. Gotta run." Giving Eddie wide berth, she circled around to the driver's door and pulled it open.

"That's cool," Eddie said, moving so close behind her that she could smell the wintergreen on his toothpick. "You been lookin' for that missing girl?"

Gracie slid into the driver's seat. "They suspended the search yesterday."

Eddie stood in the doorway and put an arm on the top of

the door. "Feel bad for that family." He looked off over the top of the truck. "Can't imagine. Got kids o' my own."

"Yeah."

Eddie looked back down at Gracie. "You into it? Search and Rescue?"

"You could say that."

"Have to stay in pretty good shape, huh?" He stretched out a hand to feel her bicep.

With a warning look, Gracie caught his forearm and moved his hand away.

Eddie held up his hands, palms out. "You look fit. That's all I'm sayin'."

"I have to go." Gracie started the engine and grabbed the armrest to pull the door closed, but Eddie's body was blocking the way.

He smiled down at her, giving her the full dazzle of perfect teeth.

Gracie tugged on the armrest, nudging him with the door. "See ya, Eddie."

He backed out of the way and saluted her with two fingers. "You take 'er easy, then, Gracie."

She closed the door and punched down the accelerator. The tires spun and spit gravel out behind the truck.

She felt Eddie grinning at her. Her cheeks flamed. She lifted her foot from the pedal, let the tires stop spinning, slowly pressed down on the accelerator, and drove out of the shop yard.

CHAPTER

4

"**W**AY to go, Devon!" Gracie shouted up to a boy standing on a steel cable far above her head. She stood beneath a rectangular system of cable elements stretching thirty feet in the air between the trunks of massive ponderosa pines.

A rope clipped to the waistband of the boy's climbing harness led to pulleylike hardware hanging from a third cable higher up, then all the way down to a belay device on Gracie's harness. She anchored the boy in place by holding the rope behind her back.

Behind her, across the expanse of bark mulch on which she stood, the middle-school group sat on log benches forming a semicircular amphitheater built into a steep hill. All eyes were trained on four climbers on the various elements throughout the course. Laughter and shouts of encouragement filled the air.

On the element nearest the amphitheater, a preteen girl with a dreadlock ponytail and wearing a canary yellow The

Sky's the Limit! T-shirt clung to a rope hanging down like a vine in front of her.

Belaying her was an Asian man named Tony. Silver flecked his short black hair and mustache. A ready smile showed even white teeth. A retired middle-school teacher from La Puente, he'd so far proven to be solid and dependable. Gracie had liked him from the start.

The girl's legs trembled, wobbling the cable and bringing a gasp from the crowd below.

"Come on, Cassie," Tony called up to her. "You can do it."

The girl regained her balance, reached out for the next rope, and grabbed it. Shouts and clapping sounded from the amphitheater.

"Nice job!" Tony yelled.

Gracie stepped sideways to stay beneath Devon as he edged along the cable above her, his hands sliding along a parallel cable even higher up. The boy had long, spindly arms and legs and feet the size of boat paddles. He wore a red climbing helmet, a bright green The Sky's the Limit! T-shirt, and canvas gloves sizes too big for him.

A high-pitched squeal drew Gracie's eyes to her left where a teenaged girl and boy with matching fire-engine red T-shirts stood on two cables forming a horizontal V. Hands interlocked, they edged away from the apex, widening the gap between them and leaning in toward each other to keep their feet on the cables. The girl's legs were shaking uncontrollably, threatening to pull her and the boy off the cable. She squealed again.

Belaying the two climbers were Abe and Madison Bonds, co-owners of Adventures "R" Us, the adventure programming company Gracie had hired for the summer to run the busy sessions of The Sky's the Limit program.

"You're doin' great, girlfriend," Madison yelled up to the girl.

"Outstanding job, Jerome," Abe shouted to his climber.

Jay had pushed Gracie to hire the couple, promoting them as "good Christian people," a description she found curious since Abe wore a Star of David on a chain around his neck.

At first, Gracie had had her doubts about hiring the couple. She found Abe's penchant for stroking his meticulously trimmed goatee and sniffing at odd times to be pompous and rehearsed. And Madison's tendency to chatter on in a voice rivaling Alvin the Chipmunk grated on her nerves.

As ever, Jett had tossed in her two cents, questioning how good a role model for kids Madison would be—a fortyish woman trying to look thirtyish for her twentyish husband. Dark eyes flashing with mischief, she had speculated loudly as to what would attract the hunky and, she assumed, virile Abe to a woman almost twice his age. Her conclusion: the Triple B-jobs—Botox, boob, and blow.

Conscious that she might be resisting hiring Madison and Abe because she didn't like to be pushed, Gracie nudged her reservations aside and hired the couple. With an office in Timber Creek, they had solid credentials, serviceable technical ropes skills, a roster of trained and certified contract facilitation staff already familiar with the camp's ropes courses, and a full slate of school and executive retreats already on the camp calendar. They were the most logical choice.

So far, the decision had proven to be the right one. The first camp session, jam-packed with nature hikes and canoeing, scavenger hunts and skits and Capture the Flag, had been, by all accounts, a rousing success.

Devon inched along the cable.

"You're almost there," Gracie called up to the boy. "Only a few more feet."

Gracie glanced over at Madison again. Even from that distance, she could see the woman's erect nipples pressing up against a size small bubblegum pink T-shirt. Khaki shorts displayed too much glossy, salon-tanned leg. For her own clients, Madison could dress as she pleased. But The Sky's the Limit campers were Gracie's responsibility. "Next item up for discussion," she said under her breath as she looked back up at Devon. "Staff dress code."

Or maybe it was just that with legs and arms still pasty white from the long Timber Creek winter, and wearing a forest green T-shirt two sizes too big and no makeup, next to Madison, Gracie felt like Grace Kinkaid, Sea Hag.

Devon stretched out a hand and touched the tree trunk.

Cheers erupted from the amphitheater.

Gracie had to yell to be heard above the din. "Okay, Devon, I'm going to lower you down. Are you ready?"

The boy looked down and nodded.

"Move away from the tree," she instructed. "And hold on to the rope with both hands." Devon did as he was told. "Now, keeping your feet on the cable as long as you can, sit back in the air and I'll lower you to the ground."

Gracie moved her brake hand forward and let the rope slide through her fingers. With the boy dangling like a spider at the end of a web, she lowered him to the ground.

Devon's feet touched the mulch to more cheers and yells from the crowd. He bowed to his audience. "Thank you. Thank you very much. I'll be here all week. Thank you."

Gracie walked up with a smile on her face and gave him a high five. "Nice job!" She unscrewed the carabiner fastening the rope to the boy's harness. "Go ahead and take off your harness and helmet and hand them to the next person in line. Walk! Don't run!"

Gracie walked across the mulch, pulling the rope along with her, the pulley skimming along the cable above. Halfway back to the access ladder, she stopped and looked around at the beehive of activity on the course. Faces brimming with uncomplicated happiness. Jubilant laughter and shouts of encouragement mingling with the songs of myriad birds in the surrounding bushes and trees. A breeze as light as a moth's wings tickled her arms, carrying with it the sweet scent of cinnamon rolls baking in the camp kitchen across the lake.

Unable to keep the grin off her face, she whispered to herself. "Is this it? Is *this* what I'm supposed to be doing with my life?" An emotion she could only identify as joy welled up inside her. Sudden tears blurred her vision, giving her the answer.

She blinked away the tears and walked the rest of the way to the access ladder where waiting for her was a tiny girl, the red helmet sitting cockeyed on her head. A powder blue camp T-shirt set off smooth chocolate skin.

Gracie crouched down in front of the girl. "Hi! What's your name?"

The sweet, soft answer: "Valeria."

"What a beautiful name. Are you ready to climb, Valeria?"

Eyes bright with excitement shone back at her. Every tooth showed in a wide smile. "I'm ready!"

IN THE COOL shadow of early evening, Gracie untied knots, unclipped carabiners, hauled down climbing ropes, and rehung haul cords.

As soon as the program had ended, Madison and Abe had disappeared, pleading the need for last-minute preparations for closing campfire that evening. Tony had helped tear down the course until Gracie had ordered him off to the dining hall to catch dinner before they stopped serving.

Far from minding doing the rest of the work alone, she

reveled in the peaceful solitude of dinnertime at camp. She removed the aluminum access ladders and padlocked them in place at the base of one of the trees, then loaded the bins of equipment into the back of her truck, reflecting again how fulfilling she was finding working with underprivileged kids, how for the first time she was contributing positively to the world while taking home a paycheck.

It was after six o'clock by the time the Ranger bumped up and around the wide, curving sweep of dirt road, emerging onto the flat area between the high course and the narrow strip of swim beach. The truck rolled slowly past Lake Ponderosa, its water smooth and still and dark in the long blue-gray shadows of trees lining the opposite bank.

Gracie stopped the Ranger at the end of the lake where Lake Road intersected with Main Road. Directly ahead, partially eclipsed by a scrabble of oak and manzanita, were the lower washrooms and three single-wide trailers set side by side—housing for Jett, Serene and her daughter, and the two women who worked in housekeeping.

Gracie turned left and followed Main Road past a steep driveway climbing up to Mojave Lodge, a wide, one-story chalet-style building with a low-pitched roof, its lights blazing through the mix of oaks and pines.

A long hill led to the upper portion of camp past the conference center on the left and, on the right, two double-wide mobile homes, one housing Jay, his wife, Elaine, and their fifteen-year-old daughter, Meaghan; the other Eddie, his wife, Amanda, and their two children.

As the Ranger topped the hill, Eddie's silver pickup was just finishing its turn onto Rec Field Road. Gracie caught a glimpse of someone in the passenger's seat, her mouth open with laughter.

Lifting her foot from the pedal, she let the Ranger slow

to a crawl as she watched the truck drive away from her. She couldn't be certain because she had never seen her with anything but a snarl on her face, but she was sure the person in Eddie's truck was the Demon Spawn herself, Jasmine.

As Gracie watched, Eddie turned and looked back over his shoulder straight at her. He grinned at her and waved.

GRACIE SET THE heavy equipment bin down on the floor of her office, straightened and yanked the string to turn on the light. The lightbulb flared on and revealed a tall girl standing in the doorway.

"Shit!" Gracie yelled, jumping back and putting a hand to her heart in a gesture of which Jane Austen would have been proud. "You scared the crap out of me."

The girl edged back into the darkened hallway.

Gracie recognized her as Meaghan, Jay and Elaine's only child. She had never been introduced to the girl but had seen her several times trudging like a duckling behind her mother and the other Camp Women on their way to the daily Bible study at the Gatehouse.

Gracie took a step forward. "I'm sorry. Meaghan, right? You startled me, that's all. Come on in if you want."

The girl's brown eyes, deer-in-the-headlights round, flicked back over her shoulder in a hunted, stealthy way. Then, without a sound, she slid into the room and perched on the edge of the metal desk chair with her hands folded in her lap, legs together, like a pageant contestant sitting on stage. Yellow butterfly barrettes held drab shoulder-length blond hair back from her face. Bangs had been scissored in a severe line. She wore an oversized yellow Camp Ponderosa sweatshirt and capri pants. Matching sneakers were smudged with camp dirt. The skin on her pudgy face and hands had a rice-paper translucence. She looked so delicate and brittle, Gracie felt, that if touched, she would shatter like a fine-glass ornament, the shards tinkling to the floor in a little pile.

Gracie bent and looked into her face. "Would you like to talk?"

Meaghan looked down at her hands, her answer the barest shaking of her head.

Everything about the girl proclaimed she was craving someone to talk to. "You sure?"

The girl nodded without looking up.

Gracie looked around the room. "Okay. I'm going to keep working then." She gestured outside. "I have more bins to unload. You're welcome to stay if you want. For as long as you want. Okay?"

Another ghost of a nod.

When Gracie walked back into the room carrying the bin of climbing rope, Meaghan hadn't moved.

Gracie set the bin on the floor and used her foot to shove it in to the wall beneath the bottom shelf. When she turned around again, Meaghan had vanished.

The girl had come and gone without a sound, without saying a single word. "Spooky," Gracie whispered, staring at the empty doorway.

CHAPTER

5

"Ahhhh." Gracie eased her body—smelling of campfire smoke, muscles stiff and sore from a half day of belaying on top of multiple days of searching—into the pink bathtub of scalding water. She leaned back and rested her head on the foam flower pillow she had snagged for a nickel at a Memorial Day garage sale. A Libbey wineglass of chilled Chardonnay rested on the bathtub ledge. Her favorite Chopin étude drifted in from the CD player in the living room.

Steam writhed upward, fogging up the mirror and one small window.

Gracie studied her legs, mottled with plum-colored bruises. "Cover up those dirty knees, Grace Louise." She could still hear her mother's voice. "Why can't you be more like your sister?"

"Miss America, you ain't, Kinkaid," she said aloud, enjoying how sonorous her voice sounded in the tiny room.

She counted the bruises on one leg. "Five, six, seven."

She lifted her head to inspect a particularly large one, still an angry maroon. "That's a doozy. How'd I get that one?" She moved to the other leg. "Eight, nine. I do remember this one. That really hurt. Stupid rock."

She lay back again, took in a long, deep breath, blew it out, and felt herself beginning to relax. Purposely avoiding Gina Ramirez, she let her thoughts meander over the events of the day, the young campers on the high ropes course, and at closing campfire, the laughter, the singing, the happy faces illuminated by firelight, the unfamiliar feeling of contentment that accompanied the revelation that she loved working at camp, loved working with underprivileged kids.

Eventually she moved toward life outside camp and settled on Ralph Hunter, Search and Rescue teammate, best friend, the man she had been avoiding. "Because you have been," she said. "Avoiding him."

The week before the search, following the SAR team's after-meeting meeting at Timber Creek's diviest bar, the Saddle Tramp, Ralph had walked her out to her truck as he always did. But this time he had surprised her by kissing her good night. Once. On the lips. Very chaste. Very nonthreatening. "No tongue even," Gracie said to herself. And here she was acting like a sixth-grader who's just been felt up for the first time. "Or are they doing that in fourth grade now?"

Ralph had kissed her once before, after the funeral of a teammate killed during the nightmare search for Rob Christian the previous Thanksgiving. In the turmoil of physical injuries and emotional trauma, Gracie had completely forgotten the kiss until, months later, Ralph had kissed her again.

She sank lower in the bathtub and evaluated the meaning of the kiss. Besides Jett, Ralph was her only real friend. He was the one person on whom she leaned, the one person she trusted to never let her down. She needed him in her life the way one needed air to breathe. The last thing she wanted was to hurt him.

Ralph's emotions were nothing to be trifled with. The death of his wife from breast cancer six years earlier had almost killed him. Pain had etched permanent lines on his sun-weathered face. In the intervening years, Gracie had never heard him laugh outright.

She knew Ralph loved her. And she loved him back. But did his kissing her mean he *love* loved her? "If it that's what it means, that's huge. *Huge*." Ever since the kiss, outside of the search, she had been avoiding him. "Maybe you should actually try to figure out why."

Because she had also said no to Rob, whose life she had saved, the man with whom, in the dark, cold confines of a snow cave, she had made the most exquisite love in her life, the man who made every nerve ending in her body come alive, the man whose presence brought the world into focus in all of its Orrefors-clear glory.

She ached to see him again. She missed the dark brown eyes—bright, intense, missing nothing. The shining hair as soft as a kitten's. The perfect smile. She yearned to feel his hard arms around her, his soft lips on hers. To breathe in his scent.

"Shit." She sank deeper into the tub and contemplated her feet—the raw blister on the outside of her little toe, the bruises covering her legs, the chipped remnants of Search and Rescue—orange nail polish.

For the first three months after their ordeal, Rob had left several messages on her answering machine and e-mailed her every week, sometimes a single line checking in, sometimes long, rambling letters. For reasons she had chosen not to explore, she had never returned his phone calls. Her responding e-mails been short, perfunctory, sharing nothing of substance. His last e-mail had come more than a month ago.

Maybe he's on location, she thought. *Somewhere remote. With no Internet. Or maybe he's just out of my life.* "Can you blame him?" she whispered aloud.

Ralph had kissed her, letting her know he was willing to take their friendship to the next level. When he had backed off to see what she would do, what had she done? Avoided him. "Chickenshit."

Rob had asked her to run away with him, a fairy-tale invitation if there ever was one. "What did you do? You said no! *Stupid* chickenshit."

With her big toe, she nudged on the faucet for hot water, let it run for a few seconds, then nudged it back off.

"You *like* living alone. *Remember?*" She took a sip of wine and carefully set the thin glass back down on the edge of the bathtub. "No muss. No—"

Beep! Beep! Beep! The piercing tones of her Search and Rescue pager sounded from the kitchen.

"Oh, *crap*!" Gracie heaved herself out of the tub, wrapped a frayed Sponge Bob beach towel around her sarong-style, and ran barefoot into the kitchen where her pager lay on the counter. She grabbed it up, pressed the readout button, and squinted at the minuscule neon green screen. "Over-the-side. Arctic Circle. Ropes certified only."

"Shit."

Vehicle over the side of the cliff. Minutes, even seconds, could mean the difference between life and death.

Grabbing up the kitchen phone, she speed-dialed the Sheriff's Office. "Kinkaid responding. ETA twenty minutes."

In the laundry room off the kitchen, she yanked sports bra, panties, and sock liners from the clothesline and out of the dryer, socks and camo pants with the back pockets still wet. She pulled everything on.

A glance at the kitchen clock told her it was 9:07 p.m.

Early June. Temperatures maybe down into the forties. Who knew how long she would be out?

She pushed her arms into the long sleeves of her orange uniform shirt.

On scene, she would be calm. Focused. Professional. But as she laced up dusty hiking boots, anxiety knotted her stomach. "Please, God," she prayed. "Don't let me screw this up." She wove her hair into a single braid and tugged on her black ball cap with the Sheriff's Department chevron on the front and *Gracie* in orange script on the back. "Please help me handle this and not have somebody get hurt because of me. Please. Please."

Gracie ran from the cabin, arms filled with fleece jacket, water bottle, floppy hat, radio chest pack, and short gaiters to be donned when she had more time. She tossed the bundle into the bed of the Ranger alongside her twenty-four-hour SAR pack and her day pack—a lighter, more compact version of the SAR pack, holding her personal ropes equipment, first-aid and survival supplies, and a hydration bladder.

Backing the truck down the steep driveway, she did a mental survey. Pager. Watch. Cell phone. Extra water bottle. There had been no time to make her usual PB&J sandwich. Her dinner of two slices of three-day-old pizza would have to do.

The pickup sped down to the bottom of the curving hill, threaded its way through abandoned cars on either side of the street, and rolled through each of four stop signs. At the Boulevard, the valley's east-west thoroughfare, she looked right, left, right. A Safeway semitruck barreled past, kicking up a flurry of pebbles. She gunned the engine, screeched left onto the Boulevard, stomped down on the pedal, and kept it there the 5.6 miles to the Sheriff's Office.

CHAPTER

6

BY the time the Ranger pulled into a parking space along the side of the Sheriff's Office, the SAR team's fifteen-seat passenger van and the Hasty Vehicle, an old converted ambulance packed with rescue equipment, sat idling and ready to roll in front of the long two-story brick building.

"Am I the last one here?" Gracie yelled to herself as she jumped out of the truck and hauled her gear out of the back. She trotted across the parking lot to where Ralph was stashing gear into the back of the van. "Hi, Ralphie."

"Hey, Gracie girl," Ralph said, blue-gray eyes crinkling back at her.

"Who's driving what?"

"You're driving the van." He lifted the pack from her shoulder and heaved it into the back of the van. "Warren's got the Hasty."

Gracie jogged up to the front of the van, hauled herself up in to the driver's seat, and clipped on her seat belt.

Lenny sat on the bench seat directly behind her, elbows on knees, blue eyes bright with excitement, Cheshire cat grin on his face. Carrie Matthews sat directly behind him.

"Hey, Lenny. Hey, Carrie," Gracie said.

"Hiya, Gracie!" Lenny at least seemed to have bounced back quickly from the search for Gina Ramirez. One advantage of being young and strong and male.

"Hi, Gracie," Carrie said in a quiet voice. Twenty-four, five-foot-five, creamy-clear complexion, dark chocolate doe eyes, dark hair pulled back into a ponytail pulled through the back of her Sheriff's Department ball cap. The newest member of the team and the only woman besides Gracie, Carrie was sharp, focused and already one hundred percent committed to the team.

Lenny and Carrie had completed their rope rescue training only two months earlier. This was their first vehicle over the side, their first technical ropes mission. Gracie didn't envy either of them the experience.

The back doors of the van slammed closed. Two seconds later, the passenger's door flew open and Ralph heaved himself into the seat. He slid a clipboard from the dash onto his lap.

"Ready?" Gracie asked.

"Ready," Ralph said. He signaled with a thumbs-up out the window over to Warren in the Hasty.

Gracie slid the side-column gear shift into Drive and pressed her foot down on the gas pedal, as mushy as a ripe plum. The van crawled forward and turned right onto the Boulevard with the Hasty lumbering behind.

Gracie stomped down on the accelerator and felt her adrenaline kick up a notch.

Ralph snapped on the blue and red lights on the light bar up top—lights, no siren. He unclipped the radio microphone from the dashboard and raised it to his mouth. "Control. Ten Rescue Forty-four."

"Go ahead, Forty-four," answered a male voice.

"En route with four SAR personnel aboard."

"At twenty-one fifty-four."

"Where we headed?" Gracie asked, swerving left to pass a slow-moving minivan.

"Glory Ridge turnout."

The van tires squealed as they crossed the double yellow highway lines on a sharp curve. Gracie let up on the pedal and hauled on the oversized steering wheel to bring the van back into its own lane, then straightened the wheel for a long straightaway. She let out a long, slow breath and tried to relax her already tightening shoulders.

A flicking of eyes over to Ralph told her he hadn't noticed her straying into the oncoming traffic lane. The dashboard lights cast a green tint over his brush-cut silver hair and lightened his eyes to ice. He was staring straight ahead, unmoving, intent, mind focused on the operation ahead.

Across the road, a granite wall rose up two feet from the edge of the pavement. On the right, a line of boulders separated the highway from a steep rocky cliff leading down to Timber Lake where the moon rising behind them skipped gleaming white coins across the dark water.

Gracie blew a bubble of strawberry gum and braked to slow the van for a tight left-hand curve. The highway straightened and she sped up again. "So what's the scoop, Ralphie?" she asked, knowing Lenny and Carrie were sufficiently intimidated by Ralph not to ask.

Her teammate turned halfway in his seat so that everyone could hear.

Lenny and Carrie leaned forward in their seats.

"Single vehicle over the side," Ralph said in the gravelly

voice Gracie loved. "Unknown number of vics. Unknown status."

Gracie stepped on the brake again and hauled on the steering wheel for a right turn. The van rumbled across the dam at the far western end of the lake.

"Somebody see it go over?" Lenny asked.

"RP called in tire tracks on the berm. CHP and CDF are already on scene. Over-the-side's confirmed."

At the end of the dam, Gracie turned left and pushed the pedal all the way down to the floor. The van gained speed and swooped onto a treacherous five-mile stretch of curving highway carved out of sheer mountain cliffs and known as the Arctic Circle.

The speedometer inched upward to fifty. Fifty-five. Sixty. Gracie's eyes flicked to the rearview mirror, then back to the road. "Warren still back there?" she asked no one in particular.

Several seconds of silence, then Carrie answered, "About a hundred yards back."

Gracie took a tight curve wide to cut the g-forces and the possibility that someone would arrive on scene needing to heave up their dinner. "Lenny and Carrie," she said. "Ralph is Ops. When we arrive on scene, he'll get a sitrep from the IC and make assignments. As soon as we stop, you haul the gear out of the back of the van. I'll guide in the Hasty. It's heavy enough to act as the main anchor."

Another curve brought into view flashing blue and red lights at the turnout a quarter mile up the highway.

Glory Ridge was a razorback ridge jutting out into the steep-walled canyon at a particularly hazardous spot in the highway—a narrow, precipitous chute with virtually no obstructions to stop a cartwheeling vehicle until it reached the bottom four hundred feet down.

Gracie lifted her foot from the gas as the van neared the wide gravel turnout jammed with vehicles—Sheriff's Department, California Highway Patrol, Department of Forestry. White spotlights cast stark eerie shadows on the sheer, rocky cliffs on the opposite side of the highway. Motorists watching the spectacle lined the pavement.

"And so the cluster begins," Ralph said so quietly that only Gracie heard him.

"At least someone thought to keep the looky-loos out of the parking lot."

Ralph raised the radio microphone to his mouth. "Control. Ten Rescue Forty-four."

"Go ahead, Forty-four," the dispatcher answered.

"We're on scene. Highway 42. Glory Ridge turnout."

"Copy. At twenty-two sixteen."

"There." Ralph pointed to where a Sheriff's deputy stood waving them into a space at the near end of the turnout.

Gracie swerved into the spot, stopped the van with a jolt, and killed the engine.

All four rescuers burst from the vehicle. Ralph walked over to a knot of three men in different agency uniforms standing close to the edge of the drop-off. Lenny ran around to the back of the van, pulled open the back doors, and hauled out packs and equipment, which he handed off to Carrie.

Gracie removed her ball cap and plunked her helmet on her head, clipping it beneath her chin. Then she trotted back to guide the Hasty Vehicle into position a dozen feet from the cliff's edge.

As soon as the Hasty stopped, Gracie opened a side compartment door and grabbed a folded-up tarp, which she shook out and spread on the ground. Warren appeared and helped her secure the corners with jumbles of pulleys and carabiners and other steel hardware.

With graying reddish brown hair and solid fields of freckles on face and arms, Warren Towne was self-possessed, a man of few words with no desire to be a leader or grab the spotlight. Content to work behind the scenes, he did whatever needed to be done in order to keep the team running smoothly.

Together, they pulled the remaining stuff sacks and duffel bags of ropes, accessory cord, steel hardware, and radios and headsets from the Hasty compartments and placed them on the tarp.

Gracie stepped into her seat harness, pulled it up around her waist, fastened the belt, doubled it back, and pulled the leg straps tight. Then she climbed into the back of the Hasty and, with Lenny on the other end, lifted out the Junkin litter—the sturdy, orange plastic basket in which they would transport any victims.

As they were placing the litter on the ground, Ralph stepped up onto the foot-high gravel berm at the edge of the turnout. "Okay, everybody," he said in a loud voice. "Listen up."

The rescuers gathered around and Ralph pointed to where tire tracks led over the side of the cliff. "Vehicle went over here. CDF has two men over the side. They've located a single vic. Deceased. About two hundred fifty feet down."

Terrific, Gracie thought. *Another body recovery.* "Are we having fun yet?" she whispered to Warren standing beside her.

Warren whispered back, "Oodles."

"They've flagged the DB," Ralph continued. "Taken pics for the Coroner. They'll continue down to the vehicle itself, most likely at the bottom another hundred, hundred fifty feet down. Don't relax yet. Until we receive confirmation that there are no live vics down there, this is still a rescue."

Four heads nodded.

"Gracie, you're Litter." As an EMT and, next to Ralph, the member with the most technical ropes experience, she was the most logical choice to go over the side with the litter to treat any remaining injured parties.

To Warren, Ralph said, "Towne. Main Line." The main line was the ropes system by which the litter, and Gracie, would be lowered.

Warren acknowledged with a deep, "On it, boss."

"We'll get some of the fire guys to help with the haul." Ralph turned to Carrie. "You okay with Belay?" Operating on its own ropes system, the belay provided backup in case the main line failed.

Wide-eyed, Carrie nodded.

"Olsen. Edge."

Lenny beamed. As Edge Tender, he would help the litter over the side and facilitate communications between Gracie and Ralph.

"Olsen," Ralph continued. "If anyone else shows, they'll work Edge and you'll be Litter with Gracie."

In less than fifteen minutes, the team constructed the complicated mechanical advantage ropes system to which the litter and rescuers would be attached. Anchored to the Hasty Vehicle, the ropes zigzagged through a series of pulleys, multiplying the force the haul team would need to bring the litter back up to the top.

As Gracie double-checked her own rigging of ropes attached to the litter, a white pickup truck skidded to a stop on the gravel across the highway.

"Jon's here," Carrie announced.

"Yay," Gracie said, meaning it. Jon was smart, experienced, and cool under pressure. And he was one more set of hands.

"Jon's Edge, then," Ralph said. "Olsen, you're Litter. You okay with that?"

"Hell, yes!" Lenny said, blue eyes shining in the light of his teammate's headlamp.

Thank God, Gracie thought. On vertical rescues, most of the litter's weight was borne by the team at the top. On a slope with a less steep incline such as this one, most of the weight would be hefted by whoever was working the litter. The more muscle on the litter, the easier on her it would be.

A wide grin on his face, Lenny moved over to the litter and unclipped himself from the edge tether. With a pang of regret, Gracie predicted the grin would be nowhere in sight by the end of the operation.

Already helmeted and harnessed, Jon jogged up to the group and dropped his pack on the tarp. Fifteen years older than Gracie and two inches shorter, Jon was wiry and tough, a former marathoner who could outhike most people half his age.

While Ralph briefed Jon, Gracie attached herself to the litter by clipping the tail of the main rope onto her seat harness with a carabiner. She backed it up with a rigging of more carabiners and a two-inch-wide strap of yellow webbing. Another webbed strap ran from her harness to the metal railing of the litter itself.

A man whom Gracie recognized as the local California Department of Forestry fire chief walked over to Ralph. The two conferred in low voices for a moment and then the fire chief walked away.

"Listen up," Ralph called out again. "CDF has reached the wreckage at the bottom. No other vics."

The entire group took a collective deep breath, relaxed, and shifted mental gears. The change from the rescue of a live victim to a body recovery slowed the entire operation, reducing the sense of urgency, the stress level, and the risk of rescuer injury.

Ralph walked up to Gracie and said in a voice meant for her ears only, "It's pretty ugly down there, Gracie girl. You still want Litter?"

Since the only victim of the accident was already dead, there was no need for an EMT. Ralph was extending her the courtesy of asking what position she wanted to work instead of assigning her to one.

She nodded. "I'll stay on Litter."

"Olsen, you still okay with Litter?"

"Hell, yes!"

Ralph turned back to Gracie. "'Bout ready?"

"Sixty seconds."

Since no other SAR team members had arrived, Ralph would also serve as Safety Officer, a nerve-wracking double duty that Gracie knew from experience was like juggling three plates, four cups, and a bowling ball with one hand tied behind his back. Ralph took it in stride.

As he made the rounds inspecting every aspect of the ropes system—anchors, knots, carabiners, pulleys—Gracie donned her day pack. She lifted off her helmet, placed on her head the radio headset Jon handed her, and replaced her helmet, buckling it beneath her chin. She pressed the little microphone button. "Radio check," she said in a normal voice to keep from blasting out everyone else's eardrums.

"Loud and clear," came Ralph's voice over the headset.

Gracie and Lenny made last-minute adjustments, wiping goggles free of dust and condensation, tightening helmet straps. Gracie turned on her headlamp to make sure the battery was still viable, then turned it off again to save the battery until she needed it.

Safety checks completed, Ralph walked over and clipped into his own safety line attached to the Hasty Vehicle. He stepped out onto the berm and blew one long, ear-shattering blast on his whistle. "Operations are ready to begin!" he shouted. "All personnel take your positions! Quiet, please!"

Immediate silence.

A gust of wind billowed dust across the parking lot and blasted the rescuers with grit.

"All safety systems have been checked," Ralph said over the radio. "We're ready for operations to begin."

Gracie turned on her headlamp. Crouching down, she wrapped her gloved fingers around the metal railing of the litter. Opposite her, Lenny did the same. "Lift on three," Gracie said. "One, two, *three.*"

The rescuers stood up, lifting the basket off the ground. The weight of the litter settled onto Gracie's hips. They would ache later, but it was better than having her knuckles drag on the ground by the end of the operation.

She and Lenny shortened the straps attached to the litter so that in spite of the disparity in their heights, the litter would stay relatively level.

"Main line, ready?" Ralph asked over the radio.

"Main line's ready," Warren's low voice answered.

"Belay, ready?"

"Belay ready," Carrie squeaked.

"Edge, ready?"

"Edge ready." Jon. Steady, reassuring.

Gracie took in a slow, deep breath.

"Litter, ready?"

"Litter ready," she said.

"Move the litter into position."

With Jon helping, Gracie and Lenny crab-walked the litter to the edge of the cliff, positioning it so they faced each other. The bottom of the litter hung out over the edge.

Ralph blew three whistle blasts, then said into the radio, "Down slow."

With her heart thudding in her chest, Gracie took a deep breath and stepped down into the darkness.

CHAPTER

7

"LIFT on three," Gracie said, repositioning her feet on the steep jumble of talus. "One, two, *three!*"

Every muscle strained as she and Lenny struggled to lift the litter up and over a granite outcropping that had been hidden by mounds of manzanita and the darkness and against which they had become wedged.

Lenny cursed under his breath as he grappled with the litter. It suddenly broke loose and Gracie scrambled to keep her footing.

"Ops," Gracie said into the radio.

"Go ahead, Litter."

"Give us about five feet of slack." To Lenny: "Move it all the way off the rock, then set it down."

The rescuers stepped sideways until the litter was clear of the manzanita and the rock, then set it down on the slope. Gracie braced one foot against a boulder to keep herself from sliding down the hill, pulling the litter and Lenny along with her.

Lenny sucked in air in gulps. "Take a breather? I need water."

"Sure." Her own breath was coming out in painful gasps and her mouth was as dry as an old bone. She pressed the microphone button. "Ops. Stand by. We're readjusting."

"Advise when ready."

Sweat trickled down between Gracie's breasts. Her shirt was damp where the waistband of her seat harness rested on her hips. "Warmer down here," she said, and took a long drink of water from the hydration pack on her back.

"I'm dyin'," Lenny said as he unzipped his jacket. "Didn't need this jacket, that's for damn sure." Lifting up his goggles, he wiped his forehead and face with his sleeve.

Gracie peered down the hillside. Somewhere between them and the bottom of the canyon lay a body. But the light of her headlamp dwindled to nothing after ten feet. She looked over at Lenny who was swallowing water from a water bottle in huge gulps. "'Bout ready?"

Lenny recapped his bottle and grinned at her across the litter. "I's born ready!"

Gracie grinned back and said, "Okay, then, lift on three. One, two, *three*."

The litter rose off the ground.

"Move down a little to take up the slack."

They stepped down the hillside until the two ropes that ran up to the top pulled taut.

"Resume lower," Gracie said into the radio.

Far above their heads, three blasts of Ralph's whistle sounded.

The next hundred feet were relatively easy going—a

straight sixty-degree pitch of dirt and rocks. The two rescuers took it slowly, placing each foot carefully before taking the next step. There were no mishaps, no stumbles, no boulders or manzanita leaping out at them from the darkness. Gracie hoped it would stay that way all the way to the bottom.

Slowly they descended. Five more feet. Ten. Fifteen.

"Fuck!" Lenny's yell split the darkness. He fell backward onto the slope, yanking Gracie forward off her feet. She landed on the litter with her shoulder in the basket. Ribs knocked against the raised metal railing. Pain snatched the breath from her lungs.

The litter pendulumed below Lenny, dragging Gracie along with it. She dug her knees and feet into the rocky soil. "Stop!" she bellowed into the radio.

A long whistle blast sounded faintly from above.

The litter stopped moving. A scrabble of pebbles rolled down the hill. No sound, but two rescuers breathing heavily.

"Litter, sitrep," Ralph said over the radio.

Grunting against the pain, Gracie pushed herself up off the litter and crouched on the steep hillside, propping herself in place by planting a hiking boot against the side of a boulder. "What the *hell*, Lenny?"

His breath coming in quick huffs, Lenny pointed down the hill and off to the left. "There."

"Litter, sitrep," came Ralph's voice again, more sharply.

"Stand by one," Gracie said in as a normal voice as she could muster. She slid around so she was facing downhill and swept the hillside below with the light of her headlamp, straining to see what Lenny had seen.

Then she saw it. "Holy shit."

A few feet below them on the slope lay a human arm.

CHAPTER

8

GRACIE and Lenny stared at the arm lying below them on the hillside.

The limb had been severed two inches above the elbow. Tendons and bone showed white in the circle of light of the two headlamps. The hand lay palm upward, fingers clawing the air.

"CDF must have missed it on the initial descent," Gracie said. She blew out a breath in one slow exhalation. "Okay, let's move down until we're even with . . . it."

Unmoving, Lenny stared down at the arm, eyes wide, his normally ruddy cheeks the color of dried clay.

"Lenny!"

His eyes jerked up to meet hers. "Yeah."

"We're gonna move down the hill until we're even with the arm."

"Yeah."

"Ops," Gracie said. "Take up a couple of feet of slack."

The ropes tightened and lifted.

"Down slow about five feet."

The rescuers walked the litter down the slope until they stood next to the arm.

"Stop," Gracie said into her headset.

"Whatcha got, Gracie?" Ralph asked over the radio.

Gracie cleared her throat to give herself an extra second to think of how to phrase what they had found. "Evidence," is what she finally said, hoping that Ralph would interpret correctly that they had found something sufficiently grisly not to relay the information over a radio system where anyone—including the victim's family members—might hear it.

"Copy."

"Flag it, will you, please?" Gracie asked Lenny. "And the bush, too, while you're at it. I'll take a waypoint."

She drew her GPS from its own little pouch on her radio pack and held it aloft to acquire the satellite signals as Lenny pulled a length of neon green flagging tape from a spool on his own radio pack. He encircled the arm with the tape, anchoring it in place with rocks and scoops of dirt. He tied another length to a branch of a nearby manzanita bush.

Coordinates gained, Gracie labeled the waypoint A-R-M, then said into her headset, "Ops. Litter."

"Go ahead, Litter."

"Evidence flagged. Ready for coordinates?"

"Stand by one." Then, "Go ahead."

Gracie read off the coordinates.

"Good copy," Ralph said, then repeated the coordinates back to her.

As Gracie zipped the GPS back into its pouch, Ralph's voice said in her ear, "Litter, resume lower on your call."

* * *

"THERE IT IS!" Lenny pointed down the hillside below to where streamers of neon orange flagging tape billowed from the branches of a clump of manzanita. The rescuers continued their slow descent until they reached a wide shelf of level ground. "Stop," Gracie said into the radio. "We've reached the scene. Will advise."

"Copy," Ralph said. Several seconds later, the rope stopped moving.

"Lower on three," Gracie said. "One, two, three." The litter settled onto the rocky ground. "Go ahead and unclip."

Detached from the litter railing, Gracie radioed, "Off belay." In her mind's eye, she could see her teammates begin the scramble to de-rig the main rope from the lower system and rig it into the haul system by which they, the litter, presumably with the victim inside, would be brought back up to the top.

"I'm takin' my pack off for now," Gracie said, unclipping the chest and waist straps. She dropped the pack on the ground and walked over to where the body lay on the ground.

The nauseating odor of rotting flesh filled her nostrils, making her stomach lurch.

Some described the smell of death as sickeningly sweet. To Gracie, there wasn't anything sweet about it. The stench pervaded everything, worming its way into every pore, every brain cell, so that the next time one smelled it, it was instantly recognizable.

Stepping back from the body, Gracie turned away and inhaled several deep breaths of fresh air. She stepped back and, breathing through her mouth, looked down on the body.

Her headlamp revealed the victim was a woman. The head, partially severed, lolled off to one side, the face turned away, features hidden by the darkness. The body was broken, disjointed, like a discarded hand puppet, the three remaining limbs flung out at awkward angles.

Lenny appeared next to Gracie. "Jesus," he whispered.

She looked over at her teammate. Wide blue eyes were fixed on the body. Then a hand flew to his mouth, he stumbled a few feet away, bent over and retched.

"Slow, deep breaths, Lenny," Gracie said with sympathy.

As her teammate followed her instructions, she turned back toward the body, adjusting her headlamp so the beam fell directly on the dead woman's head.

Black hair, dulled with dust, was close cropped on the sides and back, long up top.

Gracie's breath caught in her throat. Needing to know, anxiety growing into the horror of certainty, she peered at the remaining hand, fingers curling downward, clutching at the ground.

Crimson. Green. Purple. The stones of multiple gold rings caught the light. The ruby eye of a dragon winked back at her.

Adrenaline sizzled down to Gracie's fingertips. A yawning chasm of darkness opened at her feet and swallowed her whole.

It was Jett.

CHAPTER

9

GRACIE sat in the darkness, leaning up against the rough trunk of a Coulter pine tree. Elbows on knees, head drooping, she drew air in through her nose and blew it out through her mouth, focused solely on keeping the nausea at bay. Her stomach had been emptied of every remnant of her dinner. Each new retch shot pain into her gut.

Only vaguely aware that she was shivering, she pulled a crumpled tissue from her jacket pocket and wiped her eyes. To rid her mouth of its sour taste, she took a swig from her water bottle, swished it around, then spat it out. Not much better. She dug a piece of grape bubblegum from her radio pack and popped it into her mouth.

Male voices and the crunching of boots on gritty ground wafted into her consciousness. Less than thirty feet away, on the other side of the tree, Lenny and the CDF firefighters worked by the feeble light of their headlamps. Having found no other victims at the heap of twisted metal that was the vehicle at the bottom, the two other men had ascended their own ropes to help package the body for evacuation.

There was the sound of the long zip of the body bag. A low voice counted, followed by the sound of a heavy load being lifted and settling into the litter.

Past experience told Gracie the men would tuck hardware and packs in around the body so it wouldn't shift during the long, slow climb back up to the top, but also so they would have less to carry on their backs.

So much for respect for the dead, Gracie thought. What the hell was that anyway? Respect for the dead. The dead were dead. Respect for the survivors maybe, for the family waiting anxiously with much weeping and wringing of hands at the top.

Except Jett has no one waiting up top.

Tears burned Gracie's eyes.

Jett had been between boyfriends. There was a father somewhere, essentially nonexistent since grade school. An alcoholic mother in Pennsylvania. A teenage son in Oregon with whom she barely communicated. Those who lined the highway up top waiting for the body to be brought up were nameless strangers, craning their necks in morbid curiosity, wringing their hands in an effort to keep warm on a cool summer evening.

Not that Jett would know or care. What lay in the litter a few feet away was no longer a person. With the departure of her spirit, that mystical life force that rendered her a living, breathing human being, that inestimable gift that was Jett, no longer existed. What remained was a worthless hunk of tissue, water, blood, and bone.

Her friend was gone.

Forever.

Gracie jumped to her feet. "Lenny!" she screamed.

The sound of running feet, then Lenny skidded to a stop next to her. "Gracie? You okay?" His voice was anxious, frightened.

Gracie felt a sudden flowering of affection for the gentle giant who was her teammate. She put a hand on his arm. "Sorry. Yes. Is she . . . ? Are you . . . ?" She shuddered a breath and tried again. "Is she ready? Can I come over now?"

"Yeah." Lenny sucked in a deep breath in order to talk without panting. "We're done tyin' her in."

With Lenny's big arm around Gracie's shoulders, they walked over to where Jett's body lay in the litter, shrouded in white plastic.

"I can't remember . . . ," Gracie said. "The ratios . . . If we're all clipped into the litter . . . is it going to be too heavy?"

Too much weight on the litter would exert too much force and the entire system could be blown all to hell.

I'm already there, Gracie thought.

"They're gonna climb back up on their own ropes," Lenny said, indicating the two firefighters who, twenty feet away, were already clipping in to their own rope systems, their reflective rocker panels and striping on yellow helmets and jackets iridescent in the darkness.

"Thanks, guys," Gracie called over.

"Not a problem," one of the men responded. "See ya at the top."

"See ya," Lenny said.

Gracie turned her radio headset back on and pressed the button of the little microphone. "Ops. Litter."

"I'm right here, Gracie."

The sound of Ralph's steady voice brought fresh tears to her eyes. "The CDF guys will ascend on their own ropes. Lenny and I will come up with . . ." She stopped. *Keep it together, Kinkaid.* She took in a deep, ragged breath. "Lenny and I will come up with the litter."

"Good copy. Let me know if you change your mind. We'll switch you out."

"I want to come up with the litter."

"Copy that. Advise when ready."

Kneeling on the stony ground, Gracie clipped the tie-in strap from the litter railing onto her harness. Across the litter Lenny did the same. "Ready?" she asked.

"I's born ready."

Gracie half sobbed, half laughed. "Lift on three. One, two, *three*."

With simultaneous grunts, the rescuers rose to their feet, lifting the litter off the ground. Gracie staggered beneath the weight but managed to stay upright. *Dead weight*, she thought.

They eased the litter into position, lining it up with the ropes leading down from on top.

"Ops. Litter," Gracie said into her headset.

"Go ahead, Litter."

"Ready on your call."

"Copy."

Over the headset, she could hear Ralph make the rounds, checking off each segment of the system: Haul. Belay. Edge. Finally Litter.

"Litter ready," Gracie said, shifting her feet and flexing her fingers for a better grip.

"Taking up slack," came over the radio.

The rescuers watched the rope, waiting for the pull to travel from the top down into the canyon. Finally both ropes moved and quivered as they pulled taut.

Faintly from above came the two whistle blasts, then through the radio, Ralph's command: "Haul slow."

GRACIE SAT BACK in her harness, planted her feet above her waist on the hillside and looked up. Less than fifty feet above her head, brilliant gauzy white light poured over the black line that was the edge.

At the top, the haul team was resetting the ropes system.

Across the litter, Lenny waited, motionless except for his chest rising and falling with each breath.

Gracie thanked him silently for his presence, for his physical strength, for his inherent goodness.

On the way up the incline, the rescuers had stopped to wrap the severed arm in a black plastic garbage bag pulled from Gracie's pack and secure it in the litter.

Another hundred feet up, the last of Gracie's energy died, eaten away by adrenaline and shock. Even though she was being pulled up the mountain, the weight of the litter and its contents hauled her down at the hips. Hands, arms, and shoulders ached. Hips were bruised. Legs quivered like jelly. Every breath stabbed her lungs.

A single long whistle blast had sounded, followed by "Stop" over the radio, then "Reset." The three-to-one mechanical advantage of the ropes system provided extra pulling power, but for every two hundred feet of rope the haul team pulled, the litter was raised a little less than seventy feet. Everyone, everything, stopped and waited while the system was reset. Then the haul resumed.

Ralph's whistle blew again followed by his voice through the radio, "Haul slow." The double line of ropes dragged Gracie, Lenny, and the litter up the side of the mountain.

Gracie slipped on a loose rock and almost fell to her knees. She dug in the toes of her boots, found purchase, and took another step. She stumbled again, regained her footing, and grabbed onto rocks, branches, roots, anything she could get her hands on to keep going. Not thinking. Not feeling. Not caring. Just cursing, grunting, sweating in an agonizing fight to reach the top and have it be over.

The crushing weight of the litter suddenly lightened as two pairs of hands grabbed it from above—Jon and a man Gracie didn't know, lying belly down on the edge of the cliff.

The movement unbalanced Gracie. Her feet slipped out from under her and she went down hard on her side, landing with an unceremonious grunt. Strong hands grabbed her arms and bore her, Lenny, and the litter up and over the edge and along the flat ground next to the Hasty Vehicle.

Fighting to pull air into her lungs, Gracie unclipped from the litter, rolled away from it, and sat up. She unclipped her helmet, lifted it from her head, and dropped it on the ground. A gust of wind blasted across the turnout, stinging her with tiny stones and chilling the tendrils of dank hair plastered to her head.

"Gracie." A quiet voice on her right—Ralph crouching beside her.

Gracie wrapped her arms around his waist, nestled her face into his warm shoulder and held on.

EVERY FIBER OF every muscle ached. Gracie stood in the middle of the bedroom and stripped off all her clothes. Leaving them with their lingering smells where they landed on the floor, she donned a sweatshirt and sweatpants, climbed into bed, and pulled the blankets up, clenching them with tight fists beneath her chin.

The residual warmth of the day permeated the loft, yet beneath the sheet and lightweight comforter, Gracie shivered violently, teeth clattering together uncontrollably, as if someone had run an IV line of glacier water into a vein.

Take a hot bath scrolled past her mind's eye, but climbing out of bed, going downstairs, and undressing again seemed as insurmountable as Mount Everest.

Gracie had stood with Ralph's comforting arm around her shoulders, bathed in the pulsing blue and red emergency lights, watching as Jett's body, zipped in its bleak cocoon of white plastic, had been loaded onto the ambulance for its ride down the mountain. She had ridden back to the station with her teammates, accepted without feeling the decision to postpone the after-mission debrief, and declined Ralph's offer to drive her home, instead driving herself and remembering nothing whatsoever of the trip.

As shock and cold gradually subsided, Gracie's shivering body stilled. She reached over to snap off the lamp on the floor next to the bed, hoping that sleep might come. But along with the darkness, the horrors of the last few hours rushed back in a kaleidoscope of images and sounds and the gruesome snapshot of Jett's body gnarled in death.

Gracie catapulted from the bed, snatched her fleece robe from a hook on the door, and hurtled down the stairs to the kitchen.

For the next hour she made and ate chopped green olives and cream cheese on a sesame-seed bagel, ran the gamut of satellite TV stations a dozen times, and placed twenty-two pieces in the jigsaw puzzle that occupied one half of her kitchen table. She ate the rest of a bag of cold, soggy popcorn left over from a movie-watching marathon several nights before, washed down with the rest of the Alice White and two glasses of Carlo Rossi Sangria.

Somewhere between reruns of *All in the Family* and a home-shopping program hawking "raw tanzanite!" Gracie fell asleep on the living room couch.

IN the cool shadow of the west-facing deck of her cabin, Gracie lay on the chaise longue burrito-wrapped in her favorite purple chenille afghan. From her aerie at the top of the winding dead-end street, she looked out over the rolling patchwork of evergreens and housetops nestled between two long mountain ranges.

The day was perfect—the sky clear and blue with huge, brilliant white cumulus casting shadow mosaics across the valley. The air was filled with the sweet scent of pine and sage and the twittering gossip of birds hidden in the surrounding trees. A hummingbird whirred past Gracie's head and hovered at the feeder behind her. A chickadee called its loud three-note whistle from a nearby pine.

The world continued on.

As if nothing had happened.

As if Jett wasn't dead.

At six thirty that morning, the clock radio blaring in the

loft upstairs had snapped her awake. Ribs tender, hips bruised, every muscle protesting the effort, she had pushed herself up from the couch and plodded into the kitchen for a giant panda mug of double-strength Folgers Instant and two Extra Strength Tylenol. Bleary-eyed, still half-asleep, she had driven up to camp and waved good-bye to the departing campers with a pasted-on smile.

Back home again, she poured herself another mug of coffee and wandered out to the deck. For the next few hours she lay on the chaise contemplating life and death and Jett McKenna.

Her friend had liked things neat, orderly, compartmentalized, at one time explaining to Gracie that external order helped keep the internal demons at bay.

But there was nothing neat or orderly about the way she had died.

Why in the world had she been driving down the hill the front way? She abhorred the Arctic Circle, terrified that someday she would go over the side. To avoid the treacherous twisting stretch of highway, she would willingly tack an extra hour of driving onto a trip in order to take the "back" way up or down the mountain.

So why, this time, had she been driving the front way?

Her body ejected from the car indicated she hadn't been wearing her seat belt. If she had been, she might still be alive.

The longer Gracie thought and reminisced and evaluated, the more puzzled she became. The unanswered questions swirled inside her brain until the sun had crept high enough to flood the entire deck with light and her stomach rumbled with hunger. She creaked to her feet and, with the blanket still clutched around her shoulders, plodded back inside and into the kitchen.

Gracie lifted the last desiccated slice of Pizza Pizza from the grease-stained box in the refrigerator, picked a circle of pepperoni from the congealed cheese and popped it into her mouth.

As the refrigerator door swung closed, the blinking red light of the answering machine on the counter caught her eye.

How long had it been since she'd checked messages? Two days? Three?

She punched Play, then turned around, leaned against the counter, and took a bite of pizza.

The first message was from Ralph. "Hi, Gracie girl."

"Hey, Ralphie."

"It's Tuesday. Seventeen hundred hours. Confirming you know there's no meeting tonight because of the search."

Shit. When *was* the last time she had checked messages? *What day is it today? Who the hell knows?*

The next message was from her mother, Evelyn. "It really is a must that you call me, Grace Louise. I've left you two other messages."

Gracie took a bite of pizza.

"Gracie, love, it's Rob." The resonant baritone voice filled the room and Gracie choked on her pepperoni. "I'm in L.A. for a fortnight. Thought I'd ring you up."

Gracie sagged into one of the ladder-backed kitchen chairs, pizza drooping onto her leg.

"Uh, I wondered . . . ," Rob said. "I would love to see you, Gracie." He cleared his throat. "If you're interested, that is. In seeing me, I mean. I could take a couple of days. Drive up there to Timber Creek . . . if that would be all right with you."

Gracie smiled. Rob Christian—probably the only celebrity in the world who got tongue-tied calling a girl.

"If you'd like to ring me back," Rob continued, "my mobile is . . ." He left the number and signed off with a "Hope to hear from you, love."

Gracie set the pizza slice on the table and rubbed her greasy hands on her sweatpants. She had forgotten how the sound of Rob's voice made every nerve in her body hum like a plucked harp string, how it sent a warm—

"They're evil!" Jett's voice screeching from the machine plunged an axe through Gracie's heart. "What they're doing—"

Gracie launched from the chair, slapped an open palm on the Stop button, grabbed the Ranger keys from the counter, and ran out of the cabin.

GRACIE PUSHED HERSELF up the steep mountain road, trying to ignore her bruised ribs and sore muscles and joints. She had tried counting backward from one hundred keeping in time with every footstep. She had hummed every Disney tune she could think of, but she couldn't erase the sound of Jett's voice from her brain. "They're evil!" she had screamed. "Evil! Evil!"

Gracie reached the top of the hill where the road widened out into a large cul-de-sac at an abandoned mine. Mounds of rusted steel and mine tailings punctuated the site. A large berm of rocky dirt hid the rest of the valley from view.

At the end of the road, she jogged in place for a full minute, blowing out her breath through her mouth and feeling her heart rate slow.

Who had Jett been talking about? Who was "evil"? Who was "they"? Someone at camp? At her church? It might be someone Gracie didn't even know, but why then would Jett have left Gracie that message?

It had to be someone from camp, she decided, but who?

Certainly not Jay. He was her spiritual mentor. She loved him like a father.

Serene? The woman's animosity seemed directed at Jett, not the other way around.

Eddie was a big flirt, harmless enough. So far nothing he had done had been anywhere close to what could be considered evil.

Gracie jogged forward out of the cul-de-sac and headed back down the road into the valley, mentally ticking through the rest of the camp employees.

Emilio, who was sixteern or seventeen and helped in the kitchen, was painfully shy and always polite to Gracie.

Meaghan was a little strange but not evil.

About Jay's wife, Elaine, and Eddie's wife and kids, and the two women in housekeeping, Gracie knew almost nothing.

There was the guy Jett had been dating until recently. *What was his name?* An old-time cigarette brand. Lucky Strike? Camel? *Winston.* That was it. She knew nothing about Winston either except that Jett had been dating him hot and heavy for a couple of months. Then, suddenly, she wasn't.

Gracie held her pace down the dirt road to the bottom, hanging a right at the intersection of two trails onto the final approach to the parking lot.

All this speculation was pointless, she decided. Even though the sound of her friend's voice stabbed with a physical pain, she needed to just suck it up and listen to the entire message.

Gracie skidded to a stop.

She had heard something. Off to her left.

She held her breath and listened.

There it was again, the sound of splashing water. But that made no sense. The only water in the area was Greene's Lake, flush with spring snowmelt and glinting in the distance.

She scanned the wide swath of field with its line of pines beyond but saw nothing out of the ordinary.

The sound came again. It was definitely water. Then another sound she couldn't decipher.

Gracie stepped off the trail, bushwhacking through the field, knowing she would be picking foxtails and other pricklies out of her socks later, thankful that she hadn't changed into shorts for her run.

A hundred feet in, she stopped to listen and heard splashing again, louder this time.

She trotted in the direction of the sound until what looked like a large hole in the ground came into view. As she drew closer, the opening yawned into four-foot-square well partially obscured by tall weeds.

Gracie stepped up to the edge and looked down.

Liquid brown eyes looked back her in fear, pleading for help.

CHAPTER

11

FOUR feet down, paddling for its life in the dark, murky water was a dog. A heavy chain attached to its collar was dragging it down.

A dead mule deer floated in the water beside the dog. Milky eyes, bloated, hairless skin mottled pink and brown, the decaying carcass smelling so foul, Gracie's coffee rose as acid in her throat.

Thoughts streaked through her brain. *Climbing rope. The Ranger. Take too long. Dog would drown. Get help. Cars driving by. Take too long. Dog would drown.* "Oh, God. Hang on! I'll get you out of there." Gracie sat down at the edge of the well and swung her legs over the side. Anchoring herself in place with handfuls of weeds, she inched herself down until her toes touched the two-inch-wide wooden frame running around the well's perimeter two feet above the water's surface. She crouched down, balancing toe to heel.

The dog paddled toward her.

Letting go of the weeds with one hand, Gracie grabbed onto the collar and hauled sixty-plus pounds of panicked dog toward her.

The collar pulled off. The dog splashed back into the well and disappeared beneath the surface.

"Shit!"

Gracie wobbled on her perch and almost toppled in after. She grabbed onto weeds again and held on.

The dog's head reappeared, only just above the surface. It was foundering, the eyes losing focus.

"Hang on! I'll get you." She crouched down again. With both hands, she grabbed the dog by the ruff of its neck. Then she surged upward with a yell, pushed up with her legs, and heaved its front legs up onto the weeds.

The dog clawed with all four legs—on the wooden frame, the weeds, Gracie's arms, her legs.

She shoved its hind quarters with her shoulder.

The dog flopped full length onto the ground.

Gracie crawled out of the well and sprawled on the ground next to the dog, gasping for air, soaking wet and so vile-smelling that she gagged and vomited coffee into the weeds. She rolled away, stuck her face close to the ground, and inhaled the sweet scent of dried earth and weeds.

It took a full minute for Gracie's stomach to stop churning. She rolled back over and, breathing through her mouth, looked over at the dog lying a few feet away, dazed and panting.

It was mostly black with white paws and a white diamond on its nose. Ribs and hip bones showed beneath the long, wet fur.

"Okay, boy, girl, whatever you are," Gracie said, pushing herself up to her hands and knees. "How about we get you home for a bath and something to eat? Then we'll try to find out who belongs to you."

The brown eyes looked up at Gracie. The black tail thumped the ground, flinging an arc of water into the air.

Gracie stood up and watched the animal stagger to its feet. Then it shook itself, starting at its head and working down to the tip of the tail, flinging water in every direction.

"Ready to go now?"

The tail swished back and forth.

With the dog at her heels, Gracie cut diagonally through the open field to the parking lot where the Ranger was parked. "Whoever owns you has trained you well," Gracie said over her shoulder.

She dropped the tail gate of the truck. "I don't suppose you know to hop in." The black tail wagged again.

After several failed attempts to get the dog to jump in by itself, Gracie finally lifted the animal's front paws onto the tailgate, then hefted its rear end in. She slammed the tailgate closed and plunked down the back window.

Pulling a towel from the cargo space behind the front seat, she laid it down on the driver's seat and climbed inside. But everything about her smelled so rank that she climbed right back out.

With the truck in between her and road, Gracie stripped off her clothes, tossed them into the bed of the truck, and wrapped herself up in a paper-thin silver emergency space blanket pulled from her SAR pack.

She climbed back into the truck and drove out of the parking lot.

At the bottom of the steep, circuitous hill leading up to her cabin, Gracie stopped the truck in the middle of the street. Two junked cars were parked haphazardly in the middle of the road.

Gracie had owned her little cabin at the top of Arcturus Drive for almost ten years. For the past few years, the Lucas family had lived in a ramshackle bungalow at the bottom of the hill. The red cinder block looked as if it hadn't been painted in thirty years. Rain transformed the front yard, strewn with dirty toys, broken furniture, and car parts, into a big mud wallow. Mr. Lucas's junked cars, in various stages of disrepair, littered the neighborhood. The property was pulling down real-estate values in the neighborhood, its owners the perpetual cloudburst on Gracie's life of sunshine.

Gracie had seen Mrs. Lucas exactly three times in four years. The impression she retained was stick thin with stringy hair and a cigarette between her lips. She remembered Mr. Lucas, seen only once from a distance, as larger than mammoth. The family pickup, white and giraffe-spotted with rust, sported a Confederate flag decal and a gun rack in the back window.

So far, numerous complaints lodged by neighborhood residents to County Code Enforcement had been without result. Rumor had it that Mr. Lucas supplied the county inspector with weed.

Gracie started to plant the heel of her hand on the horn to get someone to come out and move the cars, then thought better of it. A silver blanket over bra and panties wasn't really the ideal attire for a confrontation. "Hard to be a hard-ass when you look like Chief Joseph from Another Planet," she crabbed to herself. She inched the Ranger past the cars, front and left tires a half inch from the drainage ditch. Then she roared the rest of the way up the hill to the cabin.

GRACIE KILLED TWO birds with one stone and took the foul-smelling dog into the shower with her. The animal, which she determined to be female, stood docilely, head and tail drooping, while Gracie scrubbed the black fur with her own shampoo. It took a third shampooing and a condition to completely rid the fur of the smell of rotting meat. By the time Gracie toweled the dog dry, she and the animal both smelled as flowery as a perfume-drenched blue-hair in church.

Bright eyes tracked Gracie's every move from the doorway as she grabbed sports bra and panties from the clothesline in the mudroom and pulled them on, followed by a pair of khaki shorts and a Camp Ponderosa T-shirt pulled from the dryer. She dumped her sweats, underwear, socks, sneakers, and towels into the washing machine and punched Sanitize. The wadded-up space blanket she shoved into the garbage can next to the garage.

Back in the kitchen, the dog wolfed down a half dozen eggs scrambled up with milk and a leftover turkey burger. Then she curled up on a folded towel in the corner like she owned it and went to sleep.

Looking down on the sleeping dog, Gracie realized with a pang that it felt warm and nice to have something besides death and grief to occupy her mind. "Except how the hell are you going to take care of a dog? You killed a cactus, for cripes sake."

From beneath the answering machine, she pulled the Timber Valley telephone book—the size and thickness of a cheap novel. In the past week, no dogs had been reported missing with the local animal shelter nor with the valley's one radio station, KVLY. She put in a request for a public service announcement about a found dog, hung up the phone, and looked over again at the animal, now sleeping.

"You look so cute. All curled up into a little ball," she said. "Like a big black Jelly Belly." She shook her head. "Do *not* get attached. You'll regret it when you have to give her back."

Gracie had lived alone for ten years. That's the way she liked it.

Or at least she used to.

On the search the previous Thanksgiving, she and Rob Christian had been stranded by a blizzard. Living with him for several days in a tiny makeshift shelter had forced her to interact with someone other than the men on the team, to actually hold a conversation about something other than Probability of Detection or how to assemble a nine-to-one mechanical advantage system. Since then, she had felt herself thawing, willing to risk sticking a baby toe into the maelstrom of social interaction.

Ralph was in her life, but he didn't really count because she could no more live without him than without green olives or Rachmaninoff or hummingbirds.

And then there had been Jett, a kindred restless spirit, their blossoming friendship cut short by her death.

The thought drew Gracie's eyes back to the answering machine. She still hadn't listened to Jett's message and really really didn't want to. The loss was so fresh, hearing her shrieking voice would feel like pulling off a brand-new scab.

Instead of pressing Play on the answering machine, she picked up the telephone and dialed the number for Rob's cell phone, mentally girding her loins as it rang on the other end.

She exhaled when voice mail picked up. "Hi, Rob," Gracie squeaked. *Gad. Lower your voice.* "Nice to get your message," she said in a more normal tone. "Um, I have some free days coming up. Let me know your schedule and we'll . . . um . . . see what we can do about . . . um . . . hooking up." *Um!* "Well, that was lame," she said, hanging up the phone. She heaved another sigh and studied the dog lying in the corner of the room. "What am I gonna call you?" White socks on its forepaws, sleek black fur, little white diamond on her nose. "You look like Minnie Mouse. Is that your name? Minnie?"

The dog opened her eyes and looked up at Gracie.

"Don't get too comfortable. You hear me, Minnie?"

The dog thumped the towel with her tail.

Gracie's eyes slid back to the answering machine. She sighed, pressed Play, and skipped through the messages. Then, with eyes closed and forehead pressed against the cupboard door, she listened.

"They're evil!" Jett screeched into the phone, almost unintelligible. "What they're doing is evil! I have it all down! In my journal! Goddam jackpot! You have to help me. I don't know who else to trust. I'll call you when I get home."

"I'll call you when I get home." Except Jett had never made it home. Instead it seemed she had headed down the hill by way of the Arctic Circle and launched herself over the side of the highway to her death.

THE Ranger glided up Cedar Mill Road toward camp.

That morning, Gracie had prowled around the cabin with a nervous energy, turning on the television, turning it off, lying down on the couch, getting up again, pacing the living room, trying and failing to not think about Jett until she couldn't stand herself anymore and decided to drive up to camp.

Once again, Minnie had refused to jump into the bed of the truck. This time, when Gracie lifted her inside, she jumped right out again. Resigned to the fact that the dog would have to ride on the seat next to her, Gracie opened the passenger's door. Minnie sailed inside, hopped over the seat, and lay down on the mound of gear Gracie kept piled there in case of emergency: sleeping bags, blankets, tent, gallons of water, signal flares and mirrors, containers of food, cooking utensils, and a stove. Apparently Minnie had decided the pile of gear provided her with the perfect bed.

The Ranger bounced off the asphalt onto the dirt road leading up to camp.

Minnie's warm, not entirely disagreeable breath tickled the back of Gracie's neck. She looked at the dog in the rearview mirror. "I'm not going to get sucked in by you," she said to the bright eyes looking back at her in the reflection. "I am not keeping you." She looked back at the road. "Do you hear me?"

The pickup crested the final rise before camp and rolled up to the Gatehouse. Gracie pulled into a parking space beside Jay's red pickup. Leaving the windows generously cracked for Minnie's benefit, she walked up the front walkway, into the building, and down the main hallway.

A sound from Jay's office stopped her just outside the door. She peered around the corner into the room.

Jay sat behind his desk, head bowed, hands clutching his voluminous hair, substantial body shaking with sobs.

Before Gracie could back up and leave the man with his grief, Jay looked up and saw her. "Oh, Gracie! Come in! Come in!" He waved her into the room while wiping his red-rimmed eyes with a tissue.

Gracie stepped into the room, stopping inside the doorway. "I want . . . wanted to tell you how sorry I am. About Jett. I know how much she meant to you. She said . . . she said more than once how much you meant to her, too."

"Thank you, my dear." Jay smoothed back the silver hair with both hands. "Thank you. Have a seat. Have a seat."

Gracie stayed where she was. "Are we . . . Is there going to be a . . . some kind of service for her? Here at camp, I mean?"

"Oh, yes." He searched around on his desk, moving papers around, lifting up books. "Tomorrow. In the little chapel. Eleven o'clock." He gave up the search and wiped his eyes again. "I'll be giving the eulogy, you know."

"Is there anything I can do to help?"

"No. No. Bless you for asking, but Elaine has the situation well in hand. She's very organized, you know. And efficient. Very efficient. Have a seat."

The urge to turn around and run back up the hallway was almost irresistible. But so was the need to ask the questions she had come there to ask. Gracie walked into the room and perched on the edge of one of two metal folding chairs opposite Jay.

He folded his hands on top of his desk and bowed his head.

Seconds passed. Somewhere on the other side of the building, the water heater knocked.

Gracie squirmed in her seat, looked down at her ragged fingernails, and thought about getting a manicure for the first time in her life before deciding it wasn't worth the money—they would just get ruined again on the next search. She looked up at the ceiling, then out the window. Finally she exaggeratedly cleared her throat.

No response from Jay.

What the hell? Is he asleep? "Uh, Jay?"

"Yes," he answered, without lifting his head.

"Can I ask you something?"

He looked up, took a deep breath, and smiled at her. "Of course, my dear. Of course. You should know by now you can talk to me about anything, ask me anything."

"Do you . . . do you know where Jett was going? That day? I mean, she was driving down the hill. I wondered if you knew where she was going?"

Jay's smile froze in place. "Where she was going?"

Gracie nodded. "She hated the Arctic Circle. She was scared sh . . . to death that someday she'd go over the side. You probably already knew that. I've been wondering where she was going. She had called in sick, right? Could she have been going to see a doctor or something? Did she mention anything to you?"

"Well now." He repositioned his substantial weight in his chair. "I'll have to think about that, won't I? Well. Well, I have no earthly idea where she was going. The poor girl's dead. Why could it possibly matter?"

"And why wasn't she wearing her seat belt?" Gracie continued, ignoring his question. "If she had been wearing it, she might still be alive."

"But the car . . . I heard it went . . . way down . . . way . . . down."

"It did. But I've seen it before. Two people in the same car. Over the side. Three hundred feet down. The person wearing the seat belt survived. The person who wasn't . . . didn't."

Jay leaned back in his chair, rocking slowly. "That's truly remarkable. I didn't know that. Well—"

"I just can't figure it out," Gracie said, thinking out loud. "She always wore a seat belt. She put it on to drive from one end of the Serrano parking lot to the other. Why wasn't she wearing it while driving on the Arctic Circle?"

There was something about the way Jay was staring at her that made her stop. He sat unmoving for several seconds, as if gauging, calculating. Then he jerked forward in his chair, placed his elbows on the desk, and covered his face with his open hands. "The pain is still so fresh. She was like my own daughter, you see. And I was like a father to her. She loved me, looked up to me for guidance, for strength. She struggled so with the temptations of her sex."

Gracie frowned. "The temptations of her—?"

Jay looked up at Gracie with fresh tears in his eyes. "The Lord put me before her to guide her away from the darkness and into the light. I did everything I could to save her from eternal damnation. Everything I could. But she was weak. So very weak."

"I . . . I'm . . ." *I'm outta here.* Gracie pushed herself to her feet. "I—" she tried again.

Jay dabbed at the corner of his eye with a finger. "Come. Gracie. Pray with me." He held out both hands across the desk. "Pray with me."

What was she going to say? *NFW do I want to pray with you*? She slowly sat back down, reached out, and took his hands.

Jay closed his eyes and tilted his head back as if catching the rays of the sun. "Our heavenly Father," he began. "God of God, light of light, Gracious Lord of Lords. At the end of days, in the glory of Your rapture, we shall lift our eyes to the gates of heaven and see Your holy face."

Jay prayed for Gracie, for himself, for others at camp, for those at her church who knew Jett, for their pain to be assuaged, for Jett to be delivered from her many sins and taken up into the bosom of Jesus.

At first, Gracie listened, thinking how the operatic cadences of Jay's voice would have done the Met proud. When one minute stretched into three, she stopped listening and started thinking how hard it was getting to hold on to his sweaty hands and that she was going to need a chiropractor to get the kink out of her neck.

When he launched into an appeal for the Almighty to just forgive Jett for her womanly weaknesses of the flesh, her feminine sins of immodesty and lust, Gracie jerked her hands in irritation, but Jay held on.

When he finally finished the prayer another five minutes later with an "Amen and amen" and let go of Gracie's hands, she almost leaned across the desk and punched him in the nose.

Jay opened his eyes and smiled. "How'd I do?"

"Fine," Gracie said, nodding like a bobblehead doll. She stood up and wiped her hands surreptitiously on her shorts. "Gotta run," she said, and escaped from the room.

"God bless you, Gracie," followed her up the hallway.

Holy cow, she mouthed to herself as she walked up the hallway. *Womanly weaknesses? Feminine sins? Did we do the time warp thing back to the seventeenth century?* She stopped in the middle of the front office, hands on her hips. "What a weirdo male chauvinist . . . weirdo." She looked back down the hallway. *And you're hiding something.*

Multiple telephones with different ringtones jangled throughout the building. "I'll get it," Gracie called and grabbed up the phone on the desk closest to her. "Camp Ponderosa. This is Gracie. May I help you?"

"There's a bear in here!" a voice hissed into the phone.

"Who is this? Serene?"

"There's a bear in here!"

"A bear? Where are you?"

"The dining hall! I don't know what to do. Tell me what to do!"

"Uh . . . try to scare it away. Make a lot of noise. Beat on a pan or something."

"I'm scared! I don't know what to do."

"Okay. I'll be right there." Gracie hung up the phone. Not wanting to complicate things by adding Jay into the mix, she said nothing to him, instead clumped down the basement steps and out through the shop. *Good thing camp's deserted*, she thought as she cut across the maintenance yard. The weekend groups had already left and the Adventures "R" Us ninth-grade retreat group arriving that afternoon wasn't due in to camp for another couple of hours. Things could get complicated in a hurry with a bear among campers.

Gracie walked down a wooded embankment, leapt across the creek at the bottom, then climbed the hill on the opposite side, emerging from the trees across the parking lot from Serrano Lodge.

Off to her left, Eddie on the bright orange camp tractor was disappearing down Main Road at triple the posted speed limit. "Why aren't *you* coming to Serene's rescue?" she wondered aloud.

From where she stood, she could see the front door of the lodge was propped open with a rock. No wonder there was a bear inside. An open door was an engraved invitation for all sorts of wildlife to come snooping.

She mentally scanned the layout of the building, chiding herself for not asking Serene where exactly in the huge building she was or, more significantly, where the bear was. If she went in through the front door, she might surprise the animal in the hallway, not a particularly desirable prospect.

The only bears in the valley were black, all the resident fifteen-hundred-pound grizzlies killed off by hunters in the nineteenth century. Bears in and of themselves didn't scare her, but they were incredibly strong. The previous summer she had watched a medium-sized bear rip a tree stump apart as if it were made of tissue paper. Still, for the most part, the ones that showed up in camp were big scaredy-cats looking for an easy snack.

Gracie clambered over the boulder fence onto pavement and circled around the end of the building to the back entrance of the kitchen. The screen door's rusty hinges squeaked as she slipped through. She tiptoed up the darkened hallway. "Serene?"

No response.

The kitchen was deserted. Gracie crept past the giant

prep table to the swinging door leading out into the dining room. She nudged it open a crack with an elbow, stuck her nose through, and took in the scene in a single glance.

At the far end of the fully lit room, Serene crouched on top of the upright piano. Ambling up the aisle between the long rows of tables, heading straight for Gracie, was a bear cub, its black fur dust-powdered to gray.

Gracie felt the first tingling of fear—not because a baby bear was inherently dangerous but because its presence meant the mother was somewhere nearby. A mother of any species protecting her young was arguably the most dangerous natural force on the planet. Tangling with a mother *Ursus americanus* defending her cub was dead last on Gracie's afternoon to-do list.

She ducked back into the kitchen and grabbed a large stockpot from the counter and a metal serving spoon from a drawer. Then she pushed back into the dining room and beat on the bottom of the pot with the spoon. The sudden noise blasted the room like a bass drum.

With a bleat, the bear cub swung around and loped back down the aisle and out the side patio door, which stood wide-open.

Gracie trotted down the aisle, reaching the door just in time to see the bear disappear into the trees at the bottom of the hill. "See ya, little guy." She kicked up the door stopper, pulled the door closed, and turned back toward the dining room. "It's gone, Serene."

Serene had climbed down from her perch and now stood next to the piano with her hands covering her face.

Gracie walked up to her. "The bear's gone," she said again. "Nothing like a little—" She stopped as she realized that Serene was crying. She put a tentative hand on the smaller woman's shoulder. "It's okay, Serene. The bear's gone."

"I'm sorry."

"It's not a big deal. We just won't prop open the doors from now on."

Serene threw her arms around Gracie's neck, clutching her like a life preserver, her entire body trembling. "I'm so sorry!" she said between sobs.

"It's not really that big a—"

"I didn't really mean it!"

It dawned on Gracie that Serene wasn't weeping about the bear but about something entirely different. "I'm sure you didn't really mean it," she said, patting the smaller woman's back because she didn't know what else to do and wondering exactly what it was that Serene had done that she didn't really mean and for which she was so sorry.

CHAPTER

13

SIDE by side, Gracie and Serene walked down Lake Road hill, in the cool of the shade of tall pines and oaks. Up ahead on their right, the lake, edged with tall willow bushes, came into view, green and glittering in the sun.

Gracie inhaled, preparing to ask Serene exactly what she had done that she didn't mean when the woman said in a loud voice, "I hate bears! Hate them!" Her hands were tight fists, brows furrowed. "They're *evil*!"

Gracie managed to keep walking without a hitch in her step. There was that word again: *evil*. Surely its use by Jett and now Serene was no coincidence. "Hard for me to consider bears evil," she said carefully. "They're just doing what comes naturally. That little bear was probably just looking for a snack. He was a lot more afraid of you than you were of him."

Serene looked over at Gracie as if the concept were completely foreign to her. "I don't know," she said in a quieter voice. "Maybe."

At the bottom of the hill, Serene gestured off to her left where the three single-wide mobile homes were visible only as side-by-side peaked roofs above the tops of the scrub oak. "Can . . . can I show you something, Gracie?"

There was something so hesitant, so shy about the woman's invitation, Gracie was certain if she declined, she would never get another chance. "Sure," she said, and followed the smaller woman along a path cut through a brown coverlet of fallen oak leaves and pine needles, then up the front steps of the trailer and inside.

Gracie stopped just inside the living room and looked around in surprise. With brown wall-to-wall carpet and faux-wood paneling trimmed in dark brown the tiny room might have been dreary and claustrophobic and depressing. But intricate multicolored quilts covered the sofa, an armchair, and every open space of wall, rendering the room bright and cheerful and welcoming. Flowers, animals, trees in vibrant purples, blues, greens, reds, pinks, and yellows. Braided rugs added ovals of color to the floor.

"Wow, Serene," Gracie said, peering closely at the intricate stitching of a quilt hanging on the wall next to the front door. "Did you make these?"

Serene nodded. "I make up the designs in the summer and sew them all winter." She stood in the middle of the room, brown eyes wide, arms intertwined like vines, hands tucked beneath her chin, shoulders hunched as if waiting for a blow to fall. Everything about the woman shouted an intense need for approval, for validation, for a friend.

"They're incredible," Gracie said with a smile.

The woman's wide smile transformed her dour face into beautiful. The brown eyes shone. The forehead smoothed. Her teeth were straight and white. "You do what you can with what you're given," she said.

"Do you ever sell them?"

"Oh, I could never sell them. They're not good enough."

Gracie looked over at her. "I don't know where you got that idea, but they're definitely good enough."

Serene's eyes sparkled. "Really? You really think they are?"

"I really do."

Serene bit her lower lip as if waging an internal debate. Her eyes lifted to Gracie's. "Can I, like, show you something else? A secret?"

"Okay." Genuinely curious, Gracie followed the other woman down a short hallway into a bedroom. The decor of the minuscule room echoed that of the rest of the cabin—stitched and flounced twin-bed coverlet, floor rug, and wall hangings—animals, trees, and flowers, all in gay colors.

From a cracker-box closet bursting with clothes and boxes, Serene dragged a rifle, so heavy she could barely lift the barrel off the ground.

Whatever Gracie had thought Serene's secret was going to be, this wasn't it. She took a step backward. "Holy shit, Serene. Where'd you get that?"

"Jimmy. My brother. He got it in L.A. He knows how afraid I am. It makes me feel safe, ya know?"

"Do you know how to use it?"

"You just point it and pull the trigger. That's what Jimmy said."

Oh, terrific.

The smile on Serene's face was wiped clean by something close to panic. "Nobody knows I have it. Not even Jasmine. Please don't tell Jay."

"I'm not going to tell Jay."

Serene turned away and stashed the rifle back inside the closet behind a stack of cardboard boxes. "Guns in camp are against the rules."

On that one, at least, Gracie thought, *I'm with Jay.*

"He would, like, fire me in no time flat if he ever found out I broke the rules. I need this job. It hasn't been easy for Jasmine. Living way up here. So far away from kids her own age, but I can't afford to live anywhere else, and . . ." She stopped, staring unseeing out the side window. "And I feel safer here."

"How old is Jasmine?" Gracie asked. "Eighteen?"

Serene's eyes moved back to Gracie. "Seventeen." She half smiled with exasperation. "You know. Seventeen going on, like, thirty-five. She can't wait to get out of here. Be on her own. She wants to go to college."

"Good for her," Gracie said, meaning it.

"Oh, yeah. She's that smart, you know. She wants to be a chemical engineer."

"That's impressive."

"A chemical engineer. Whatever that is." Serene gave a little laugh. "Yeah, she's that smart. She doesn't get that from me. I'm not very smart. She gets that . . ." She stopped.

The room was so silent Gracie could hear the sound of the tractor outside somewhere.

Then, with a visible shake of her head as if to derail her thoughts, Serene asked, "You want something to drink? You want some lemonade?"

"Sure. That'd be nice."

Gracie followed the smaller woman out of the room.

"I like you, Gracie," Serene said over her shoulder as she walked back up the hallway. "I mean, you're nice." She thought for a moment. "I'm glad you're here."

"Thanks. I'm glad I'm here, too."

In the kitchen, Gracie pulled out a chair and sat down at the oval table.

Serene fussed about the room, opening and closing the

refrigerator, opening and closing the cupboards. "Jay didn't want to hire you, you know."

"Oh, yeah?"

"I heard Eddie and him, like, yelling about it one time. Eddie's been running the ropes courses. Did you know that? But the church told Jay he had to hire you to do it instead. Something to do with training and insurance and risk or something like that. I didn't understand it all." She poured pink lemonade from a plastic pitcher into purple plastic glasses. "Eddie was pretty mad 'cause he likes doing it—the ropes course. I don't know why Jay was mad. Maybe because Eddie didn't like it."

"I wondered about that," Gracie said. "About how he felt about it." She fingered the ceramic owl salt and pepper shakers sitting on top of a pile of paper napkins in the middle of the table. "Jay doesn't seem to like women very much, does he?" she asked finally. "Or at least he seems to think they're all weak. Don't you think?"

Serene stopped picking out little wafer cookies from the package and looked over her shoulder at Gracie, an enigmatic expression on her face. "I don't know," she said. "Maybe. Eddie's not that way." Then she turned away again and concentrated on arranging the cookies into a multicolored pinwheel on the plastic plate.

"I think he doesn't quite know what to do with me . . . about me working here. I don't quite . . . fit in with—"

"I do know he told Eddie they just needed to get through the summer." She straightened a single cookie, then another. "I don't think I should have said that."

"Can I ask you a question?" Gracie asked.

"Okay."

"About Jett?"

Serene slammed her fist on the counter and swung around

to face Gracie. Her eyes sparked with sudden anger. "No! I don't want to talk about *her*."

"Sorry. I know you and Jett didn't get along . . ."

"Didn't get along? Right! She was a bitch! And a . . . a . . ."

A slut? "But," Gracie continued, "do you know where she might have been going when—"

"She was *doing* it with Eddie, you know!"

"Buhhh," Gracie spluttered. She shook her head, frowning. "I don't think . . ."

Serene's fingers bit into the edge of the counter behind her. "They were, like, *doing* it," she spat. "I *know*. I found . . . I found—"

Gracie didn't really want to know what Serene had found. "Maybe. Once. But that was a while ago. Jett doesn't . . . didn't really like Eddie. In fact, I think she—"

Serene grabbed up the glasses of lemonade and banged them down on the table so hard that the pink liquid splashed onto Gracie's shirt. "She just couldn't keep her dirty hands off him!" She practically threw the plate of wafer cookies onto the table. Several slid off the plate, across the table, and onto the floor.

Serene's in love with Eddie. The realization hit Gracie with the force of a two-by-four. Of course. That was it. "I'm sorry," she said, bending to pick up the cookies and place them on the table. "I never should have brought it up."

Serene scraped the other chair back and sat down hard, chest heaving, sucking air in through her nostrils. Then she banged her elbows on the tabletop and pressed her knuckles to her eyes. "No, I'm sorry," she said, her voice breaking. "I'm sorry. Can I talk to you, Gracie?" she asked in a whisper. "About something that's been weighing on my heart?"

"Of course."

The screen door in the living room creaked open, then banged closed.

Both women froze. Footsteps stomped through the living room and down the hall. A door slammed.

Silence.

"Jasmine," Serene whispered.

Gracie nodded and squeezed out a smile.

Serene pushed her chair back and stood up. "I have to get back to the kitchen."

GRACIE SAT CROSS-LEGGED on top of a tower of granite boulders as high as a ten-story building. With her eyes closed, head tipped back, she breathed deeply, drinking in her surroundings. The gentle, cool air brushing her arms. The pungent scent of dried sage. Blue sky ceiling. The music of wind whispering through pine needles. Below her, towering spires of pine and spruce and fir. Beyond the valley a tapestry of russet and brown, gray and green, encircled by dark green mountains. Timber Lake, shimmering like a sapphire garland.

This was Gracie's cathedral. More than any man-made edifice ever could, this was what brought her closer to her God.

She breathed peace deep into her lungs.

The sound of voices sifted into her consciousness, growing louder until, with maximum maneuvering, talking and laughing, a group of what sounded like college students climbed up onto the boulder behind her.

She didn't move, keeping her eyes closed, trying to ignore them, trying to hang on to the mood.

"Hi, Rachel," a women yelled. "Guess where we are right now? Castle Rock! I know, right?"

"It's awesome!" a man shouted.

Someone picked up a rock and tossed it over the side. It bounced once, twice, then disappeared into the brush below.

"Back up, Josh." Others chimed in. "Yeah, back up, moron. Farther. Farther." More talking. Laughter. Jostling. "Cut it out. That's not funny." A squeal. More laughter.

"Excuse me," a female voice said. A pause, then more insistently, "Excuse me."

Gracie opened her eyes and looked up at a young face a foot from her own. "Can you take a picture of us?" The young woman was holding out a cell phone.

Gracie smiled up at her. "Sure," she said, and pushed herself to her feet.

GRACIE AMBLED ALONG the sun-dappled dirt road, heavily timbered with oak and yellow pine, that meandered through the back acreage of camp. She reveled in the cool shade of the trees and thought of how, in an hour, the one-dimensional paper doll that had been the Sourpuss in the Camp Kitchen had blossomed into Serene, a three-dimensional woman with fears and secrets and an incredible creative talent, marveling especially that someone with such a dour exterior could produce something—so many things—bright and cheerful.

She wandered past the Tent Village, a collection of large white canvas tents built on permanent wooden platforms, and wondered about the secret Serene had wanted to share, what it was she hadn't meant to do and was so sorry about, and how she was, Gracie was certain, in love with Eddie.

Back at the high ropes course, Gracie turned off the soaker hoses she had left watering the giant pines that held the element cables. She climbed the wooden steps up to the flats, waded across the soft sandy rectangle of the swim beach, and stood looking out over Lake Ponderosa.

A long wooden dock, overdue for a fresh coat of white paint, jutted out into the lake. Three canoes tethered to one side reflected red oblongs onto dark water. A pair of mallard ducks paddled casually away, the drake's head feathers an iridescent emerald.

Gracie pushed the long sleeves of her T-shirt up over her elbows and felt the high-altitude sun burning the virgin skin on her arms. By the end of the summer, all the little freckles would have merged into one big freckle presenting a reasonable semblance of a tan. A feather breeze blew pine-scented air past her nose. All was calm, peaceful, quiet. *I'm in heaven*, she thought. *I could stand here forever and never get tired of it. I'm* happy *here.*

Gracie left the swim beach and walked down Lake Road to where, at the intersection with Main, water gushed out of a pipe in the ground. She swallowed an icy handful, then sauntered along Main Road past the end of the lake.

Somewhere up the hill on her right, a tractor started up, intruding on the afternoon quiet. There was a crashing of underbrush. Gracie turned her head in time to see a black bear lope out of the woods straight at her.

CHAPTER 14

GRACIE froze.

The bear was small for a black bear, but it was big enough. It had slowed to a lumber and was heading straight for Gracie.

Shit!

Running away would only attract the animal's attention. If it was already agitated, no telling what might happen.

In slow motion, Gracie stepped backward into the lake shallows and ducked out of sight behind a bank of willows. She waited. Seconds later, the bear chuffed past her into the lake, sending the ducks paddling furiously away. It emerged onto the swim beach, dripped across the sand, and disappeared down the treed embankment of the high ropes course.

Well, that was interesting, Gracie thought. *Kinda early for bears to be coming down out of the high country in search of water.* She waited another half minute until she felt positively ridiculous standing in ankle-deep water, then splashed out of the lake, leaving a trail of muddy footprints in the dirt.

With water puddling around her boots, she stood on the road looking up the hill toward the sound of the tractor. Her eyes slid over to where the roofs of the side-by-side single-wide trailers showed among the trees. She considered for a moment, then sloshed across the road, through the leaves and up onto the little porch of Jett's trailer.

The front doorknob was loose, the latch stiff, but it was unlocked. She pushed the door open. First wiping the mud and grit from her boots on the mat, the word *Welcome* worn to a shadow, she stepped into the living room and stood just inside the doorway.

The trailer's layout mirrored Serene's, but the contrast between the two couldn't have been greater.

Diffused light filtered in through fly-specked windows. Dark brown carpet and wood paneling. Sagging furniture. Heaps of clothes, piles of magazines and books, dishes, CDs, and DVDs. The dark room felt morose, depressing, a window into Jett's tortured spirit. Gracie's shoulders sagged.

Without turning on the lights, she wandered into the kitchen and opened the refrigerator, studying the contents: a half loaf of white bread, two eight-packs of cheap diet cola, a half-consumed box of Velveeta cheese. In the tiny bathroom, she inhaled the lilac scent of a bar of cheap soap lifted from the sink. In the bedroom, she fingered a rhinestone-studded scarf draped over a dented lamp shade next to the bed. Then she sank onto the rumpled, unmade bed. With hands covering her face, Gracie wept.

GRACIE WALKED SLOWLY along the path leading from Jett's trailer and turned onto Main Road, thinking somber thoughts until she found it impossible to ignore the growling of the tractor up the hill on her right.

What's Eddie doing up there anyway?

Leaving the road, she climbed diagonally up the hill, pushing through thick stands of scrub oak, stepping over fallen logs, homing in on the noise until she stopped next to a ponderosa pine three feet in diameter.

She peeked out from behind the tree.

Two hundred feet away, at the far end of a large rectangle of bare earth, Eddie rode away from her on the tractor, its back blade scraping the dirt smooth.

As Gracie watched, the tractor swung around and headed in her direction. Cold tendrils of apprehension tickled the back of her neck and she ducked back out of sight. Leaning against the rust-colored plates of bark, she listened as the tractor chugged to the near end of the field, swung around and headed away again.

She peeked out again and watched the tractor bounce across the field, then leave it altogether. The chugging grew louder as it passed by on the road below, presumably on its way back to the shop yard.

When all was silent, Gracie picked up a sturdy stick from the ground and walked out onto the dirt. Kneeling down, she dug at the soil with the stick.

Finally, with sweat trickling down her temples, she sat back on her heels and stared down at what she had uncarthed.

Banana and orange peels. Foam packing peanuts. Food cans. Plastic water bottles. Coffee grounds. The handlebar of a girl's bicycle. An open paint can oozing celery green.

"No wonder there are bears in camp," Gracie said aloud. Eddie was burying the camp's trash—some of it hazardous waste—on camp property. "They have their own private smorgasbord courtesy of one Eddie Wilson."

"Hulloooo, Gracie."

Gracie yelped at the caramel voice so close behind her and stiff-armed the ground to keep from toppling over sideways.

This time there was no doubt in her mind. Eddie had crept up behind her in stealth mode with the express purpose of scaring her.

Gracie pushed herself to her feet, turned around and glowered at Eddie head-on. "You have a bad habit of sneaking up behind people," she snapped. "Don't *ever* do that to me again."

Standing only six feet away, Eddie looked like a Marlboro cigarette ad. Glaring white T-shirt rolled up at the sleeves showed off tanned biceps, hands thrust in the back pockets of his Levi's, straw cowboy hat pushed back on his head, toothpick in the corner of his mouth.

The green eyes flicked down to Gracie's muddy boots, then inched up her body, taking in her droopy wet socks, scratched legs, dirt-covered knees, shorts, and T-shirt, finally moving up to meet her blazing brown eyes.

"I didn't sneak, darlin'," he drawled, dimples showing. "I walked. I can't help it you didn't hear me comin'. What're you doin' here, Gracie?" The question held only mild interest.

Gracie's cheeks flamed with anger. "I guess I could ask you the same question." She waved a hand at the dirt field behind her. "What are you doing here?"

Eyebrows lifted in feigned ignorance.

"You're burying trash."

A single shoulder shrugged as if to say, "So?"

"*Why?*"

"Why?" Eddie looked around as if to an audience. "It saves the camp money?"

"It saves . . . Aren't there dumping laws?"

"Pro'ly." The grin was cocked off to the side of his mouth. "But who's gonna find out?"

"What about runoff into the lake?"

"There ain't no runoff."

"People swim in the lake. *Kids* swim in the lake. They drink the water out of the pipe." *I drink the friggin' water out of the friggin' pipe.* "It could be a health risk."

"Don't worry about it, Gracie."

"Isn't this private land? The church's land?"

Eddie blinked back at her.

"Do they know what you're doing?"

The green eyes narrowed. The cocky grin vanished. The toothpick moved to the other side of his mouth. Eddie took a step closer.

The image of a snake coiling, readying itself for the strike, flashed in Gracie's brain. She had pushed Eddie too far.

CHAPTER

15

THE image of a snake coiling faded back into Eddie standing so close in front of Gracie that she had to tip her head back to look up at him. She smelled aftershave along with a hint of wintergreen from his toothpick. He smiled down at her and drawled, "What're you gettin' yourself all worked up for, Gracie?"

Alarm bells clanged in her ears. She had no illusions about being able to win a wrestling match with Eddie. It always stunned her how physically strong the average man with average-sized muscles was. Eddie wasn't average-sized. And neither were his muscles.

She took a step backward. Then another. And another. She lifted the heavy stick. "See ya, Eddie."

Eddie didn't move. He just grinned back at her, giving her the two-fingered salute. "See ya 'round then, Gracie."

On Gumby legs, she turned and started walking down the hill. When she was sure Eddie couldn't see her through the trees, she ran the rest of the way down the hill and jumped down onto Main Road.

Anger spurred Gracie up the hill leading to the upper portion of camp. Whether he had intended to or not, whether she had imagined it or not, Eddie had scared her and she didn't like it. Heavy stick still in hand, feet squishing inside her boots, she glanced over her shoulder every twenty feet or so to make certain that he wasn't following.

She stormed past the rec field and the Serrano parking lot where a yellow school bus and several cars were disgorging a laughing, highly charged group of ninth-graders and adult chaperones in the throes of moving into the lodge.

By the time Gracie climbed the hill leading up to the Gatehouse, she was breathing hard from fast-walking a quarter mile uphill at over eight thousand feet.

Madison Bonds's silver and white Toyota FJ was parked where Jay's truck had been.

The adrenaline rush from fear and anger had bled off leaving her exhausted and cranky and wondering if Jay wasn't there, why the hell was Madison?

She walked up to the Ranger, remembering suddenly that Minnie had been waiting for her in the truck all this time. "Shit." Gracie wasn't used to having a being other than herself to care for. So far, she decided, she sucked at it.

But the dog seemed no worse for wear for her time spent on her little bed behind the driver's seat. When Gracie opened the door, she peeked out from her bed, tail thumping the blanket. When Gracie said, "Come on, little girl," the dog jumped over the back of the seat and out of the truck.

With one eye on Minnie attending to her doggie needs across the road, Gracie sat on the tailgate of the truck and exchanged waterlogged socks and boots for a pair of Tevas, which left her pruny feet feeling light and cool and airy.

When Gracie whistled, Minnie trotted back across the road and hopped right back inside the truck, over the back of the seat and lay down on her bed. Gracie closed the door after her and leaned in through the open window. "Good girl," she said. "I'm not keeping you."

Gracie found Madison sitting behind the desk in Jay's office, perky blond ponytail pulled through the back of a khaki-colored Adventures "R" Us baseball cap, blue nail polish matching an Adventures polo shirt.

"Hi, Madison," Gracie said from the doorway.

"Oh! Hi, Gracie," the woman chirped an octave too high. "I'm just leaving this for Jay. He said it was okay. He has to spend a lot of time in the kitchen now that . . . nowadays." She drew her pink tongue across the flap of a large manila envelope, sealed it by pounding it with the heel of her hand, scribbled something on the front with a blue marker, and propped the envelope up against the stem of the desk lamp. Then she stood up and brushed past Gracie in the doorway, smiling into her face. "See ya! Wouldn't want to be ya!"

I need a drink, Gracie thought. *A fruity rum drink. With a little purple umbrella.* She watched the substantial hips in too-tight khaki shorts bada-boom up the hallway, belatedly remembering the conversation she was going to have with Madison about dress code with The Sky's the Limit campers. She sighed, walked into the office and plopped down into the warm chair Madison had just vacated. Too bad alcohol wasn't allowed in camp. She would keep a stash of those little airplane bottles in her desk downstairs.

She leaned back in the chair and rocked and thought about Eddie. Eddie dumping trash on camp property. Eddie with his bulging muscles standing way too close.

Was Eddie dumping trash the evil Jett had talked about in her telephone message? Was that the jackpot? Dumping trash on someone else's property was probably criminal. And while die-hard environmentalists might call it evil, Gracie was fairly certain that wasn't what Jett meant.

Plus, Jett had said "they." Who was they? The Brothers Wilson?

To Gracie, the camp was like a thoroughbred to be pampered, nurtured, coaxed to its full glory. Instead it was unkempt, just shy of seedy. Jay didn't seem to care about the camp of which he was steward or for the environment in general. Maybe he knew what his brother was doing and he simply didn't care.

Jett had said she had everything written down in a journal. "I wonder where that journal is," Gracie said. Her eyes traveled over the clutter on her boss's desk, alighting on the manila envelope Madison had left propped up against the lamp and on which she had written the name of the ninth-grade retreat group in a flowery script, the i's dotted with little daisies.

Names and meal schedules and other boring retreaty-type stuff, Gracie figured.

Her eyes moved to a single sheet of paper resting on top of a pile of camp brochures. She leaned forward and picked it up and scanned Jay's scribbled thoughts about Jett for her memorial service. She replaced the paper and leaned back in the chair again, studying the knots in the pine ceiling.

Go home, Kinkaid.

She didn't move. Usually the thought of being home in her little cabin offered comfort, warmth, peace. Today being at camp made her feel closer to Jett.

The phone on the desk rang. Gracie grabbed up the receiver and barely listened to a woman from All Seasons Ice wondering when they were going to get paid. She scribbled down the name and number on a message pad for Jay, hung up the phone, and leaned back in the chair again.

Where might Jett have kept a journal?

Jett had dyslexia and hated writing anything by hand. Something as extensive as a journal she probably would have kept on a computer. Since Jett didn't own one, the most likely would be the computer in the kitchen office in Serrano Lodge.

CHAPTER

16

GRACIE turned on the desk lamp on Jett's desk, thought better of it, and snapped it off again. Enough light filtered through the closed miniblinds on the window opposite for her to see.

What if someone finds me in here snooping around? she wondered, and felt her palms begin to sweat.

She had moved the Ranger from in front of the Gatehouse down the road leading away from camp, parking it out of sight in the shade of a boulder the size of a small house. Then she had circled back behind the Gatehouse, taking the shortcut through the woods to Serrano where she pushed through the noisy, milling crowd still moving into the lodge, ducked around the corner into Jett's office, eased the door closed, and locked it.

Sitting in the armless secretarial chair, she pushed aside the enveloping sadness by reminding herself that she was doing exactly what Jett would have wanted and turned on the computer. With toes tapping the carpet, she waited as the pre-Cambrian system booted up.

None of the documents were password-protected, a pretty good indication that nothing of real value was stored on the computer. Jett might have been a high-school dropout, but she was savvy. A journal about camp was too potentially explosive to keep on an office computer without protecting it from prying eyes. Still, not wanting to take the chance of missing anything, Gracie methodically opened every file of every folder, scanning the contents, closing it, and moving down the list to the next one. She found nothing anyone might remotely consider evil, except possibly a recipe for calf's brains.

A check of every drawer in the desk uncovered no flash drive or CD or anything else on which a journal might be stored.

Gracie glanced at her watch. She had been in the office for more than an hour. Time was pressing in on her. *Think, Kinkaid. Think.*

Somewhere in the building doors slammed, making Gracie jump. Feet pounded up the hallway. "Come on. We're late!" Voices and laughter gradually diminished to silence.

Gracie exhaled and leaned back in the chair.

Maybe Jett didn't leave the journal around the office at all. Maybe she kept it with her in the suitcase-sized satchel she carried everywhere.

But where was the satchel?

Odds were Jett had it with her when she was driving down the hill at the time of her accident. But how was Gracie going to find out for sure?

Her stomach growled audibly, reminding her that she hadn't eaten anything since breakfast. Leftover roast beef sounded perfect.

Gracie turned off the computer and slipped into the

hallway, now deserted and silent. The farther she got from
Jett's office, the greater her relief and the straighter her back.
By the time she pushed through into the dining room, she felt
as if, in fifty feet, she had evolved from *Australopithecus
africanus* back into modern woman.

She pushed into the kitchen itself and stood in the open
doorway.

Every light was on, the radio on a shelf opposite the door
was blaring, but the room was empty.

Gracie let the door swing closed. "Serene?"

No answer. Or at least nothing she could hear above the
din. She walked around the butcher block table and turned
the radio down to the decibel level of an acid rock concert.

She hauled open the door of the walk-in refrigerator and,
not liking to close herself completely inside, propped the
door open with a box of paper towels. If she was lucky, there
would still be leftovers from Sunday's dinner. If Eddie had
already been there, the shelves would be picked clean.

It was apparent that Eddie felt the camp benefit of feeding
its employees during work hours included transporting home
most of the leftovers along with large quantities of toilet
paper, cereal, and soda.

When Gracie had contemplated aloud to Jett about speaking with someone at the church about Eddie's light fingers,
her friend had flown into a tizzy, subjecting Gracie to a
thirty-minute tirade about how this had been going on for
years and no one at the church gave a rat's ass about what
went on at the camp and the only result of her saying anything would be that she would be out on her ear in a blink.
Compelling argument to keep one's mouth shut.

Feeling mildly guilty that she hadn't done enough work
that day to warrant a meal herself and vowing to go without
some other day to make up for it, Gracie loaded her arms with

industrial-sized containers of butter and horseradish, a half loaf of Wonder white bread, a Saran-wrapped plate of sliced roast beef, and a single Dr Pepper and backed out of the walk-in. She dropped the food on the prep table and slapped together a sandwich, then returned the rest of the food back inside the walk-in.

She took a bite of sandwich and washed it down with a sip of soda. Mid-chew, she froze.

She had heard something. Down the back hallway. A thump of some kind.

She swallowed. "Serene?"

She held her breath to listen. No answer. She reached back and turned down the radio even further.

She heard the noise again—a muffled bump.

Gracie's heart started a loud, steady pounding in her ears, making her realize with irritation how skittish her encounter with Eddie had left her.

She looked down the dimly lit hallway leading to the back door.

Empty.

She heard another bump and what sounded like a groan.

Goose bumps shivered down Gracie's arms.

There was definitely someone—or something—in the closet near the back door.

She tiptoed down the hallway and stopped. Another step brought into view a foot wearing a jellied lime green flip-flop. It was pressed flat against the doorjamb at waist level.

Another step. Gracie's eyebrows shot up. Her mouth dropped open.

A tiny butterfly tattoo showed on the outside of the woman's ankle. A twist of white cotton panties dangled from a slender thigh. A small feminine hand clutched the back of the startlingly white T-shirt with the sleeves rolled up. Levi's bagged around white muscular legs. A bare butt pumped rhythmically.

Sonofabitch!

Serene and Eddie. Going at it in the storage closet.

Gracie turned and shot back up the hallway. Grabbing up the soda and sandwich, she raced out of the kitchen, through the dining room and out the side patio door. "Friggin' hell! I wish I hadn't seen that! Eddie's white ass forever imprinted on my brain! Friggin' *hell*!"

GRACIE TURNED THE Ranger off the Boulevard and onto Arcturus. She drove up several blocks of straightaway leading up to her cabin for the umpteenth time, seeing nothing in front of her but Eddie's startlingly white butt cheeks.

She jammed on the brakes and drooped in her seat.

The road in front of Lucas house was totally blocked again, this time by a bright red Firebird with tinted windows and an old dented black pickup parked so far out on the pavement that she couldn't even edge the Ranger past without putting a tire into the drainage ditch.

She felt Minnie's cold, wet nose touch the back of her neck and reached back to scratch the dog's ear. "A drug deal," Gracie informed her. "Or two."

Over the past several years, there had been multiple raids on the Lucas house, but so far, much to the frustration of local law enforcement and the residents on Arcturus, no drugs had been found.

Gracie slipped the Ranger into Reverse, backed down the road and turned onto a cross street. Driving through adjoining neighborhood streets, she reemerged ten feet up from the offending vehicles, turned back onto Arcturus, and drove up the road to her cabin.

GRACIE sat on the living room couch, enveloped in the purple afghan and the halo of light from an antique floor lamp, with Minnie curled up on an old blanket at her feet. Occasional strains of Vivaldi crescendoed from the CD player in the far corner. A half-drunk Coors Light sat in a puddle of condensation on the sea chest serving as a coffee table.

Outside the temperature was already in the low fifties; inside, the cabin was warm from the day's solar gain. Even so, Gracie shivered and pulled the afghan up around her shoulders.

So Serene is screwing Eddie.

Serene was having sex with a coworker, the brother of her boss, a married man, the husband of someone with whom she attended daily Bible Study.

So Eddie is screwing Serene.

Mousy Serene with the perpetual scowl. Eddie was

married to Amanda, tall and graceful with her shining strawberry blond hair and sparkling blue eyes. And while, according to Jett, not the sharpest pin in the sewing box, Gracie had thought, on meeting her, she seemed a genuinely nice person.

So why would Eddie tipple moonshine when he had Chivas Regal at home?

Because he can, that's why. And because he's a skank.

Once again, Eddie's white ass pumped in her mind's eye. "Ick!" She shook her head to try to dislodge the vision from her brain once and for all. "Visualize something better than that."

What was better?

Anything.

A tinny piano playing "Für Elise" sounded from Gracie's cell phone atop the sea chest. She ignored it, not even bothering to see who was calling. Balancing on one foot on the northwest corner of the deck railing fifteen feet above the ground was the only way she could use her cell phone at home. Even then she could maybe hear only every third word. Anyone she would want to talk to knew to try the landline first.

The phone stopped ringing. Five seconds later the telephone in the kitchen rang. Gracie waited until the answering machine picked up and listened as her mother left an urgent sounding, "Grace Louise. I need to talk to you."

Gracie stayed where she was.

With Evelyn, everything was a calamity. A ding in the Lexus was cause for a double Dewar's on the rocks. The groundskeeper missing a leaf on the expansive Grosse Pointe Farms lawn could prompt a crimson-faced tantrum, naturally out of earshot of the neighbors.

Evelyn's crisis du jour could wait.

Gracie realized that the roast beef sandwich gobbled

down on the drive home from camp had already worn off
and she was hungry again. She flipped off the afghan and
padded into the kitchen. Minnie trailed after her and curled
up on the towel in the corner.

Gracie yanked open the freezer, pulled out a chicken
alfredo and broccoli dinner, threw it into the microwave,
and punched the 1 Minute button twice.

Glancing over at the answering machine, she noticed the
little red message light was blinking again. She leaned over
and pressed Play.

"Gracie, love." Rob's rich baritone filled the kitchen.

Crap. When did that one come in? She needed to check
her messages more often.

She listened to Rob telling her he was working the next
couple of days but would be free for several days after that.
Was there any way they could get together? He would be
happy to drive up to Timber Creek. Or she could come down
to the city. All she needed to do was tell him when and where.

The message ended and Gracie considered driving down
to see Rob on her day off.

The microwave dinged. She pulled out the little tray,
stirred the steaming noodles with a fork, and put it back in
to cook for another couple of minutes.

"Grace Louise," came her mother's voice from the
machine. "I need to talk—"

Gracie hit Next, skipping over the rest of the message.

With an emotion suspiciously similar to relief, she noted
there was no message from anyone claiming Minnie.

The microwave dinged a second time. Gracie grabbed
the tray of food and another Coors Light from the refrigerator and sat down with her dinner at the kitchen table.

As she ate, thoughts and events from the last week
whirled in Brownian motion inside her head. Jett's death.

Bears in camp. Serene in love with Eddie. Jay lying about something. Eddie burying trash. Serene and Eddie going at it in the storage closet. Jett's message. The spooky Meaghan.

There were so many disparate pieces she wasn't sure how they all fit together. Or if they were even all from the same puzzle.

But there was something—a *lot* of somethings—going on at camp. Maybe it was sitting on some kind of magnetic anomaly that caused everyone to act whacky. Or maybe it was just that everyone there was a close-knit bunch of dysfunctional misfits. Or maybe she had just forgotten what it was like to work in close proximity to . . . people.

The telephone on the counter rang again. Again Gracie waited until the answering machine picked up. Ralph's voice said, "Hi, Gracie girl."

She jumped up from the table and snatched up the receiver. "Hi, Ralphie."

"I don't want to talk to some shrink," Gracie said, and took another swig of her Coors Light.

She and Ralph sat on the sprawling deck of the Evergreen Restaurant, looking out over Timber Lake and reveling in the cool air of a summer night in the mountains.

When Ralph suggested they meet for a beer, Gracie agreed, even though she was certain he would force the issue of the kiss and their relationship, not letting her ignore the issue until it went away on its own.

But as they talked, comfortably catching up on mundane things, discussing SAR team business, without the subject of the kiss ever being broached, Gracie began to relax and enjoy the evening.

Ralph had listened with an amused half smile on his face as she acted out finding Minnie and detailed her unsuccessful efforts to locate her owner.

"So where's the dog now?"

"In my truck." She added with an indulgent smile, "Lying on the gear behind the front seat. I think she likes it there." She shot Ralph a look. "I'm not getting too attached to her if that's what you're thinking."

"Whatever you say," he said, tipping back his bottle of Stroh's.

Halfway through their second round of beers, the real reason for the invitation out became clear when Ralph steered the conversation to the body recovery and Gracie's mental well-being.

"I don't need to talk to some shrink," she said again, and stretched out her long legs, crossing one sandaled foot over the other.

The light from the faux lantern on the café table between them sharpened the angles of Ralph's sun-weathered face. On the lake, the lights from boats out after dark appeared as starbursts of color on liquid satin. The bright orb of a nearly full moon rising in the east tossed white ribbons across the water.

"We should come here more often," Gracie said. "The Saddle Tramp is too smoky. And crowded. And loud."

"You're covered by the Sheriff's Department's workers' comp," Ralph began.

"I know that," Gracie said, annoyed that her attempt at changing the subject hadn't worked. "I can talk to you."

Pushing the candle lantern aside, Ralph reached across the table and took Gracie's hand in his. He looked at her, his eyes kind. The lines his wife's death had carved into his face made it somehow even more beautiful. The calluses on his fingers felt hard and rough on her palm. "You need to talk to a professional about this," he said. "The woman was your friend."

"I'm fine," she said with finality, pulling her hand away

and concentrating on peeling the silver label from her beer bottle. "Have you talked to Lenny? How's he doing?"

Ralph looked at her for several seconds, then leaned back in his chair. "Lenny'll be fine. He, at least, was smart enough to realize he needed to talk to a professional."

"It was his first over-the-side. So did he say anything to you about it?"

"Are you sure you want to hear this?"

"I wouldn't ask if I didn't."

"He was okay with everything. Even finding the arm. What was giving him trouble was putting the . . . her . . . in the body bag."

"Oh. They had to break . . . it . . . her . . . to fit her in?" Why the hell was she asking that? She *really* didn't want to know the answer.

"No. She had already lost rigor."

Gracie shook her head. "You're right. I don't want to hear about it. Do you know if they hauled the car up out of the canyon? Or did they just leave it down there?"

"They hauled it up."

Gracie looked over at Ralph. "Really? Do you know if they found her purse, a big satchel?"

"Her purse? No. I don't know. Why?"

"No particular reason." She drained her bottle and set it on the little table, knowing without seeing that Ralph was watching her, waiting. "Jett kept a diary—a journal. I think it may have been in her purse. I want to read it."

"Why?"

Gracie opened her mouth to answer, then closed it again, uncertain of how much she wanted to reveal to Ralph about Jett, about what was going on at camp. She finally told him about the answering machine message Jett had left. "There are too many unanswered questions about . . . everything.

About why Jett was driving on the Arctic Circle. Without a seat belt. About where she was going." She stared off into the distance, her thoughts leading her down a dark path she didn't want to travel. "Too much of it doesn't make sense."

"Let it go."

"But—"

"Don't let your imagination run away with you."

"I'm not." Gracie frowned again and said more to herself than Ralph, "I need to find that damn journal."

Ralph was looking at her. "What are you thinking about doing?"

"Nothing," she said too quickly. "I'm not thinking about doing anything." She didn't sound convincing even to herself. *I have to bone up on my lying skills*, she thought.

"Don't go out and do anything impetuous."

"When do I ever do anything impetuous?"

Ralph gave her a look.

"Quit looking at me like that. I'm not gonna do anything, okay?"

Ralph looked at her for another moment, then turned to look out over the lake. He took another swig of beer and said in a measured voice, "I do know there were no skid marks at the scene."

"What do you mean?"

"They're treating the accident as a possible suicide."

"No way!" Gracie yelled, sitting up in her chair and drawing looks from a couple sitting on the other end of the deck. She leaned over the table toward Ralph and hissed, "There is no way Jett killed herself. Not in a million years. Besides, why leave me that message, then turn around and kill herself? It makes no sense."

"CHP's still investigating. Let them do their jobs."

"They're not doing their damn job if they decided Jett killed herself."

"Nothing's been decided yet. If it makes you feel better, I'll talk to Krueger—"

"I like Krueger."

Ralph nodded. "He's a good man. I'll talk to him about the answering machine message."

"I still have it. I didn't delete it."

"He can determine if it's relevant or not, whether he wants to pass it on or not."

"Okay." Suddenly unable to sit still, Gracie stood up.

Ralph pushed himself out of his chair, stepped around to face her, and put his hands on her upper arms. "They'll figure it out."

She slid her arms around his waist and mumbled into his neck, "Don't ever leave me. I don't know what I would do without you in my life."

"I'm not going anywhere," Ralph said in a quiet voice. He lifted her chin with a finger and kissed her. His lips were dry and hard.

Ralph moved his head so he could see Gracie's face in the dim light.

Disappointed in some way, she half smiled at him.

"This isn't the way I wanted to do this," he said.

"Do what?"

He looked around as if distracted by something, then down at her again. "I love you, Gracie. I want you to be my wife."

Her mouth dropped open. She clapped it shut.

"I'm not rushing you," he said, with the barest hint of a chuckle in his voice. "God knows if I did, you'd run away like I'd set your hair on fire. I don't need an answer right now. But I couldn't go any longer without telling you how I feel."

Ralph looked at her with such warmth and tender love that

she almost said yes right then and there. Instead, she looked down, pretending to examine her fingernails. She couldn't look into his eyes and say what she needed to say, what she had known she would have to say, but for the life of her didn't want to. "I love you, too," was what she finally managed, her voice hoarse. "But I don't . . . I don't think . . ." She rushed through the rest. "I don't think I love you in that way." It felt like her heart was being ripped out of her chest. "But I don't know." She lifted her eyes to his. "I just don't want to hurt you. I just couldn't stand it if you were hurt again."

She knew in an instant she had made a mistake.

Ralph took a step backward. His arms dropped to his sides. The heavy black eyebrows merged into a single line. The blue-gray eyes sparked with an anger so strong it slammed into Gracie with the force of a baseball bat. "I'm only going to say this once," he said in a low voice. "I want you to be happy. I want you to be with the person who makes you happy. If I'm not that person, I'm truly sorry because I believe in my heart that you're the last person on this earth I will love. But it's your love I want, not your *goddam* pity." He turned away and dug his wallet out of the back pocket of his jeans.

"Ralphie . . . ," Gracie croaked.

Ralph threw a twenty on the table and walked away across the deck.

By the time Gracie mobilized her feet and ran after him out to the parking lot, he was already inside his truck and peeling out onto the Boulevard.

CHAPTER

19

JETT leaned back in the plastic chair, bare feet with their black-lacquered toenails propped up on the porch railing of Gracie's deck, black BDU pants ripped short above the knees, black T-shirt dotted with white skeletons. "Don't get much better'n dis," she crooned, holding her face up to the afternoon sun and blowing smoke rings from her Swisher Sweets cigarillo into the air. She looked over at Gracie and grinned.

As Gracie smiled back, Jett's face dissolved into a bare skull, shredded skin hanging from the chin and ears, eyeballs dangling from their orbits.

Gracie yelled.

The skull shifted into Ralph's face in death—skin a dull yellow, milky eyes open, seeing nothing, mouth gaping wide in a silent scream.

Gracie yelled again and sat straight up in bed.

Wet ropes of hair clung to her cheeks and neck. Terror

exploded the breath from her lungs. Minnie sat a foot from the bed, panting with anxiety.

Gracie heard nothing, but a voice in her head telling her that Ralph was dead. "His heart. I killed him."

She kicked loose from the grasping tentacle of twisted sheet and scrambled up from the bed. Stripping off her sweat-soaked T-shirt, she threw on a sweatshirt and jeans. She shoved her feet into Tevas and flapped down the wooden stairs with the dog at her heels.

"Stay here, Minnie," she managed to say in a calm voice, and sprinted outside to the truck.

THE RANGER SPED along the meandering highway which ran along the north shore of the lake, crossing the double yellow lines to cut the curves, flying past a middle-of-the-night driver putting along at thirty miles an hour. Just before the VILLAGE LIMIT sign, the truck hung a sharp right and screamed up the side of the mountain through the twisting maze of roads. It screeched to a stop at the foot of a steep stairway leading up to Ralph's log cabin.

The cabin was dark, the garage door closed.

Leaving the engine running, Gracie jumped out, leapt up the cement steps three at a time, and hammered on the wooden front door with the side of her fist. "Ralphie!"

She waited, heart throbbing in her temples, terror squeezing her throat.

She thumped on the door again. "Ralph! I need to know you're there!" *I need to know you're alive.*

The front porch light flared on like an airport beacon. Relief so intense flooded Gracie's body that she grabbed onto the pipe hand railing to keep from sinking to her knees.

The door was yanked open. Ralph stood in the doorway,

wearing only a pair of gray sweatpants with the word *Army* running down one leg. He held a revolver down at his side. The blue-gray eyes were steel, displaying no sign of love, not even anger, but something infinitely worse—indifference.

"Ralphie," Gracie panted, barely able to draw in a breath. "I had a . . ." She dug away the tears with the heel of her hand. "I had to . . . I'm sorry. I'm so sorry." She swung around and stumbled back down the steps to the idling truck.

She climbed inside, slammed the gear shift into Drive, and fishtailed away from the cabin.

20

GRACIE'S feet thudded on the trail, her breath keeping rhythm with each step. Minnie trotted behind, her black nose inches from Gracie's heel.

Behind her, the sun nudged above the rolling hills—a brilliant fireball shooting fingers of orange light the length of the valley. In spite of the early-morning chill, Gracie was sweating. She pushed the hood back from her head and peeled damp stands of hair away from her forehead.

Returning home from Ralph's, she had fallen back into bed, asleep almost immediately. At 4:26, she awoke with a start.

As dawn lifted the night's veil from the valley, as birds in the trees outside chirped morning greetings to the world, Gracie had sat on the lumpy couch in the living room, wrapped in the purple afghan, Minnie's heavy chin on her knee, trying to write Ralph an apology. Two panda mugs of instant coffee and five crumpled-up attempts later, she had given up, tossing the pen and paper onto the sea chest.

The indifference she had seen on Ralph's face stabbed her with a physical pain. "My heart hurts," she whispered.

The whip of a tail thumped the couch.

Gracie looked down at Minnie. "You still love me, don't you?"

The black head lifted, brown eyes bright. The ears perked up.

She stroked the silky black fur. "Not that I love you." She laid her head back against the couch and closed her eyes. "And my head feels like Henry Higgins's cotton, hay, and rags."

She threw off the blanket and stood up. "Come on, Minnie. Let's go for a run."

NOW AS GRACIE ran, thoughts tossed around inside her head like rocks in a tumbler. Ralph's proposal. Her own blundering response. Jett's death. Eddie dumping trash. Serene having sex with Eddie. Jay lying. Or at least hiding something. Ralph. Jett. Meaghan. Eddie. Ralph. Serene. Jett. Eddie.

"Quit thinking!" she shouted. "Focus on your breathing!" She concentrated on breathing in and breathing out for ten whole seconds before the dust devil of thoughts whirled back again. Something in the back of her brain was nagging at her, insistent, trying to break through into her consciousness, something vitally important that had been overshadowed by everything else that had been happening.

What was it?

Gracie skidded to a stop. Minnie sat down at her feet and stared up at her.

A memory swirled to the forefront. Sitting on the deck of the Evergreen Restaurant. Ralph saying that by the time she and Lenny had reached Jett's body at the bottom of the canyon, it had lost its rigor.

Gracie frowned, staring off into the distance.

The search for Gina Ramirez had been called off on Monday afternoon. Tuesday Gracie had returned to work at camp. Tuesday Jay had told her that Jett had called in sick to work. That night they had recovered Jett's body.

Thinking back now, she realized that, in a state of shock over finding her friend's body, she hadn't noticed that the smell of decay at the scene of the wreckage had been strong, much stronger than it should have been if Jett had been dead only a few hours. The advanced state of decomposition and the loss of rigor mortis meant that, by the time they had found Jett, she had been dead at least twenty-four, maybe even thirty-six hours. Which meant that Jett had died some-time on Monday, possibly even Sunday.

Gracie thought back trying to remember exactly what Jay had said. She was almost positive he had said Jett had called in sick again that morning, Tuesday morning.

There was no way Jett could have called in that morning because she was already dead.

Jay must have been mistaken.

Or he had been lying.

Gracie sat down cross-legged in the middle of the trail. Minnie lay down in the dirt beside her.

Had Jay actually said he had talked with Jett? Gracie couldn't remember his exact words. Maybe Jett had left a message on the answering machine in the camp office and Jay had only gotten it that morning.

That had to be it.

Because what else could it be?

Gracie's breathing slowed. Her heart rate dropped.

Tentacles of apprehension crept up her back as thoughts she had been pushing down, refusing to acknowledge, crowded their way in.

What if Jett's death *wasn't* accidental? What if Jett had discovered something, something evil? What if she had hit the jackpot, whatever it was, and been sent over the side in her car for it? "That would explain a lot of things."

At the sound of her voice, Minnie's tail swished the dirt.

Gracie glanced at her watch. "Dammit." Jett's memorial service started in less than two hours. "Come on, Minnie," she said, pushing herself to her feet and dusting off her behind. "We better go home now or we're gonna be late."

21

OBLIQUE shafts of sunlight poured in through three floor-to-ceiling windows across the wood floor and rows of rough-hewn log pews. At the front of the little chapel, four windows in the shape of a cross looked out onto towering ponderosa pines. Bouquets of flowers—sunbursts of lemon and pink and turquoise—encircled a rustic podium. In the back, a stone fireplace rose up to the wood-beam ceiling. The room smelled of cedar with overtones of wood smoke.

Gracie sat alone in the back pew nearest the door, self-conscious in the first dress she had worn in she couldn't remember how many years.

Finding nothing appropriate to wear among drawers of polypropylene, Polartec, and Gore-Tex, she had climbed the folding ladder into the cabin's attic and dug through multiple boxes of office clothes—remnants of her former life as a Detroit ad exec. She unearthed a slinky black dress, now three sizes too big, disguised the plunging neckline with a purple scarf, and topped it with a black blazer. Since hiking boots or Tevas didn't seem suitable footwear, she dug out a pair of strappy sandals.

Gracie squirmed on the hard wooden pew and plucked at the itchy waistband of the panty hose she had bought at the Quik-Trip on her way through town and stretched on while sitting in her truck parked in front of Serrano Lodge. Forced inactivity made her antsy under the best of circumstances, and the tiny chapel felt claustrophobic and artificial.

She looked around the room, almost full with people, most of whom she didn't recognize, and wondered if someone in the room had murdered Jett.

Jay sat in the front pew diagonally across from her. A fold of neck fat draped over his shirt collar, bright white against his coal black suit. His luxuriant silver hair had been newly cut and coiffed.

Had he said Jett called in sick when she, in fact, was already dead? She might be remembering his words incorrectly. Could he have killed Jett? She had been like a daughter to him. Or at least Jett had thought so.

More fitting with Jay's personality was that someone else had killed her and he was covering up for that someone. Someone like his brother. Jay seemed to look the other way for Eddie all the time. Would he go so far as looking the other way at murder?

Gracie's eyes moved a fraction to the right to Elaine sitting next to her husband. Dull blond hair in a severe Dutch boy cut. Back ramrod straight. Muffins of fat pouring out of the armholes and tugging the seams of her pea green shift.

Meaghan sat beside her mother, looking years younger

than fifteen in a loose-fitting white sweater worn over a navy blue dress. Her head was bowed so that her stringy hair fell forward to obscure her face.

As if sensing Gracie's eyes on her, Meaghan jerked her head around and focused the deer-in-the-headlights eyes directly on Gracie. Then she jerked her head back, swinging the ropey hair back over her face.

Elaine turned to see who her daughter was looking at and fixed beady brown eyes on Gracie. She returned Gracie's smile with a tightening of pale lips, then turned back around to face the front.

Could either Elaine or her daughter have killed Jett? The idea was so farfetched as to be ludicrous.

Serene sat a row behind and a little to the left of the Wilsons. Wearing a plain blue top with a long floral skirt, she sat with her hands clasped tightly in her lap. Her cheeks were splotchy as if from prolonged crying.

Did Serene kill Jett? Gracie wondered. She was in love with Eddie. Or at least she was having sex with him. Serene believed Eddie had also been having sex with Jett and therefore hated her. But had she actually killed her? Was that the thing she had done for which she was so sorry? Serene just didn't seem capable of killing another person.

Jasmine sat next to Serene, wearing a relatively modest black T-shirt and hip-hugging jeans and looking older than her own mother. Her hair was a decidedly unfuneral shade of electric blue. The young woman radiated defiance and hostility—heavily lined, laser-beam eyes focused straight ahead, jaw thrust forward, shoulders hunched, arms crossed over substantial breasts. The general air of hatefulness aside, what motive for murder would the seventeen-year-old have?

And what about the rest of the camp staff?

At the far end of the pew ahead sat Emilio, looking barely

old enough to be shaving. The young man's shining black hair was brushed straight back and he wore a bright white button-down shirt. Staring straight ahead and sitting so still, he looked like a teak statue.

Emilio was always so quiet, his movements so deliberate, almost stealthy, appearing at odd times in odd places around camp, so much so that Gracie had wondered before whether he was up to something, whether he was hiding something.

Maybe Serene and Emilio were in it together, Gracie thought, cooking up their boss's murder along with the chili and corn bread. But, again, what motive would either of them have for killing Jett?

Gracie looked around the room again. The twin sisters from housekeeping, about which Gracie knew next to nothing, weren't present.

Seeing everyone in the flesh made the possibility that any of them had anything to do with Jett's death seem far-fetched. In fact, it made the whole idea of Jett being murdered seem outrageous and improbable.

The chapel door opened. All eyes turned to watch a huge man enter the room and pull the door quietly closed behind him.

The man's arms were the circumference of small trees, his thighs three times that. He was dressed in a white long-sleeved button-down shirt, a gray-and-blue striped tie, and black pants held up by red suspenders. He had a long, bushy beard with no mustache. A New York Yankees baseball cap was pulled down low over his forehead.

Wafting aftershave, the man walked along the aisle behind Gracie and took a seat at the other end of her pew.

A moment later, the chapel door burst open as if it had been kicked from outside and Eddie's wife, Amanda, walked in. Tall with shoulder-length, strawberry blond hair and a

peaches-and-cream complexion. By Timber Creek standards, she was elegantly dressed in a sleeveless black shift
and black sandals. By anyone's standards, she was stunningly beautiful.

But, Gracie noticed, her blue eyes held no vibrancy of
life. It occurred to her suddenly that the woman knew about
her husband's philandering.

Amanda held the hand of the couple's son, Dylan. The boy
was dressed in blue slacks, white shirt, red tie, and black
lace-up shoes. With irresistible dimples, long-lashed eyes,
large and green, and a mop top of chestnut curls, he was a
miniature version of his father. *Nothing but trouble*, Gracie
thought.

Amanda put a light hand on Gracie's shoulder as she passed.

Gracie smiled after her, thinking, *You're too good for
that rat.*

Eddie followed his wife into the chapel. Natty in a black
western-cut suit, bolo tie with a turquoise slide, and black
cowboy boots, he carried his daughter, Sophie, in his arms.

The girl was the spitting image of her mother with reddish blond hair and long-lashed blue eyes. Dressed in a frilly
pink dress, lace-trimmed anklets, and patent-leather Mary
Janes, Sophie's arms were wrapped around her father's neck,
her cheek pressed close to his.

Eddie slammed the chapel door, making everyone in the
room jump. He walked so closely behind Gracie that his hip
would have brushed her back if she hadn't leaned forward.

Amanda led the family up the center aisle to the front of
the chapel. Eddie, deferential to his wife, loving and affec-
tionate with his children, gave the impression of a devoted
husband and father. As he took his seat, he glanced back at
Gracie, caught her watching, and winked at her.

With no effort, she retained her stony glare.

Did Eddie kill Jett? He slept around on his wife. But being an adulterer didn't make him a killer.

As soon as Eddie and Amanda sat down, Jay stood and walked up to the wooden podium at the front of the chapel.

His coloring looks bad, Gracie thought. As though a pink overlay hadn't quite covered up a gray underwash, as though he was going to have a heart attack right then and there.

Accompanied by a young man on an electric piano, Jay led the congregation in the singing of two contemporary, thoroughly unfamiliar songs after which Elaine read a flat, emotionless Psalm 23.

When Jay launched into a meditation that had nothing whatsoever to do with celebrating Jett and her life of faith and redemption, and everything to do with guilt and condemnation and listening to the sound of his own voice, Gracie sent her mind off to wander.

GRACIE LEANED BACK from the little bar table so she wouldn't inhale the chocolate-scented smoke from Jett's Swisher Sweets.

Even though California law dictated no smoking in bars, Saddle Tramp patrons, including Jett, were smoking, paying homage to the law by blowing the smoke in the general direction of the front door, which had been propped open with a large stone.

A red neon Fat Tire bicycle hung in the window and posters for Foster's Lager and Coors lined the wood paneling. Ceiling fans swayed bras hanging from the rafters like wisteria clusters and rippled Jett's plume of hair, an eye-popping fuchsia, which, according to Jett, had nearly given Jay a heart attack the first time he saw it.

Garth Brooks sang at earsplitting volume about spurs

and latigo from a jukebox next to which Jett had insisted on sitting. She played with the straw of her gin and tonic with one hand. The other rested on a Bible lying on the bar table. Jett was the only person Gracie had ever met who saw nothing ironic or wrong with bringing a Bible to a bar. "My life preserver," she had yelled into Gracie's ear when she had mentioned it. "Sink without it!"

Gracie took a sip of vodka and cranberry and leaned forward to try to catch at least every other word of what her friend was saying. Reading her lips filled in some of the other words.

"Jay . . . I'm weak . . . ," Jett yelled, causing several heads to swivel in their direction. "Consumed . . . evil thoughts . . . womanly . . . the flesh . . . need to pray . . . Almighty . . . forgive . . . ho like me."

"Jay called you a ho?"

"As much as."

"You are *not* a ho."

"Unless I repent . . . off the bonds of sinful . . . going to hell . . . burn forever." Her face was contorted in pain. The ruby stud in her left nostril flashed in the light of the jukebox. "Trying so hard! . . . you think . . . to hell?"

"Of course not!" Gracie said, suddenly angry at Jay for foisting his fear-inducing, unforgiving religion on others, especially women, especially someone as emotionally and spiritually vulnerable as Jett. "I think God is loving," she said, deciding it right then and there. "I think He . . . or maybe She . . . is accepting. Of everyone. No matter who you are. No matter what you've done. Why do you believe everything Jay says is the Gospel truth? He just wants to make himself look good and everyone else look bad. He likes calling himself a pastor. Where did he go to seminary anyway? And where's his congregation? I think he's a fraud with a capital *F*. I think a lot of what he says is a big pile of horseshit."

Jett's eyes shot open wide. ". . . spiritual leader."

"Where's the love, Jett? Where's the compassion? Where's the forgiveness?"

"But . . . child of . . ."

Gracie took another sip of vodka and cranberry, then said, "Cat has kittens in the oven, doesn't make 'em muffins."

"WE COME TO you on bended knee, Almighty Father," Jay intoned.

Gracie jerked back to the present and looked around the chapel. All heads were bowed in prayer.

She looked up at Jay. A single tear glistened on his cheek.

Crocodile tears, Gracie thought, still filled with the anger conjured by the memory of her friend's spiritual torment.

"We beseech You that You just forgive our sister, Jett," Jay prayed on. "That You just take her, a lost sheep, full of feminine weakness and sin, into Your loving arms."

22

GRACIE stood in the side patio doorway leading into the Serrano dining room. The relief she felt at the end of the memorial service had lasted as long as the hundred-yard totter in three-inch heels up the dirt pathway from the chapel to the lodge

Small groups of people talking in reverential tones dotted the dining room. Halfway across the room, Jay stood with Elaine beside him, working the room like a politician running for office, smiling, shaking hands, grasping shoulders.

Off to the right, a half dozen teenage girls huddled in a tight circle with Jasmine as its focal point. Several feet back from the cluster of girls was Meaghan, standing alone, head lowered, hands clasped in front of her.

Gracie took a step forward to go over to talk to the girl, but stopped. Directly behind Meaghan, Eddie stood with his arm around Amanda's waist, chatting with another couple, but eyes flicking toward her.

Dylan and another boy a year or so younger dashed past Gracie and into the room, weaving in and out of the crowd. A second later, Sophie followed, pink tongue showing at the corner of her mouth as she struggled to keep up.

Gracie hesitated in the doorway. At the moment, talking with either Wilson brother was as high on her priority list as sucking on a lime without the Cuervo.

Immediately to Gracie's left stretched a banquet table covered with a white paper tablecloth and holding platters of homemade cookies and a large faux-crystal punch bowl with matching cups. The huge man in the baseball cap stood alone at the far end of the table looking mildly ridiculous holding a urine specimen–sized cup in his beefy hand.

Suck it up, Kinkaid, she told herself. *If you can jump out of a helicopter into five feet of snow on the side of a mountain, you can certainly socialize with someone you don't know for two minutes.* She sidestepped over to the banquet table, scooped out a thimbleful of pink punch, and sidled over to the giant man with the teacup. "Hi," she said.

"Hello," the man said in an incongruously high voice. He held out his free hand. "Winston Ferguson."

"Grace Kinkaid," she said, feeling downright Lilliputian standing next to the man who she estimated was at least six foot six.

His warm hand, the size of a bear paw, engulfed hers. "Grace Kinkaid," he repeated as if to cement the name to memory. "Pleasure to meet you." For a moment, he studied Gracie with soft blue eyes. Then he leaned down and looked her full in the face. "I'm Jett's fiancé." He swallowed hard, straightening and shuffling his feet. "Er . . . was . . . her fiancé."

Gracie blinked, unable to think of single response. "Uh . . . I'm sorry for your loss" was what came out of her mouth. Then the Rubik's cube of information clicked into place.

Winston. Jett's boyfriend. *Ex*-boyfriend. Except that Jett had never mentioned anything at all about marrying the guy.

"I loved her very much," Winston continued. In what seemed to be an unconscious gesture, he lifted the brim of his ball cap, wiped his sweat-dampened forehead with a napkin, then settled the cap back onto his head. He drank his punch in one gulp and looked down at Gracie again. "You work here?

"Yeah. For this summer at least. Jett—"

Winston leaned over so that his mouth was a foot from Gracie's ear and asked in a lowered tone. "Are you married?"

What the heck? Is he hitting on me? "No. Not married." *Time to leave.* Her eyes shifted toward Eddie, who, she noticed, was watching her from across the room. He caught her eye, whispered something in Amanda's ear, shook the hand of the man across from him, and headed in Gracie's direction.

Definitely time to leave.

"Nice to meet you," Gracie said, giving Winston's hand another squeeze. "Gotta run." She placed her cup on the table, and made a beeline out of the room.

As the door swung closed behind her, she reflected that Jett had been uncharacteristically closed-mouthed about why she had broken up with Winston except to say that the man scared her. Gracie had met some scary characters. In spite of his size, the soft-spoken giant reminded her more of a really big teddy bear.

What she found strange, however, was that Winston, who had called Jett his fiancée, had seemed to be hitting on her. Even stranger was that he had already been wearing a wedding band.

"**S**AYONARA and good riddance." Gracie wadded her panty hose into a ball and shoved them into the ladies' room trash can. Standing barefoot on the cool tile, she leaned over the counter and squinted at her reflection in the mirror.

Light coming in through frosted-glass bathroom windows and reflecting off walls rendered her skin a sickly green and deepened the hollows of her cheeks. Gray smudges encircled her eyes. "Yow," she said. "Why don't you just change your name to Rocky Raccoon? Or Moaning Myrtle. Or—"

Three girls in their early teens burst into the room and huddled just inside the doorway, whispering and giggling over what Gracie presumed was a cell phone.

"Hi, ladies," Gracie said, bending over to pull her sandals back on.

Two heads surfaced to chirp "Hi!" in unison, then returned to the huddle.

The third girl, the tallest of the group and obviously the leader, turned her back to Gracie, focused on what appeared to be a smartphone in her hands. Blond hair pulled back into a long, sleek ponytail, wearing a yellow long-sleeved hoodie with *St. Kitts* written in white on the front, a curving row of tiny, probably genuine, diamond studs in her left ear. "I only have one bar," she said, stretching the last word into two syllables.

"You're in the mountains," Gracie butted in with a smile. "There's almost no reception anywhere on camp property. And aren't you girls supposed to be doing Chutes and Ladders this morning?"

"Forget it then," the tall girl snapped. "This is *such* a fucking bore!" She spun around and steamed out of the room with the other girls in tow.

Nice, Gracie thought as the door closed behind them. *Madison's ninth-grade group, Madison's problem.* Looks like her facilitators needed to be reminded about the importance of keeping a closer eye on their campers and especially of taking head counts.

She turned back and sighed at her reflection in the mirror.

A click sounded behind her.

Gracie whirled around.

Meaghan stood in the doorway of the toilet stall. Gracie hadn't seen her leave the dining room. She must have slipped past when she was talking with Winston.

The entire time Gracie had been in the bathroom, the girl hadn't made a sound. And there hadn't been any feet showing beneath the stall door. She must have been crouched on the toilet seat, hiding.

"Hi, Meaghan," Gracie said. "Are you all right?"

No response.

Any number of things might be bothering the girl, Gracie

figured. She might just need to talk to somebody, anybody. Even Gracie. She peered into the girl's face. "Do you want to talk?"

The barest nodding of the head.

"Why don't we go and sit outside somewhere?" Gracie said, grabbing the handle of the outer door. "It's a beautiful day."

But instead of walking outside, Meaghan backed up, wedging herself between the wooden partition and the toilet. She motioned for Gracie to come into the stall along with her.

"Okay, let's talk in the world's tiniest bathroom stall," Gracie said as she slid in next to the girl. "Close the door?"

Again, the barest of the nods.

Gracie closed the wooden door behind her.

Meaghan reached around Gracie and slid the latch home. She sat down on the toilet seat, knees off to the side, head lowered, hair hanging forward, hiding her face.

Gracie waited.

Meaghan looked up. A single tear slid down her porcelain cheek. In a soft voice barely louder than a whisper, she said, "I'm going to die."

"What?"

"I'm going to die."

Gracie peered into her face. While she was pale, her coloring in general seemed good. Her breathing wasn't rapid or shallow. "Why do you think you're going to die?"

The head dropped. The hair fell forward. "It's my wages," she mumbled.

"Your what?"

" 'For the wages of sin is death.' Romans 6:23. I'm going to die and go to hell."

"Ah," Gracie breathed, so relieved she almost smiled.

Meaghan wasn't speaking physiologically. She was spouting her father's theology.

Gracie reached out a tentative hand to touch the girl's hair, afraid she might shy away like a skittish colt.

But Meaghan responded like a wilted violet to water, rising to cling to Gracie with her arms around her neck.

Gracie stroked her soft hair. "I'm reasonably certain you're not going to die anytime soon as a result of something you've done."

Meaghan looked up at Gracie, her face clearing. "I—I'm not?"

"No."

"Oh. But I'm weak and I've sinned."

"Everybody sins." Gracie harked back to her years of Sunday school. "I think what that verse means is that if you do something wrong or bad, you're sorry for it and try not to do it again."

"Oh." Meaghan frowned, then said, "You don't think I'm going to hell?"

Gracie smiled. "No. I don't think you're going to hell."

Meaghan thought again for a moment. "Please don't tell anybody what I said."

"Who would I—?"

"Meaghan!" Elaine's shriek out in the hallway pierced the restroom like a dentist's drill.

The girl jerked away from Gracie, eyes wide with what could only be terror. "Don't tell her anything. Please!"

"Meaghan!"

Gracie ripped off several squares of toilet paper and handed them to the girl. "Dry your eyes." She unlatched the door, stepped out of the stall, and into the outer hallway.

Like a bat, Elaine flew down the corridor and stopped in

front of Gracie. "Where's Meaghan?" The woman spat the words, beady eyes blazing, body visibly shaking.

"Hi, Elaine," Gracie said.

"Where's my daughter?"

"In the bathroom."

"What's she doing in there?"

Resisting "What does one normally do in the bathroom?" Gracie answered, "We were just having a chat. Woman to woman."

"Woman to . . . she's a *child*!" Elaine's eyes narrowed with suspicion. "What were you talking about?"

Gracie shrugged. "Periods. Boyfriends. You know."

"She's too young to have a boyfriend!"

The woman's voice was so shrill that Gracie almost clapped her hands over her ears. "I was talking hypotheticals."

Elaine narrowed her eyes even further in a way that reminded Gracie of Eddie. "What were you doing in there with my daughter?"

Gracie's eyes narrowed in return. "I was *talking* with her."

The restroom door opened and Meaghan slipped out into the hallway, eyes round as soccer balls, face drained of color, arms of her sweater clenched in her fists. "Hi, Mommy," she said in a voice much younger than the one she had used with Gracie.

Elaine jabbed a finger at the floor next to her. "Meaghan. Now."

The girl slid past Gracie and stood next to her mother.

"What did she tell you?" Elaine demanded.

Before Gracie could think of an answer, the woman said, "Whatever she told you was a lie. It doesn't concern you."

"I . . ." Gracie fumbled. "She just needed someone to talk to."

"She can talk to her mother. This is family business. *My*

family's business." Elaine swung around, pinched the fleshy part of Meaghan's upper arm and marched the girl back up the hallway toward the dining hall.

"You can call me anytime, Meaghan," Gracie said. "Just to talk."

"She will *not* be calling you," Elaine said, without looking around.

It was possible that Elaine truly thought her daughter would obey her order not to call Gracie. But the look Meaghan shot her over her shoulder told her otherwise.

POOR MEAGHAN, GRACIE thought as she drove the Ranger up the little hill to the Gatehouse. How horribly sad to be raised in that kind of emotionally debilitating, unforgiving environment. According to Jett, the girl was homeschooled, living in a tightly controlled vacuum with no television, no Internet, isolated from her peers. Instead of introducing their daughter to the outside world, guiding her and teaching her how to recognize the wolves lying in wait, Jay and Elaine were raising the girl to be vulnerable and socially inept, to believe she was weak and relegated to second-class citizenship because of her gender. Instead of helping her build the confidence and insight to flourish on her own, they were stacking the deck against her, setting her up to fail.

Gracie wondered again what the girl's "sin" was, what she could have done for which she had been so certain of her own death, both spiritual and corporeal.

Let it go, Kinkaid, she instructed herself. *You don't need to fight that particular battle. What you need to do is keep your head down, your mouth shut, and hang on to your job.*

A rustle of paper drew Gracie's attention to the

passenger's-side floor. *What's that? A mouse? How'd a mouse get inside my truck?*

She pulled the Ranger into a parking space in front of the Gatehouse, leaned over, and lifted the Taco Bell bag lying on the floor.

Triangular head. Unblinking eyes with elliptical pupils. Coiled up in the corner was a rattlesnake.

With a yell, Gracie shoved her door open and half fell, half jumped out of the truck, landing on her hands and knees on the pavement. "Shit! Ow! Hell! Shit!" Rolling over so she was sitting on the asphalt, she examined an abrasion stinging one knee. "Ow!" Then, *"What the hell's a rattler doing in my truck?"*

She picked a stone out of the scrape and flicked it away.

It wasn't that she hated snakes. She loved them, in fact, thinking they were beautiful, mysterious, elegant, and totally cool. She just didn't like them surprising her in her truck. Or anywhere else for that matter.

Gracie kicked off the spikey sandals again, pushed herself to her feet, limped around to the opposite side of the truck, and peered in through the open window.

The snake, tan with brown diamonds running along its back, was still coiled in the cool, dark corner of the floor.

How the hell am I going to get you out of there?

Reaching in through the back window of the shell, Gracie unclipped her trekking pole from her SAR pack. She extended two of the sections to their full length, tightening them in place, then unscrewed the end section altogether. She unclipped a pair of heavy leather gloves from an outside loop and pulled them on.

Grace Kinkaid, Snake Handler. "More like Snake Dinker," she muttered, returning to the passenger's window again.

"Snake Harasser. Snake Don't-know-what-the-*hell*-I'm-doing-and-am-going-to-get-bit . . . -er."

Standing as far away from the truck as possible, she leaned over and pulled the door open. Leaving it ajar, she circled around to the driver's side, climbed in and knelt down on the seat, sucking in breath through her teeth as the rough fabric scraped the raw abrasion on her knee.

Gracie studied the snake, motionless except for its forked tongue flicking in and out of its mouth. It looked about three and a half feet long, not very long for a rattlesnake.

Long enough.

From a Bites and Stings class she had taken for Search and Rescue, she remembered the striking distance for this size snake would be about two feet.

She gently nudged the blunt end of the trekking pole among the coils.

The snake's rattle buzzed. Its head moved back.

"I know I'm scaring you, Mr. Snake," Gracie said in her best snake-soothing voice. "I'm not going to hurt you. I'm just trying to get you the *hell* out of my truck."

With both hands, she lifted a single coil. The weight surprised her. The stick drooped and the coil dropped off the end.

The snake struck, hitting the metal pole.

Gracie reared back in the seat. "Shit!"

Its tail buzzing, the snake recoiled for another strike.

Blowing out a breath, Gracie pushed the end of the pole among the coils again.

The snake struck the pole again.

This time Gracie was ready. With a grunt, she lifted the coils with both hands, moved them off to the side, tipped the end of the pole down, and let the snake slide off out the door. The head followed the body and disappeared.

Leaning forward, Gracie watched the snake glide across the pavement and disappear into the leafy ground cover edging the parking lot.

She sat back and blew out a breath.

While rattlesnakes were indigenous to the area, they weren't that common. Gracie had only seen three in the ten years she had been living in the valley. If the snake had been there when she had driven across town to camp, she was pretty sure she would have noticed.

Someone must have put it in her truck while it was parked in front of Serrano Lodge. That someone was probably Eddie. Because who else would do it?

Was this another one of his so-called practical jokes? If it was, it definitely wasn't very funny. Or was it a warning of some kind? "Whatever it is," Gracie said, backing out of the truck. "Wait'll I get my hands around his neck."

She reclipped her gloves and the collapsed trekking pole to her pack. Still barefoot, she walked up the front sidewalk and into the office to wash the remaining grit out of the scrape on her knee.

In the doorway of the little bathroom, Gracie stopped. From the end of the hallway came the sound of a woman sobbing.

She tiptoed down the hallway and looked into the room on the left.

Serene sat in one of a circle of metal folding chairs, elbows on knees, hands with nails chewed to the quick covering her face.

"Serene?" Gracie said in a soft voice.

Serene's head snapped up, eyes round, fists clenched.

"Sorry I startled you," Gracie said, walking into the room and sitting down in a chair next to her.

Serene dropped her head in her hands again.

"What's wrong?" Gracie asked. "What can I do to help you?"

Serene shook her head. "Nothing. It's too late."

"Too late for what?"

"She hates me."

"She who? Who are we talking about, Serene?"

"Jasmine." Serene looked up at Gracie with red-rimmed eyes, her face splotched with tears. "We had a big fight this morning."

"I'm sure she doesn't hate you. She loves you. You'll work it out with her."

Serene shook her head back and forth. "No. *No*. You just don't understand. She hates me because of him."

"Him? Him who?"

"Jason."

Who's Jason?

As if in response to her unspoken question, Serene said, "Jasmine's daddy. She doesn't understand what he did, why I left him, what happened."

"What"—*Not your business, Kinkaid!*— "did he do?"

"Hit me. He used to hit me." Serene's words tumbled out fast, unstoppable, like whitewater over river rock. "Sometimes for no reason. When he was drinking. When he wasn't drinking. When his coffee wasn't hot enough. When supper wasn't ready when he got home. He called me stupid. All the time. Stupid bitch. Stupid shit. Stupid. Stupid. Stupid. He peed in the toilet, then held my head down in the water. I almost drowned. He hit me with the telephone. Broke this tooth out." She tapped a space where a tooth was missing in front on the bottom. "Once he even threw my Bible out into the backyard."

Gracie blew out a long, slow breath. "Where's Jason now?" she asked. "I hope he's in jail."

"No. He's dead."

"Oh. Shit. What—"

"I killed him."

Oh, shit!

Serene focused her eyes on Gracie. "We were in the kitchen. He was, like, punching me. Punching my head. My stomach. He kept yelling he was going to kill me. 'Once and for all.' He kept saying that. 'Once and for all.' I remember grabbing this knife."

Gracie held her breath.

"It was a pretty big one. Lying on the counter. I got him with it. Like this." As if holding a knife, Serene lifted her hand and jabbed sharply downward. "Only one time. Right here." She pointed to the middle of her chest.

Probably severed his aorta, Gracie thought. *Once was all it took.*

"I don't remember a whole lot after that. He just stood there with his hands out like this on either side. There was a lot of blood coming out. A lot. This big puddle on the floor. I remember him saying, 'You killed me, Serene.' Like he was so surprised. And then he fell down. Kind of like in slow motion. And then he was just . . . like . . . dead."

"Then, uh," Gracie said. "What . . . what happened?"

"Somebody . . . I don't remember who . . . maybe it was me . . . called the police. They came. I got arrested. There was a trial and everything. But they found me not guilty. Self-defense. Because we were in my house. And he was attacking me. Because he had been arrested for hitting me before." Serene put her hands over her face. "But I'm not not guilty! I did it. I killed him. I killed Jasmine's daddy."

Gracie leaned forward and said in a quiet voice, "Serene, I'm so sorry."

"Nobody knows. Not even Jasmine. She was so little

when it happened. She knows her daddy's dead but doesn't know what really happened. I told her he had a heart attack. She blames me for that, too. She thinks he died of a broken heart because I left him. But someday she'll find out what really happened. On the Internet or something. And then she'll hate me even more than she does already. *Oh, God!* You won't tell Jay, will you, Gracie? Please don't tell him. I'll really lose my job."

"I'm not going to tell Jay."

Serene tipped her head back, fists still pressed to her eyes. "And now I've killed her, too," Serene moaned.

"Who are you talking about now, Serene?"

Serene dropped her hands and looked over at Gracie, her face twisted with pain. "Jett. I killed her."

Gracie sat up straight in the chair. *Holy shit! Did Serene just confess to killing Jett?* "Serene," she said in a low voice. "How . . . how did you kill Jett?"

"I prayed for her to die. But I didn't mean it. Not really. I just wanted her gone. Away from here. And now she's dead!"

Gracie sank back in her chair. *Ahhh*, she thought. The guilt that was eating Serene alive wasn't from having committed murder but the good old-fashioned guilt that comes from having prayed for the death of her rival and having her rival actually die. "Serene," she said again, reaching out to touch the woman's arm with her fingers. "I don't know much about how prayer works, but I don't believe that's why Jett is dead."

"Yes, it is."

"No, Serene. It's not."

"But when I asked Jay, he said I was . . ." She stopped and stared at Gracie. "He said that Jett was dead because of my weakness and that I needed to pray for forgiveness and that maybe, someday, the Almighty would forgive me and I wouldn't go to hell."

He would say that, Gracie thought.

"You really don't think it's my fault?" Serene asked, with tears in her eyes. "That she's dead because I prayed for it?"

"No. I don't."

Apparently relief brought a new burst of tears. Elbows on knees, hands covering her face, Serene sobbed.

Shifting in her chair, uncomfortable, not knowing exactly what to do, Gracie put a hand on Serene's back. "I'm sorry, Serene," she said. "What can I do for you?"

"Be here with me?" Serene reached out and squeezed Gracie's hand. "Be my friend?"

"I'm already your friend, Serene," Gracie whispered. "I'm not going anywhere."

CHAPTER

24

AN SUV behind the Ranger honked.

Gracie looked up from her hands gripping the steering wheel, saw that the traffic light had turned green, and pressed down on the accelerator. The Ranger moved forward, third in a long line of east-bound boulevard traffic.

Once again she hadn't been paying attention to her driving. "Someday you're going to hit someone," she chided herself aloud, and tried to concentrate on steering the truck around the long curve of two-lane highway that ran along the southern edge of Timber Lake.

But all she could think about was Jason using his diminutive wife for a perpetual punching bag and eventually paying for it with his life.

Gracie rubbed the round scar on her side with the inside of her elbow. Of their own accord, her thoughts turned east, to Michigan, to Detroit, to Morris, her stepfather, sitting in his favorite chair in the den, Lions football blaring from the flat screen, stinking cigar in one hand, Johnnie Walker Blue Label on the rocks in the other.

Gracie was ten years old when Evelyn married Morris. Initially words had been her new stepfather's weapons of choice—cutting, demeaning, sneering, aimed toward Gracie and her older half brother and sister, Harold and Lenora. Eventually, over time, the abuse had turned physical and increasingly violent—a hand, a fist, a shoe, a belt. And once, finally, when Morris had managed to catch Gracie, the glowing end of a cigar.

"I am never getting married," Gracie said, hands wringing the steering wheel.

She turned off the boulevard and drove up Arcturus. At the bottom of the hill leading up to her cabin, she stopped the truck. "Well, Minnie," she said to the dog lying behind her. "Didn't this day just get a whole lot suckier."

The same red Firebird and a pickup truck with mottled gray and blue paint were parked haphazardly in the middle of the street, again completely blocking the way.

Deliberately engaging in a confrontation with the Lucases was like picking a fight with a mother grizzly defending her cubs—a bad idea at any time. An even worse one now when a red mist of residual anger hung in front of Gracie's eyes.

There wasn't a doubt in her mind that the owners of the two vehicles were taking part in a drug transaction. It was common knowledge throughout the entire valley that if you wanted drugs of almost any quantity or kind, the red cinderblock bungalow on Arcturus was the place to go.

Nothing and no one was visible behind the heavily curtained front windows. Gracie honked the horn, a single toot with the heel of her hand.

No acknowledgment. Her normally low blood pressure inched upward. "I really, *really* don't need this."

She knew she should just drive meekly around again. Or to where she had cell phone reception so she could call the Sheriff's Office and request a deputy.

"Those deputies have more important things to do than come to my rescue." And, with her luck today, it would probably be her nemesis, Sergeant Ron Gardner, who showed up and chewed her ass for wasting his time. "Arrogant windbag blowhard jerkface."

Gracie's ongoing feud with the sergeant had ballooned out of a single mission several years before—the body recovery of a pilot from the burned wreckage of a downed single-engine airplane. At the crash site, the smell and the sight of the only uncharred part of the dead pilot—a hand still gripping the yoke—had made Gracie lose her lunch. Since there were plenty of personnel at the scene, Ralph, as Operations Section Chief, had given her and another male member of the team who had also upchucked his lunch a pass on extricating and carrying out the pilot's remains, assigning them instead to complete the voluminous Incident Command System paperwork back at the Command Post.

Ignoring that a male SAR member had also gotten sick, Sergeant Gardner had decided the incident was further evidence in support of his unofficial belief—legendary within the Department— that women didn't belong in positions of real responsibility or authority over men. It didn't matter that Gracie was an indispensable part of the SAR team, more than carrying her weight, responding to more call-outs and putting in more hours than anyone else. She was a woman and she had fallen down on the job. In Gardner's eyes, nothing she could do would ever make up for it.

Gracie knew that, ever since, the sergeant had been gunning for her, and she had done everything she could to avoid running into him.

Gracie wrung the steering wheel with her hands. She honked the horn again, more insistently.

Another minute crawled with no response from the Lucas house.

"Shit!" She shoved her door open and dropped down onto the gravel.

It wasn't until she rounded the front of the truck, teetering in heels on the nubby asphalt, that she noticed a boy no more than five years old sitting on a rusty tricycle in the middle of the sidewalk leading up to the house. Dirt-smudged face and arms. Haystack of dusty brown hair. Dull, vacant blue eyes.

"Hi there," Gracie said as she walked up. "Is your mom or dad home?"

The child simply looked at her and said nothing.

She stepped around him and up onto the cement porch. She rapped on the screen door and waited, staring through the sagging, rusty screen at the front door—chipped white paint smeared with greasy fingerprints.

Ten seconds ticked by. Twenty. "Hello?" she called. Another ten seconds. She put her mouth next to the door. "Your vehicles are blocking the road. I can't get through. Would you move them, please?"

Ten more seconds of silence. Then the front door was yanked open with such force it strained the hinges. Mr. Lucas glowered down at Gracie through the screen.

Greasy shoulder-length hair, holey black Harley-Davidson T-shirt, six inches of hairy white paunch, an inch of boxer shorts, filthy low-riding jeans, Doc Marten boots. A hand with tattooed fingers and black half-moon nails held a can of Budweiser. His lower lip bulged with a wad of chewing tobacco.

"Hi!" Gracie piped in her best Pollyanna voice. "I was just wondering if you could move your vehicles." She gestured back to the road. "I can't get past."

"Get the fuck away from my house."

Strappy sandals adhered to the porch. "Your cars are parked in the middle of the street. I can't get past. I live at the top of the road." *Probably shouldn't have told him that.*

"We'll fuckin' move 'em when we're goddam good and ready. Get the fuck off my porch."

Gracie didn't move. "They're blocking the road."

The door slammed.

With her mouth next to the keyhole, she bellowed, "Then I guess I'm going to have to call the Sheriff's Office and have a deputy come over and *make* you move them!"

The front door was yanked open and the screen door shoved open so hard it smacked Gracie in the nose. She tottered backward, almost tipping over the porch railing.

The screen door banged against the railing and stayed there.

Mr. Lucas scowled from the doorway, this time with a shotgun cradled in the crook of his meaty arm, this time with Mrs. Lucas peering out from behind her husband.

Deep-set eyes set against pale skin; sunken, pockmarked cheeks; stringy dishwater blond hair. A black midriff top revealed a pale concave stomach where a crude tattoo just below her belly button disappeared into a ratty pair of cut-offs. Skeletal legs with dirty knob knees led down to even dirtier feet. Long yellowed toenails hung over the ends of once-white flip-flops. "You call the fuckin' cops," she snarled in a harsh, phlegmy voice, "you'll regret it." She put a Salem cigarette between thin lips, inhaled the smoke deep into her lungs, and blew a thin stream directly at Gracie.

I already regret it. "I don't want trouble," Gracie said, unable to keep her voice from quivering. "I asked you civilly. All I want is for you to move your vehicles so I can get past."

A stream of brown tobacco juice splatted on the porch an inch from Gracie's foot.

The three glared at one another until Mr. Lucas yelled over his shoulder. "DeMay! Mason! Get out here and move your fuckin' cars!"

Gracie swung around and escaped back to the Ranger on legs shaking so badly she could hardly walk. She hiked her dress up to her thighs, climbed into the truck, slammed the door, and waited, sucking in deep breaths through her nose.

Eventually two men, as stunningly groomed as their pals, emerged from the house and strolled to their vehicles.

"Could you move any more slowly without actually standing still?" Gracie griped from the safety of the truck.

With maximum engine revving and squealing of tires, the two men drove away.

Gracie tore up the hill the rest of the way to the cabin. She stalked inside, dialed the number for the Sheriff's Office and reported witnessing possible drug activity. The Lucas residence. 10269 Arcturus Drive.

GRACIE sank down into the armchair in Jay's office and drummed her fingers on the desk.

The day after the Lucas encounter, back at camp to help with an afternoon hike to Castle Rock with the ninth-graders, Gracie had checked that everything was in order for the hike, then found herself with an hour and a half to spare.

The timing of Jett's death, in particular when exactly, or even if, she had called in sick to Jay, had been nagging at Gracie. Since everyone was down at Serrano for lunch and she had the office to herself, she decided a little snooping was in order.

The telephone answering system in Jay's office saved the numbers, dates, and times of the last thirty incoming calls. Digitally paging back through every saved call, Gracie had hoped to find some indication if and when Jett had left a message calling in sick to work. But enough people had called into camp over the past several days that the furthest-back the calls recorded were from the day after Jett's body had been recovered.

So that idea was a bust, Gracie thought. Rocking in Jay's chair, she thought for a moment, then grabbed the telephone book from the top of the desk, looked up the California Highway Patrol, and dialed the number. In a voice wavering with tears, she worked her way through the system, explaining with increasing dramatics and embellishments to several different people in several different agencies about how Jett had been her best friend and she needed to know if anyone had found a large satchel in the wreckage because Jett had some pictures of the two of them that she would love to have. At the Coroner's office, she finally found a sympathetic ear in what sounded like a very young man who left her on hold for ten minutes of cloying music. When he finally returned on the line, he told Grace in a hushed voice that no satchel had been found.

With a fresh burst of boo-hoo-hooing, Gracie thanked the man and hung up the phone.

Another dead end. Jett carried the suitcase-sized satchel everywhere. There was no way she didn't have it with her when she was driving down the hill.

Maybe, like Jett, it had been ejected from the tumbling car on its way down into the canyon and now lay somewhere among the thousand shrubs, trees, and boulders along its scarred path. Gracie considered descending into the canyon to look for the satchel, then dismissed the idea as too risky and harebrained—too impetuous—even for her.

She leaned back in the chair again and wondered what to do for the next hour. *How about nothing?* She was tired. She could use a little break in order to do absolutely nothing.

Head resting on the back of the chair, rocking slightly,

she let her eyes wander the room until they finally settled
on the giant annual calendar filling the opposite wall.

For the first time, she actually studied the calendar on
which Jay recorded the names and numbers of all guests
and the lodges in which they were scheduled to stay. The
names written in blue marker were the camp's own clients,
mostly various types of church groups. Names in green
indicated Adventures "R" Us clients, mostly school and
corporate executive groups. Those in red were clients of
other adventure programming companies.

Gracie did a cursory count of Madison and Abe's
clients—more than thirty-five. But there were only three
clients for all other outdoor programming companies in
Southern California, odd given the camp's proximity to the
L.A. metropolitan area, its unparalleled beauty, and the high
quality of the high and low ropes courses.

Why was Madison and Abe's relationship with Jay so
cozy that it precluded almost all competitors from using the
camp? She could understand how a deal for almost exclusive
use of the camp would benefit the Adventures couple. But
what was in it for the camp?

What if, she mused, it didn't have anything to do with
what benefited the camp and everything to do with what
benefited Jay personally?

Gracie reached over to a large metal rolling filing cabinet
sitting next to the desk. Pushing aside the half-empty bag
of mini–Hershey bars, she pulled out the manila file folders
for several Adventures clients, laid them on the desk, and
paged through them.

Nothing out of the ordinary jumped out at her.

From an upright file holder on the top of the desk, she
extracted the file for the school group currently in camp and
studied the contents. Finally she zeroed in on the contract

itself. The minimum number of campers required by the contract was twenty-four. There were a total of sixty-five ninth-graders plus ten adult chaperones in the group.

From the pile of files she had just examined, she pulled the file for a recent church family retreat. The minimum number of campers required by that contract was eighteen.

Gracie had worked the group's high-course program with two other belayers. With one belayer for every twelve or so climbers, there would have been about thirty-six people on the high course. At least a dozen had chosen to not participate, sitting in the amphitheater and cheering everyone else on. That totaled a minimum of forty-eight people.

She flipped open the file of a men's church retreat three weeks earlier. The contract minimum was twenty.

Gracie had watched the group's talent show from the back of the camp's upper amphitheater, laughing at men dressed in grass skirts and half-coconut bras playing ukuleles and singing a song from *South Pacific*. The program had listed more than a dozen acts and skits. The amphitheater, which could hold two hundred people, had been at least a quarter full. Gracie figured the lowest ballpark figure for the group was fifty, most likely twenty more.

She rocked back in the chair again and thought.

Actual numbers far exceeding the minimums seemed to be a pattern but in and of itself indicated nothing nefarious. Was there actually something unethical or illegal going on? Or was she just being paranoid and suspicious, wanting to find something where nothing existed simply because she thought Jay was a putz and a phony.

She needed to compare the actual group numbers against how many guests had been paid for or at least how many Jay had reported to the church.

But all those records were kept password-protected on the computer.

Or were they?

Had Madison already paid for the ninth-grade retreat? Maybe that was what was in the envelope she had left on Jay's desk a couple of days earlier.

Every week Jay mailed an envelope down to the church office in L.A. with an accounting of that week's camp guests.

Gracie stood up and slid open the sliding door to the closet containing the floor safe and office supplies. On a shelf above the safe was a large manila envelope, unsealed.

Fearful of leaving telltale wrinkles on the pristine envelope, she lifted it out and carried it to the desk on her open palms as if presenting a gift to the gods. Drawing out the contents, she sifted through the papers until she found a one-page spreadsheet listing that week's bank deposits. Three deposit slips were paper-clipped to one corner, along with a list of clients, their numbers, and payment amounts, including the ninth-grade group and the Korean Methodist Church.

Tires rolled on gravel outside.

Gracie froze, listening as a car drove past the Gatehouse on its way out of camp.

She exhaled, irritated that her hands were now shaking, and chided herself that she needed to pay more attention to keeping an eye out or she'd be caught red-handed and having to explain why she was snooping around Jay's office.

She examined the spreadsheet in her hands, entered some numbers on the desktop calculator, and studied the totals. Her heartbeat kicked up a notch.

For the ninth-grade group, Jay had received and recorded a deposit and final payment for only sixty-four campers.

There were seventy-five people currently in camp, a difference totaling more than three thousand dollars.

He had recorded Korean Methodist's payment as a little more than thirty-two hundred dollars. Three times Gracie had counted out the wad of cash she had received from the tiny Asian woman. And she had handwritten the receipt— for a little more than four thousand dollars.

A difference of more than eight hundred dollars.

Gracie stared down at the spreadsheet. She could think of no reason for the discrepancies other than Jay was under-reporting to the church how much money he was taking into the camp and pocketing the difference.

Because where else was the money going?

Gracie looked up at the calendar. More than 150 church groups had already stayed at camp that year. Most of the clients paid by credit card or check. But, Gracie figured, if even a small percentage of those clients—say five percent— paid in cash, and if Jay skimmed off only five hundred dollars per client, that alone would total more than thirty-five hundred dollars.

And adding in a little bit from each of the thirty-five Adventures clients?

Gracie sorted back through the Adventures "R" Us client contracts and confirmed what she already suspected—the per person rates were far lower than other camp clients, lower even than normal wholesale rates. Even if Abe and Madison Bonds paid a portion to Jay, they still would be making a tidy sum with every client.

As far as embezzlements went, it was nothing sophisticated or elaborate or ambitious. But it was effective. And whether Jay and possibly Madison and Abe were bilking the church out of a hundred dollars or ten thousand dollars, it didn't really matter. A fiddle was a fiddle was a fiddle.

"Jay, you hypocrite," Gracie whispered. "You charlatan. You sanctimonious sack of shit. You arrogant, self-serving . . ." She stopped, unable to think of a word bad enough.

Jay had been managing the camp for almost twenty years. It was possible that for that entire time he had been diverting away from the church and into his own pockets, possibly as much as hundreds of thousands of dollars.

Gracie couldn't believe no one had caught on to him before this. But nobody outside Jay and his family ever worked in the camp office. Maybe that was one reason, if not *the* reason, he had resisted Gracie coming in to work at the camp. The church's bookkeeper worked in the church office a hundred miles away in Los Angeles, seldom, if ever, coming up to the camp to look at the books, much less conduct any kind of thorough audit. The reason was plain and simple. The church trusted Jay.

So where's the money going? Gracie wondered. It wasn't like Jay drove a Mercedes or wore Armani suits.

The house in the desert.

Had to be.

Jay and Elaine's house in Cathedral City where the family lived during the winter months.

Which meant Elaine had to know. And probably Eddie. Possibly even Amanda.

Gracie pulled out her cell phone and took a picture of the wall calendar. She checked her watch. She had already been in Jay's office for more than a half hour. Feeling a sudden urgency to finish what she was doing and get out of there, she made copies of the spreadsheet and deposit slips, then worked her way through the files in the rolling cabinet, copying receipts, contracts, and anything else potentially incriminating.

As she placed a contract on the glass and pressed Copy, a sudden thought sent goose bumps rippling up her arms.

Was embezzlement enough to kill for?

Gracie stared at her hands on the glass.

People were killed for a lot less every damn day.

Outside in the parking lot, a car door slammed.

Gracie sprang to the window and peered out through the slit in the curtains. Elaine was walking across the parking lot from her car to the front sidewalk.

Shit!

She slid the spreadsheet and receipts back into the manila envelope, laid it back on the shelf in the closet, and closed the door. She dropped the files back into the file holder on the desk and the rolling cabinet, hopefully in the right order. With a lightning glance around for anything she might have missed, she gathered up the copies she had made, ran up the hallway into the kitchen and tossed the copies into the refrigerator.

The refrigerator door closed just as the front door opened, ringing the little bell.

Elaine stopped when Gracie appeared in the kitchen doorway. Her eyes narrowed into the familiar squint, measuring, calculating. "I'm looking for Serene," she said in a tight voice.

"Not here," Gracie answered, her heart beating a pile driver in her chest. "Haven't seen her today. Try the kitchen."

Elaine gave Gracie a thin smile. She turned away, then turned back. "A group of us are driving down the hill to picket the abortion mill in Riverside. Come with us." An order, not a request.

"The . . . uh . . . what?"

"Come with us."

Gracie stared back at Elaine. "Um, thanks for the offer.

But. I can't. I have to work." She looked at her watch. "In fact, it's high time I was down at the dining hall meeting my group." Her smile was received with a cold stare.

Without a word, Elaine spun around and walked back outside, slamming the door behind her and sending the little bell doing its thing.

Guess that bit in the Bible about the speck and the beam doesn't apply to the Wilsons, Gracie thought as she watched Elaine back the car out of the parking spot.

In the backseat, Meaghan looked woefully out the window.

And why aren't you paying closer attention to your own daughter?

Gracie checked her watch again. It really was time for her to be down at the Serrano dining room.

Hell's bells, she thought as she gathered up the papers from the refrigerator. Climbing around on rocks a hundred feet high was infinitely more sane and safe and uplifting than dealing with the people at camp.

GRACIE peeled back the lid of the third little Moo Juice container and poured the white liquid into her coffee cup. She felt as if she could fall asleep where she stood in the dining room in spite of the din of the students and adults still high from an afternoon hike in the mountains.

The events of the past week on top of her late-night escapade to Ralph's punctuated by her certainty that, with Madison and Abe's help, Jay was embezzling money from the church that owned the camp left her feeling as if she had been fed through the rollers of a ringer washing machine, every ounce of energy wrung from her body. At that moment, she cared about nothing in the entire world except climbing into her little bed in her little cabin with her little dog curled up at her feet.

She leaned against the counter, took a sip of coffee, and watched Jasmine back out of the kitchen door lugging three large trays of plastic cups.

Big load for such a tiny person, Gracie thought, and was impressed when Jasmine heaved the trays on top of a four-foot-high stack. She pulled a wet rag from her back pocket and began wiping down the counter against which Gracie was leaning.

Gracie studied the sullen face. It hit her with fresh shock that Jasmine didn't know her mother had killed her father. "Hi, Jasmine," Gracie said, not expecting an answer and not receiving one. Her eyes traveled from the electric blue hair to the black T-shirt and white short shorts down the long legs to lime green flip-flops and a tiny butterfly tattoo just above her ankle.

Gracie's stomach did a ten-story elevator drop. She spit the mouthful of coffee back into her cup.

Her eyes shot all the way back up to find Jasmine's bored, half-closed eyes watching her.

The person she had seen Eddie screwing in the back kitchen closet hadn't been Serene at all. The person she had seen Eddie screwing was Serene's seventeen-year-old daughter.

ROOM noise swirled around Gracie, but she didn't hear it. The knowledge that Eddie was having sex with Jasmine, someone less than half his age, had twisted her stomach into a pretzel.

Jasmine flipped back her hair and stared with insolence back at Gracie. "What?" she demanded.

Gracie took in a deep breath and set her coffee cup down onto the counter. "Nice tattoo," she said.

Jasmine's eyes filled with such hatred that Gracie took a step backward. "It's no big deal," she hissed. "A lot of kids at school have 'em."

Gracie shrugged. "*I* never said it was a big deal."

No response, then a sulky, "You don't . . . *disapprove*? You're not going to say it's . . . *evil*? That I'm, like, *weak* and full of sin and am going to . . . *die* and go to . . . *hell*?"

Gracie had to clear her throat before she could manage,

"No to all of the above. I was just handing you a compliment. I think it's pretty."

Jasmine stared back, her face wiped clean of animosity with something else in its place—pain. Then she snapped the washcloth on the edge of the counter, grumbled what sounded like "That's a first," and stalked into the kitchen.

Gracie grabbed up her day pack and headed out of the dining hall, narrowly missing a head-on collision with Emilio emerging from a storage closet. She jogged down the long corridor and out the front door. Out in the parking lot, she tipped her head back and sucked the cool evening air deep into her lungs, then blew it out as if with it she could cleanse herself of the knowledge that Eddie was having sex with someone young enough to be his daughter.

I have to tell Serene, Gracie thought as she walked across the parking lot to where she had left the truck parked in the shade of a grouping of tall pines.

Except how did one tell a mother that her seventeen-year-old daughter was having sex with a forty-one-year-old man she thought she loved?

At that moment, Serene was working in the kitchen where Jasmine was. And Jay. Waiting until she could speak with Serene privately would allow her a little time to plan her words carefully. And the last thing anyone needed was for Serene to go berserk and strangle Eddie in front of a room of ninth-graders.

Gracie threw her pack onto the passenger's seat and climbed into the truck, greeted by Minnie's welcoming tail wagging and gaining no small amount of comfort by scratching the silky black head.

She drove down to Serene's trailer and tucked into the screen door a note written in a pen on a Taco Bell napkin. *Serene, we need to talk. Right away. Private!* Underlined twice. *Important. Call me!* At the bottom, she scribbled her name along with her home and cell phone numbers.

Gracie was already halfway down Cedar Mill Road when her thoughts cleared enough for her to remember that she hadn't retrieved her paycheck, which should be sitting on the desk in her basement office.

The Ranger skidded to a stop on a pullout. Gracie wanted nothing more than to leave camp, to be rid of the knot in her stomach, to escape the hypocrites and embezzlers and general hatefulness.

Except she needed to pay her bills. If she didn't go back now, she would have to drive all the way back across the valley the next day—on her day off—to retrieve it.

She made a three-point turn on the narrow road and headed back up the hill to camp.

GRACIE HELD HER paycheck up to the light of the window in the front office, grimacing at the amount.

A sound behind her made her jump and drop the check. She spun around.

Eddie leaned against the door leading to the hallway.

"*Dammit*, Eddie!"

Smiling at her, Eddie pushed himself away from the door and walked over to the desk nearest Gracie and settled a hip on the corner, swinging his foot.

She realized with a jolt that with one move he had effectively blocked her escape. Her mind raced to think of a way to get past him, out to her truck and away from camp.

Eddie's tight black T-shirt accentuated his tan face and well-muscled arms. He leaned forward, resting his forearm on his thigh, automatically flexing the bicep. "Kinda jumpy, aren'tcha there, Gracie?"

"I don't like people sneaking up on me," she said, careful to keep her tone even, calm.

"I didn't sneak, darlin'," he said, dimples showing. "I walked."

Gracie noted the exact words he had spoken a few days before and wondered how many times he had said those same words before with other women.

Her eyes flicked down to his booted foot swinging back and forth, then up to his face. There was no way she wouldn't have heard him clunking up the basement steps in those big old work boots, even if she had been distracted.

"You don't like me much, do ya, Gracie?" He cocked his head and looked at her, his green eyes wide and innocent.

"I wouldn't say that," Gracie answered. "Don't like" was too mild for what she felt about Eddie.

"You and me," Eddie continued. "We just got us off to a bad start somehow. I was tryin' to think on how we could get along a little better from now on, mend some fences, ya know?"

Gracie said nothing. She sucked air in through her nose and out through her mouth in an attempt to stay focused and not allow the fear rising in her throat to take hold.

"I'm not such a bad sort," he drawled. He pulled a toothpick from the front pocket of his shirt and stuck it in the corner of his mouth. "Maybe you and me could go out some time. Tip a few. You could tell me all about that Search and Rescue."

"I need to get going, Eddie." Keeping as far away from him as she could, Gracie moved to walk past him.

But he stretched out the swinging leg and planted his boot on the ledge of the stone fireplace, blocking her way. "What's your hurry, Gracie? We're just gettin' warmed up."

Gracie backed up a step so she wouldn't be standing in the V of Eddie's crotch. "I need to go. Move your leg."

"Come *on*, Gracie. What's wrong with a little . . ."

"Move your leg," she said. "Now."

The foot dropped to the ground. He stood up, only a foot away from Gracie.

"I'm warning you, Eddie. Move aside and let me leave."

His green eyes twinkled. "*You're* warnin' *me*?" He leaned in toward her.

Gracie bunched her leg muscles and put her hands on the desk to vault over the top away from him, but Eddie grabbed her arm, cementing her in place.

"Let go," she said between clenched teeth.

"Aw, come on—"

Anger coursed through Gracie's body. She jerked her arm out of his hand. "I'm not some little girl you can push around. I *know*, Eddie."

Something flashed across his face. Doubt perhaps. Or fear. He cocked his head again. "Exactly what is it you think you know?"

"Seventeen, Eddie? And you're how old?"

The machinery inside his head turned. Then his face cleared and he shrugged. "She came on to me."

"She's seventeen."

"Yeah? So?"

He still doesn't get it. "In some states, like, for instance, New Jersey," Gracie said, "being seventeen means you're a consenting adult. But you're in California, Eddie. The age of consent is eighteen."

"Oh, yeah?" He leaned in toward Gracie. "She came on to me. What was I supposed to do? Disappoint her?"

"She's underage, you moron." Gracie just couldn't stop herself. "I wonder how much jail time you'll get for having sex with a minor?"

Every muscle in Eddie's body tensed. His green eyes iced and narrowed. So quickly Gracie didn't have time to react, he moved forward, crowding her with his body, forcing her to back up against the window. "Who's gonna tell? You?" He flicked away the toothpick and leaned in so that his mouth almost touched hers. "Gracie?"

"Get away from me." With both hands on his chest, she pushed with all her strength.

He barely moved. Instead he leaned in and put a hand on her breast.

Gracie slugged him in the side of the head with her fist.

In the movies, Eddie would have gone down. But the blow hardly seemed to faze him. He caught both of Gracie's wrists and forced them down to her sides. He shifted his feet to redistribute his weight and pressed his body full length against hers, sandwiching her against the heavy glass, his face an inch from hers.

"Let me go, Eddie." Gracie's voice was low. Her teeth were bared like a cornered animal.

"Now that I finally have you where I want you?"

He kissed her suddenly and hard, banging her head against the window. He thrust his tongue so deeply into her mouth she gagged and shoved his legs between hers so that she was off balance, defenseless.

She hadn't the leverage to stomp on his instep or knee him in the groin. It flashed through her brain that Eddie knew exactly what he was doing. He had done it before.

Gracie squealed, opened her mouth wide and bit down. She caught his tongue between her teeth and held on.

Eddie yelled, let go of her, and tried to wrestle free. "Lehgo! Lehgo!"

She clamped down tighter, grinding her teeth until she tasted blood. Then she opened her mouth.

Eddie stumbled back, falling hard against the stone fireplace, his mouth smeared with bright red blood.

Gracie's feet barely touched the ground as she sprinted past him.

"You bith!" Eddie screamed after her. "You thucking *bith*!"

Gracie threw the front door open and lurched outside.

THE RANGER ROCKETED down Cedar Mill Road.

Gracie threw water from her water bottle into her mouth, swished it around, and spat it out the window.

Her entire body shook. A wrist smearing away tears came away bloodied. Her own blood? Or Eddie's?

The thought of HIV flooded her body with fear.

As soon as three bars appeared on her cell phone, she called Ralph's house. No answer. She left a message: "I need to talk to you! Please?" She left the same message on his cell phone adding, "You're my only friend. Please don't be mad at me anymore. I need you."

The Ranger careened crazily into the Sheriff's Office parking lot and into a spot. Gracie half ran up to the building and fumbled to insert her key into the doorknob of the heavy steel door of the employees' entrance. Inside, she stumbled down the long corridor and around the corner. In the doorway of the Watch Commander's office, she stopped.

Sergeant Gardner was alone in the room. His substantial frame overwhelmed the tiny desk behind which he was sitting. Red hair buzzed to nonexistent. Pale, freckled skin. Porcine eyes, upturned nose. Beefy hands gripping a single sheet of paper.

The two stared at each other, Gracie taking in great gulps of air, not able to draw enough into her lungs.

The sergeant frowned, an inscrutable look on his face. "What do you want, Kinkaid?"

"Krueger?" was what Gracie managed to say.

"Not in."

Gracie spun around and staggered back up the corridor and out of the building. No way in *hell* was she going to talk to Gardner and be assaulted twice in one hour by having him tell her she asked for it because her T-shirt was too tight or that she deserved it because she was born with breasts instead of a dick.

Somehow Gracie made it the rest of the way across town and up to her cabin unimpeded by idiot flatlanders hogging her lane or junked cars blocking the road. Or without killing anyone.

Unable to think clearly, she didn't know what to do about Eddie, about his attack on her. She wanted nothing more than to take a long, hot bath to rid her body of the brutal taste, smell, and feel of the man, then climb into bed and sleep for a month. Hyperaware she had been traumatized, emotionally and physically, she grabbed her camera and took pictures from every conceivable angle of her bloodied mouth and the bruises already visible on her face, wrists, arms, and breast.

Then, with Minnie watching with her head on her paws, Gracie climbed into a bathtub of scalding water. Thirty minutes, two tumblers of Gallo sangria, two Tylenol, and two generic over-the-counter sleep aids later, she staggered up to the loft bedroom and fell into bed.

FOR HOURS, GRACIE drifted in and out of sleep. Every time she closed her eyes, Eddie's mouth crushed hers, his hands groped her body. The fist she had punched into the side of his head was sore and stiff. Her lips were swollen and split at one corner. A dull ache persisted behind her eyes. The skin around her mouth was chafed and raw with razor burn. Her pubic bone felt bruised where Eddie had pinned her hands with the full weight of his body.

Somewhere close to midnight, she finally fell asleep. At four thirty-three the next morning her eyes shot open. She kicked off the sheet and burst up from the bed. With Minnie on her heels, she padded downstairs to the kitchen. While the dog attended to her business in the backyard, Gracie filled the teakettle with water, slapped it on the burner, and turned on the gas.

Shock had evolved into rage as hot as a blacksmith's forge, and images of Eddie danced in front of her eyes. "I'm going to bring him down," she whispered, staring into the flickering blue flame of the burner. "And his hypocritical, lying sack of chickenshit charlatan brother along with him."

The kettle whistled. She turned the burner off and poured the hot water into her mug, stirring in the instant coffee crystals.

Embezzlement. Statutory rape. Jett had uncovered at least some of what was going on at camp and been murdered for it. She needed to find out exactly what it was that Jett had discovered and exactly what had happened to her. She needed to act methodically, strategically, and very, very carefully. She needed to find Jett's journal.

CHAPTER

28

GRACIE stood on the Glory Ridge Trail, steeped in cold blue shadow a third of the way down into the canyon. At her feet, the ground dropped sharply away, plunging another thousand feet down to the winding gray ribbon that was Boulder Creek at the bottom. Across the yawning divide, the tree-studded wall of granite rose up to a long, vertical scar in the rock three hundred feet higher that where Gracie stood on the trail—the highway cut that was the Arctic Circle. The first rays of morning flushed the overlooking peaks with a pink glow. There was no sound except the occasional hum of tires on the highway overhead and the wind whispering in the canyon.

It was still fully dark when Gracie left a woeful Minnie tied up in the backyard of the cabin. Better for the dog to spend the day alone on a little bed in the shade of the deck with plenty of room and toys and water than baking inside the Ranger for an indeterminate amount of time.

Rather than follow the steep, treacherous route which Jett's car had taken in its spectacular tumble down from the turnout, Gracie had chosen instead to follow the Glory Ridge Trail, a less steep, but much longer, more monotonous series of switchbacks descending into the canyon.

Even though the thought of being rescued by her own team galled Gracie, hiking alone into steep, rugged territory presented the real possibility of a sprained ankle or twisted knee. Before leaving the cabin, she had e-mailed her SAR teammate Jon, telling him that if she didn't call him by the appointed time that afternoon, a note taped to her front door described exactly where she was going.

An icy breeze riffled the brim of Gracie's floppy hat, cut right through the twin layers of black T-shirt and fleece jacket and raised goose bumps on her bare legs. Shivering, she zipped the jacket the rest of the way up to her chin, humped her day pack higher up onto her shoulders, and cinched the waistband tighter. She took another long draw of water from the hydration bladder inside the pack, tucked the little tube away beneath the chest strap, and continued down the trail into the canyon.

WORKING HER WAY out from the shattered glass and scattered pieces of chrome and steel—all that remained of Jett's station wagon at the bottom of the canyon, Gracie searched the surrounding area.

She climbed up the side of the canyon opposite the trail following the path of broken tree branches and white-scarred boulders, the path the car had taken both in its fall from the turnout and on the long haul out. Her eyes swept back and forth along the oatmeal-colored ground, over and behind smaller rocks and boulders, light green sage and leafy mounds of manzanita.

No satchel.

There was a real possibility that the trip into the canyon was a wild goose chase. If Jett had been killed somewhere else and put into her car and sent over the side to make her death look like an accident, there was no telling where the satchel or the journal might be. Perhaps it had been disposed of all altogether—sent to the dump. Or buried in the camp trash. The idea of clawing through the half acre of trash at camp to look for the satchel almost brought Gracie to her knees in despair. She shook the thought away with the stubborn determination that she would cross that tottering footbridge when she needed to and continued her search along the steep canyon hillside.

A hundred feet up from the remnants of the vehicle, she stopped. Pulling off a glove, she wiped the sweat from her forehead with the back of her hand. She tugged the glove back on, looked around, and gasped.

There it was.

Ten feet away, lying in plain sight on the rocky ground: a large square satchel of turquoise, black and white fabric woven in a Mexican pattern.

Sidestepping over, Gracie slung off her pack and sank to the ground. She picked up the bag, upzipped it, and dumped the contents onto her lap.

Hairbrush. Comb. Mirror, cracked. A tampon, the wrapper slightly worse for wear. Makeup bag with orange blusher and blue eye shadow reduced to powder. A single condom. Three pens. A butter knife. The world's tiniest address book, page corners dog-eared. A two-inch metal cross. A wallet of navy blue fabric carrying a California driver's license with a West Covina address, a single debit card from a local credit union, seven dollar bills.

Gracie shook out the bag one more time to make sure it was empty, then dropped it on the ground.

No hidden pockets.

No journal.

"Shit." She closed her eyes and dropped her head forward onto her knees. She stayed there for several minutes.

Then, rousing herself with a physical shake, she dropped the contents back into the satchel, stuffed it into her day pack, and zipped it closed.

Then she slung the pack onto her back, pushed herself to her feet, and started down the hill for the long hike back across the bottom of the canyon and up the trail to her truck.

CHAPTER

29

"**M**INNIE?"

Gracie stood at the sliding-glass door leading out from the living room onto a narrow deck that ran along the south side of the cabin.

Already she and the dog had an established routine. When Gracie returned home, Minnie would be sitting on the deck. When the door slid open, she would jump around with joy like a little bucking bronco until Gracie knelt down. Then the dog would stand with her front paws on Gracie's knees and cover her face with doggie kisses.

But this time there was no Minnie welcoming committee.

"Minnie!" Gracie called. "Where are you, silly girl?" She walked out onto the deck and looked up and down the long, narrow portion of the deck. She walked toward the back, fear growing that Minnie had gotten out of the yard and disappeared forever.

She rounded the corner.

The dog lay motionless on her side in the far corner of the deck.

"Minnie!" Gracie ran over and knelt next to the dog. Her breathing was fast and shallow. The tail thumped the deck. Once.

The black fur looked wet. Gracie placed her fingers on the spot. They came away bright red.

Blood.

She gently parted the long fur, searching the skin until she found what she was looking for—a round hole the size of a pea, oozing blood.

A bullet hole.

Someone had shot Minnie.

Gracie surged to her feet and ran into the house. She grabbed up a pink bath towel from a pile on the dryer and a first-aid kit from atop the refrigerator. From the kitchen table, she picked up a rectangular piece of Masonite holding a half-completed jigsaw puzzle and flipped the pieces off onto the table.

Back out on the deck, she knelt beside Minnie again and placed a heavy square of gauze on top of the wound, taping it in place on the fur. Then she gently slid the Masonite board beneath the dog's body while whispering, "Stay, Minnie. That's a good girl." Except for the brown eyes following her every move, the dog lay perfectly still.

Gracie draped the towel over the animal, then straining already-aching muscles, she lifted the entire board and carried it across to the side deck, down the steps and out to the driveway. "What a good girl," she said in a soft voice. Tears ran down her cheeks and dripped onto bare arms. "You're such a good dog, aren't you, Minnie? You're my little girl."

* * *

WITH FINGERS SQUEEZING the stainless-steel counter, Gracie stood in the sterile examination room staring at the spot on the X ray to which the veterinarian was pointing. "It entered here," she said. She moved her finger to where the bullet showed up as a bright white lozenge. "And ended up here. We're going to have to remove it surgically and repair any damage. There's no other way."

"Do it. Whatever you have to do." Dreading the answer, Gracie asked, "Is she going to die?"

"Let's see how the surgery goes," the veterinarian said, her eyes kind, sympathetic. "We'll have a better idea then of how much, if any, permanent damage was done."

"Thanks, Dr. Peterson," Gracie whispered.

In a daze, she walked through the outer lobby and out of the building to her truck.

30

GRACIE walked down the steps leading from the deck of the cabin to the backyard. At first glance, she found no tracks but her own and Minnie's anywhere in the tiny yard or along the chain-link fence delineating the yard from the rest of the property, which ran down to the road below. Slipping through the gate, she studied the ground below the fence, rewarded ten minutes later by a muddle of footprints on a level area of bare dirt eight feet up from the road. A break between two five-foot-tall mountain mahogany bushes provided a clear line of sight up to the deck. Minnie, looking down through the slats of the railing, black tail swishing back and forth in welcome, couldn't have presented a more perfect target.

Almost invisible in the mottled shadows at the base of one of the bushes lay a single small-caliber bullet casing. Gracie left it untouched. She crouched and examined a single footprint apart from the others, pressed into the soft dirt as clearly as if it had been made with a rubber stamp.

Gracie's first thoughts upon finding Minnie wounded had been that Eddie had driven all the way across the valley from camp. But instead of the lug sole of a work boot, the print sole had a zigzag pattern, possibly that of a flip-flop, the outside edges blurred as if with wear. Although there was no way to tell exactly what size or brand the shoe was, Gracie was certain the print, two inches shorter and an inch narrower than her own hiking boot, had been laid by a woman.

Back inside the cabin, Gracie stuffed her camera into the day pack along with a full bottle of water. She grabbed up her tracking pole leaning against the door in the mudroom, plopped the floppy hat onto her head, and pulled on a pair of pliable nylon and leather rappel gloves.

The shooting of an innocent animal, the dog she now loved, had drop-kicked Gracie into Search and Rescue mode. A pervasive sense of calm had taken hold. The tears were gone, as were the lump in her throat and the bone-deep fatigue. The internal foundry had reenergized her and crystallized into a laser beam of purpose.

No longer a victim, she was on the hunt.

GRACIE DROPPED DOWN onto the gravel shoulder of the road and looked around, the brim of her hat shading her eyes from the dazzling midday sun. Most of the houses at the top of the dead-end road where her cabin was perched were vacation homes, empty the majority of the year. Her one full-time neighbor was on vacation in Alaska with her new partner.

There was no one else around.

Gracie had flagged as evidence and taken several pictures of the bullet casing and the footprints on her property. Now, stooped over like an old woman, eyes trained on the ground, she searched for more tracks. Stealthily, as keenly focused as a cheetah stalking a gazelle, she moved down the winding road, crisscrossing back and forth, scouring every inch of shoulder, leaving nothing unsearched, until, at a point, on the opposite side of the road and several yards down where the hillside dropped off yet again, she found a half-inch-long portion of the same zigzag tread in the dirt.

Gracie slid down the steep embankment, cut through the thicket of pines and scrub oak, and came out directly across the road from the Lucas house. There she found a semicircle of the zigzag tread in the dirt, a toe dig headed in the direction of the Lucas house.

Crouching next to a telephone pole, she studied the scene.

Mr. Lucas's pickup, usually parked on the shoulder in front of the house, was nowhere in sight. The lot on the uphill side was empty and weed-choked. The house downhill was vacant, its screen door hanging from one hinge, the front windows smashed. Several blocks down Arcturus, a car turned off onto another street.

Gracie waited.

A squirrel chattered a harangue from a tree limb behind her. A mountain chickadee called its loud whistle from somewhere over her head.

Five minutes stretched into ten.

A ponderosa pinecone dropped like a missile, thudded on the ground next to Gracie, and rolled to a stop at her feet.

Ten more minutes crawled by with no visible movement from within or around the Lucas house.

"Screw with my dog, screw with me," Gracie whispered, and made her move. She secreted her tracking pole beneath the bushes next to the telephone pole, scooted across the road, and dropped into the yard. There in the dirt were a multitude of footprints with the zigzag tread.

Hugging the cement brick wall, Gracie slunk along the side of the house to the back where an eight-foot-high solid board fence jutted, blocking the way. There was no gate. The only intended way into the backyard was through the house.

Gracie tossed her pack over the fence. "Now you're committed," she said, and mashed herself through the tiny gap between the fence and cement wall.

At the back corner of the house, she stopped.

Tin cans. Plastic and beer bottles and cans. Broken dishes. A television set. Even a couch with the stuffing exposed. All had been tossed into a pile reaching taller than Gracie. A whirligig of flies buzzed above the mound.

A raven the size of a small cat flew up from the pile to hop along the board fence running the perimeter of the yard. Shiny blue-black feathers ruffling with the breeze, the huge bird croaked its disapproval of its snack interrupted.

Gracie stepped farther into the yard.

The rest of the area was a dump of scrap metal, an entire car engine, scattered tires. A single dingy gray sock and a Harley-Davidson T-shirt caught by a single clothespin hung from a green plastic clothesline stretching from the far corner of the house to the fence.

"Well, whaddya know," Gracie said. Propped up against the fence were her own pink-and-mint green cross-country skis, missing from her storage shed since the previous winter. "Those sons of bitches." She pulled her camera from the day pack and took a picture of the skis and, for good measure, the rest of the yard.

Not wanting to make it a dead giveaway as to who had

come calling that afternoon, she left the skis where they were.

She crossed to the back door and tested the knob. Locked. The windows in back and on the opposite side of the house were also all closed and locked.

Gracie squeezed back through the gap between the fence and the cement wall and stood looking up at a narrow window open a quarter of an inch. "She came in through the bathroom window," she sang to herself.

CHAPTER

31

GRACIE dropped her pack into the bathtub and, wriggling feetfirst through the narrow window, followed it inside. She looked around the bathroom and almost climbed right back outside again.

The grout in the pale orange floor and wall tile and around the base of the matching sink and toilet was black with mildew. The odor of stale urine, vomit, and feces hung as an almost palpable mist in the air. Imaginary microscopic creepy crawlies climbed up her arms and into her hair. "Eeesh," she whispered and pulled the neck of her T-shirt up over her nose and breathed through her mouth.

Slinging her day pack over a shoulder, she stepped from the bathtub and out of the room, turning left up a long hallway toward the kitchen at the back of the house. She stopped in the doorway, stunned by the squalor of the room. The stench of stale cigarettes, beer, and decaying animal was almost overpowering.

With her shirt still covering her nose, Gracie nudged on the light with an elbow, pulled out her camera, and took pictures from where she stood. The lens caught a cockroach skittering out of sight on the counter. Plates with congealing food sat stacked in the sink and on every inch of counter space. Bloated pink and green marshmallows and cigarette butts floating in a bowl of gray milk on a giant electrical spool table. Cupboard doors hanging open displayed mismatched plastic dishes and a stack of jumbo 7-Eleven cups. Ground-in food and dirt hid what color the vinyl flooring was supposed to be. A desiccated mouse carcass lay in a trap beneath the one metal folding chair beside the table.

Gracie walked into the room, her boots sticking to the floor. Thankful for her gloves, she pulled open the refrigerator door.

Well stocked . . . with beer. And a half-consumed summer sausage. Not a drop of milk in sight. Not a vegetable. Not a piece of fruit. Or anything remotely healthy for a child to eat.

Gracie tiptoed back down the hall to the first room on the left, a large bedroom.

A single bare king-sized mattress stained with blood and other fluids Gracie didn't want to think about lay on a rust orange shag carpet so tamped down as to be a solid piece of felt. Clothes and hangers were strewn everywhere.

Not a single storybook or toy. Not a single child's blanket. The only sign of a child's presence was a tiny Donald Duck T-shirt in a sad little pile on the floor.

Gracie stepped into the room and grabbed ahold of the closet doorknob, grateful for her gloves. As if velocity would make the revelation of its contents any less repugnant, she yanked it wide-open. Instead of clothes on hangers and maybe a pair or two of shoes, the small space was filled floor to ceiling with cardboard cartons of all shapes and sizes with REMINGTON printed on the sides. "Wow," Gracie whispered. "There's enough here for an army."

Along with larger-caliber weapons propped up against the wall in one corner was a .22 rifle. "Bingo."

She snapped close-up shots of the box labels and the firearms, including the rifle, and then crept down the hallway, taking pictures as she went. A second bedroom held only two dirty mattresses with greasy pillows. The closet was completely empty, except for a single beer bottle lying on its side.

The heavily curtained living room was a transformation with every type of electronic gadget drug money could buy: PlayStations, computers, a monster plasma television, and a pristine velour sectional couch.

A fly landed on the cut on Gracie's mouth. She slapped it away and walked across the room to the front door where she stopped again, looking down.

At her feet, chained to the floor and set to spring, was the largest animal trap she had ever seen. The steel jaws looked large and strong enough to snap a human bone, especially the small, relatively delicate metatarsals of a foot. Anyone entering the house without invitation would have stepped right onto the trigger. Simple. Effective. And downright nasty.

Gracie leaned across the trap and tested the front doorknob. Unlocked, practically inviting intruders—or nosy neighbors—in.

She broke out in a cold sweat. A booby trap had never occurred to her. If she had walked in the front door, at this moment she would be lying on the floor in agonizing pain, possibly unable to escape and permanently maimed.

GRACIE LEFT THE Lucas house the way she had come—through the bathroom window. She dropped down into the side yard, edged along the side of the house, and at the all-clear, scurried across the road at a crouch and retrieved her tracking pole from the base of the telephone pole. Then, in plain sight, she walked up the winding road to her cabin.

The bullet casing, the tracks, and the presence of the .22 possibly might be enough to nail Mrs. Lucas for shooting Minnie. Or the presence of her skis for some kind of burglary charge. And the armament in the bedroom closet just might get someone charged with domestic terrorism or some related crime. But aiding and abetting the removal of the pathetic little boy with the dirty face and dull eyes from that sewage pit of a home might prove infinitely more satisfying.

Back at the cabin, which in contrast to the Lucas' house, seemed light and fresh and spic-and-span, Gracie donned a pair of purple latex gloves. She transferred the pictures she had taken from her camera onto four separate CDs. She wrote up a detailed description of the condition of the house and the yard along with the suggestion to check the backyard pile of trash for a drug stash. She put a copy of the letter and a CD into four separate manila envelopes addressed in turn to the Timber Creek branch of the Sheriff's Department, the L.A. office of the FBI and county social services down the hill. No return address. The fourth envelope she addressed to herself.

While she was at it, she stuffed the papers she had copied in the camp office into another envelope addressed to the church in L.A., along with a note recommending they conduct a thorough audit of the camp's books, paying close attention to guests paying in cash and Adventures "R" Us clients.

That completed, she sat back in the chair, motionless, staring into space, hands in her lap, thinking. She had no idea who to call about the events at camp and their relationship to Jett's accident, which was being handled by California

Highway Patrol. She didn't know enough about the different law enforcement agencies and how they interacted with one another, and while she'd heard the names of several California Highway Patrol officers bandied about, they in essence remained nameless faces to her. Finally she dialed the Sheriff's Office and asked for the one person in law enforcement she actually liked Detective Krueger. When a female voice told her the detective was in the field and unavailable, she left her name, her cell and home phone numbers, and a message saying that she would like to talk to him in reference to the automobile accident of Jett McKenna and that she believed she had information that might prove helpful to the case and didn't know who else to call.

With the envelopes sitting in a pile on the kitchen counter waiting to be stamped and mailed, Gracie stood in the middle of the kitchen, exhausted but restless, unable to sit still.

Only two weeks before, the cabin had been her comfort, her refuge. Now it felt hollow, a shell, bereft of life. And love. Bereft of Minnie. Gracie had never experienced such absolute trust, such unconditional love.

If Minnie died . . .

Gracie jumped into the shower to rid herself of the stench of the Lucas house. Five minutes later she jumped out again and threw on a cotton button-down shirt and a pair of khaki shorts. She picked out another change of clothes from the clean clothes pile on top of the dryer, stuffed them into a duffel bag, and tossed a toothbrush in on top.

Then she ran out of the cabin and out to the truck.

32

GRACIE stood just inside the heavy glass front door of La Maison de Francois and rubbed away the beads of sweat on her upper lip with the tip of her finger. The humidity at what was, for all intents and purposes, sea level had laid a sheen of moisture on her face and arms. The air inside the restaurant cradled the heavy scent of baking pastry.

Gracie had left her cabin with no clear purpose, no definitive destination, only the single, driving need to be away. Almost too late, she texted Jon to let him know she had made it safely out of the canyon. She had called Rob's cell phone, leaving him a message that she was driving to L.A. that evening and that he could call or text her on her cell phone if he was available to meet her for dinner.

The drive to Los Angeles had been typically grueling— an hour of winding, mostly two-lane highway down the mountain followed by almost two hours of squinting into the setting sun on the 10 Freeway, eight lanes of traffic traveling seventy miles per hour.

In Pomona, where the Ranger had sat at a dead standstill for ten minutes, Gracie had called the animal hospital on her cell phone, learning that Minnie had made it through her surgery and was in recovery. The real test would be if she made it through the night. Gracie spent the next thirty minutes swiping away the tears blurring her vision in order to avoid a multicar pileup.

Rob had texted back saying he would make himself available to meet her for dinner. Following directions he had provided, a half hour along surface streets brought her from the interstate to a chichi restaurant on Wilshire Avenue.

Two women sailed past Gracie and into the restaurant. Tall and willowy, like ethereal woodland beings with rivers of gleaming wheat-colored hair streaming down their backs. Gauzy floor-length dresses billowing behind them.

Gracie looked down at her scratched and bruised legs. Fingernails and toenails clipped short. No-label button-down shirt, shorts, and Tevas. Why hadn't she at least thought to wear the little black dress she had worn to Jett's memorial service?

That was the problem. She hadn't been thinking.

She looked back up and watched the two women disappear into the depths of the restaurant. Their botanical garden scent hovered in the air.

She bought Patagonia and North Face from sale racks and outlet malls, not Hermès and Dolce & Gabbana from boutiques in Paris or Milan. She was beer and take-out pizza, not French wine and whatever-the-French-ate.

I don't belong here.

With near panic, Gracie turned to push out through the front door.

The maître d' glided up behind her. "May I help you, madam?" he asked.

Gracie stopped, turning back. "No. Thank you. No, I'm . . ."

"She's with me." Rob appeared out of nowhere, took Gracie's hand, and kissed both cheeks.

"Very good, sir," the maître d' said, and melted away.

When Rob straightened and looked Gracie full in the face, she almost gasped.

Had it really been six months since she had last seen him on that horrible November day, at the funeral of one of her teammates killed on a search, the day he had offered to whisk her away to London and a life of unimaginable wealth and luxury? The day she, in a moment of insanity, had turned him down, choosing instead to stay in her dreary little life in Timber Creek?

Except for his curling mop of hair, which had been restored from dyed black to its natural corn-silk blond and a tan, a total reversal from the pasty white of the previous winter, Rob hadn't changed. Dark eyes, thick-lashed. Wide shoulders. Narrow hips. More than six inches taller than Gracie. And a magnetic power that still knocked Gracie sideways.

He wore a creamy white long-sleeved shirt and faded Levi's with a braided brown leather belt and brown suede Pumas.

And that perfect golden smile.

Seeing his face again, feeling the warmth, the caring, Gracie decided it didn't matter if she was attracted to him because he was a truly nice person or because he was so friggin' gorgeous. She was there with him now and that was all that mattered.

Gracie looked down at his feet, then up into his face.

"Glad to see you lost those butt-ugly roach-killer city shoes," she said.

"Glad to see you finally washed your hair," he said. He cocked his head. "You seem taller."

"That's 'cause I'm standing up, dolt, not lying in your smelly armpit in an itty-bitty plastic shelter. Or sitting in an idiotic wheelchair."

His dark eyes were shining down at her. "You look as tired as a ruttin' bull-cat after an all-night prowl through the mud."

Gracie grinned at Rob's penchant for cowboy slang, as familiar and comfortable as a childhood smell. "Any other brilliant observations?"

"Just that I'm so happy you called," he said, and enfolded her into his arms, breathing in her scent.

"Yeah, uh . . . Sorry about the short notice. I . . . And sorry I haven't been very good about . . . keeping in touch."

Rob whispered something that sounded like, "You're here now. That's what matters." Then he kissed her earlobe, a lingering of soft lips that sent fire shooting down the length of Gracie's body.

With a hand on her back, Rob guided her back through greenery, wrought iron, and red brick to a high-backed, black leather booth in a private alcove that announced privacy and movie deals and lots and lots of money.

Conversation was immediate, easy, as soft and comfortable as an old baseball glove, as if no time at all had passed and during which Gracie felt no need for pretense, no pressure to present herself in the most flattering light. Rob had already seen her at her worst.

Over goat cheese and garlic soup with lobster, Rob regaled Gracie with stories about the movie he had shot in Kenya, of living in tents in the bush with volcanic dust in every crack and crevice, of no outside contact for days, of bull elephants in camp and cheetahs and hyenas and lions out on the savannah, and hippos in the Mara River.

As Gracie sampled the black truffle risotto—one bite was enough—Rob asked her about The Sky's the Limit program.

"It's fantastic!" she said, leaning toward him. "I love it! Thank you! So much."

During dinner of tenderloin with grapefruit polenta, broccolini, and beurre rouge, Gracie described scavenger hunts and Capture the Flag and hikes through the woods, identifying flowers and birds along the way. She told him about sprained ankles and homesickness and mosquito bites and nighttime pranks, about the glowing faces, the laughter, and the goofy antics of camp staff at closing campfire. Throughout it all, Rob listened, his bright eyes never leaving her face, a half smile on his lips.

Finally when she had run out of stories, he asked, "And Search and Rescue? Of course, you're still doing that."

"Of course."

"Tell me."

Gracie leaned back, the leather seat creaking with the movement. She examined the glass of Pinot Noir in her hand, considering whether she should tell him about Jett's death, about her suspicions that her friend might have been murdered. In the end, not wanting to break the spell but deciding that she would tell him the entire sordid story someday, maybe, she described for Rob the unsuccessful search for Gina Ramirez, and the vehicle over-the-side recovery operation, explaining everything carefully, slowly, leaving nothing out except that she had known the victim.

When she had finished, Rob took her hand and looked into her face. "Have I ever told you how amazing I think you are?"

Gracie squirmed in her seat, unable to meet his eyes. "Smoke and mirrors," she said under her breath.

"Haven't changed a bit, have you?"

She looked back up at him. "A little. Maybe."

"Don't change too much, love," he said with a twinkle in his eyes that made Gracie's stomach do a somersault. "I love you just the way you are."

MARROW-DEEP EXHAUSTION SENT the heavy meal, crème brûlée, three glasses of Pinot and an orange liqueur straight to Gracie's head.

She sank low in the supple leather seat of Rob's Mercedes, barely aware of the quiet, smooth-as-silk glide out of the city, up through a dark, winding maze of streets to the top of Hollywood Hills, through a ten-foot-high gate of wrought iron and onto a property more closely resembling the Amazonian jungle than a yard.

She now stood facing Rob on a thick Persian rug larger than a lake in the center of a palatial living room. Through the haze of fatigue, she absorbed only vague impressions of recessed lighting, saddle-brown leather, vases exploding with white orchids and roses and gladiolas. The mantel of a gargantuan stone fireplace was crowded with gold orbs and angels and picture frames flanked by a pair of gold statuettes. A solid wall of glass doors opened up onto a deck floating above a sea of lights.

"This your house? 'Sbig."

"A friend's."

"Friggin' Prince of Wales?"

Rob touched the scab on the corner of her mouth with the tip of his finger. "How did you get this?" he asked.

"Dunno," Gracie said, purposely vague. "Search?"

"Bullshit," Rob said in a quiet voice. He took her hand and turned her arm to the light, exposing dark purple circles on her wrist where Eddie's fingers had bitten into her skin. "These, too? Are you going to tell me you got these on a search?"

Gracie frowned down at the bruises. Her brain was fuzzy. She couldn't think of a single plausible answer except the truth, so she shook her head and whispered, "No." She swayed on her feet.

Rob steadied with a hand on her elbow and bent to look into her face, brows furrowed above gentle eyes. "You look all in, love."

"Yeah. Sorry. Too much . . . t'drink."

Without another word, Rob led her down a long darkened hallway, past alcoves of artwork and pottery, to a bedroom with a bed the size of a swimming pool. She stood like a child as, with great care, he unbuttoned her shirt, un-Velcroed her Tevas, and slid off her shorts. Then, tossing a mound of decorative pillows onto an armchair, he drew back the covers and helped her into bed, pulling the Egyptian cotton sheet and blanket up beneath her chin.

"Not ver' romantic," she mumbled, unable to keep her eyes open.

"Shut up, twit," he whispered in her ear. He kissed her gently on the mouth and reached over and turned out the bedside lamp.

In an instant, Gracie was unconscious and slept like the dead.

GRACIE stared up at an exquisite mural of cherubs and flowers and clouds and thought, *Where the hell am I?*

She sat up in bed and looked around the room.

Morning light and a symphony of chirping birds poured through the sheer white drapes of a floor-to-ceiling window. The other side of the enormous bed had been slept in, its pillow dented, but it was now empty.

Gracie drew on the silk robe that had been draped over the armchair beside the bed. From her pack on the floor next to the bed, she dug out her cell phone and called the animal hospital.

With a relief so intense she had to sit down on the bed, she listened to Dr. Peterson telling her that Minnie had survived the night, recovered enough to lap up some water and wag her tail, but that she would like to keep her for a couple of more days.

Gracie spent several minutes in the marble-everything

bathroom large enough for a Roman emperor, amazed at how resonant and beautiful her own voice sounded when singing "Pour, Oh Pour the Pirate Sherry" in the cavernous shower.

She then wandered through the massive house, passing media and music rooms and a wood-paneled library in search of Rob.

She found him sitting on an outdoor terrace, orange bougainvillea cascading behind him, drinking what she surmised was tea and reading a script. The terrace overlooked a canopy of palm trees and lavender jacaranda. The humid air was bursting with birdsong and unfamiliar semitropical smells. The sun burned through the gray marine layer as a gauzy orb.

When Gracie appeared, Rob stood up with a smile and kissed her on the mouth. "Morning, love." He was barefoot, wearing the same Levi's as the night before, but with a red-, green-, and white-striped rugby shirt. Gracie realized with a start that, for all she and Rob had been through together, this was the first time she was seeing Rob Christian as his true self in the light of day.

"I'm sorry about last night," she said. "I mean for falling asleep. I was . . ."

"Knackered?"

Gracie huffed a laugh. "Yeah. Knackered." She sat in the cushioned chair across the glass table from Rob and gestured to the mansion behind her. "Nice digs. Think they got enough room here? The friggin' bathroom's bigger'n my friggin' cabin."

"I haven't seen your cabin."

Gracie let that one slide. "You always live like this?"

"Only when I'm trying to impress a girl." He grinned at her over his teacup.

Gracie snorted. "You don't need to impress me."

"Payback then."

Gracie squinted back at him. "You know that isn't why I'm on the team."

"Of course it isn't. But sharing this with you makes me happy. So shut that beautiful mouth and allow me to indulge you. Please?"

Breakfast for two, prepared by an anonymous someone in the cavernous kitchen that Gracie had caught only a glimpse of the night before, was rolled out on a silver cart: eggs Benedict with juicy slabs of ham, thick slices of whole-wheat toast, fresh blackberry preserves, real butter, freshly squeezed orange juice, little crystal bowls containing chunks of real Hawaiian pineapple and guava and passion fruit, and coffee topped with a dollop of heavy whipped cream.

By the time Gracie and Rob left the mansion, the Ranger had miraculously appeared, keys inside, on the circle drive in front.

They drove up the Pacific Coast Highway in the Mercedes with the top down, on their left ocean breakers brilliant white against deep Pacific blue, and reveling in the pleasure of each other's company.

Late lunch was perched on teetery chairs at a dumpy shack across the highway from a wide strip of white beach, studded here and there with boulders. Gracie was shocked at how shocked she was at the sight of young women with bits of string barely holding triangles of fabric over breasts, unnaturally high and rounded, and other parts lower. Men with machine-molded chests and arms sun-roasted to golden brown played beach volleyball and other mating-dance sand sports. Umbrellas in yellow and green and red and blue. Kids with balls and shovels and buckets in the shade of palm trees swaying the hula in the breeze.

Rising up in the curving distance, misty cliffs crowded with houses of white stucco and terra-cotta intertwined throughout with palms and flaming fuchsia bougainvillea.

The air tanged with ocean salt. Seagulls wheeled overhead, their mournful cries heard above the laughter, the talk, the noise of passing cars, the constant thudding of the aquamarine surf.

All the while Gracie was aware that she was in a state of suspended animation, living in the present with no past and no future, as if she had pressed the Pause button on her life and lost herself in the dream that was Rob Christian. For a few short hours, nothing and no one else mattered.

Gracie bit into her cheeseburger, so large she could barely get her mouth around it. Across the rickety table from her, Rob slathered a greasy French fry with ketchup and popped into his mouth. Then he grinned and reached over to wipe off the juice running down her chin with a napkin.

Gracie could see a fish-eye version of herself in the lenses of his sunglasses.

"So," Rob said, "Remember when . . . during . . . back in November, I said that I had changed, that that whole . . . experience had changed me, my life?"

Gracie almost said that it had changed hers indelibly, forever, as well, but she kept silent and just nodded, still chewing.

"That you had changed me, my life?"

She swallowed. "The circumstances did. It would have changed anyone."

"Be quiet and listen to me, please."

"Yes, boss," Gracie said, and took another bite of her burger.

"I remember that at the time I waxed lyrical about having

lived in two dimensions up until then, and I was then seeing things in three."

"I remember."

"That things had simplified while at the same time becoming more complex, richer somehow."

How could Gracie forget? She remembered everything about the last time she had seen him as if it was happening at that very moment.

After her teammate's funeral, Rob had come to see her where she sat in a stuffy little room off the sanctuary. She remembered the subtle, husky scent of his cologne, the shushing sound his suit made as he pulled a chair next to her wheelchair and sat down, the way his hair, then still dyed black for the movie, curled a certain way above his ears, the microscopic stitches closing cuts on his cheekbone and above his eye, the bruises, the scrapes, his warm hands taking hers, his soft lips pressed to hers. But mostly she remembered his eyes, dark brown and shining at her. "I haven't forgotten," she said.

"That feeling hasn't faded," Rob said. "If anything, it's intensified. I see things, my life, the people around me with a clarity I didn't think possible. You were the one who brought me here . . . to this point. I want to thank you, again, for that."

AS THE REST of the afternoon sped by, Gracie shed the ten years she had aged over the last two weeks. Her world righted and stabilized as if she had time to finally catch her breath and regain her balance. The thunderclouds gathering on the horizon dissipated.

Finally, with the sun a memory of swirling deep purple clouds above the silver satin Pacific, the Mercedes wended its way south along the coast toward the city. When Rob glanced over at Gracie, placed his warm hand on hers, and said, "I want to make love with you," she only just managed not to spray her Double Chocolaty Chip Frappuccino all over the leather dashboard.

"Properly," Rob continued, frowning at the road ahead. "Not in a bloody cold snow cave with layers of bloody clothing in between."

As nonchalantly as she could muster, Gracie shrugged and said, "Who am I to argue?"

ANGLED STREAMERS OF early evening light filtered in through the gauzy white drapes. Gracie and Rob stood in the middle of the sumptuous bedroom, feet sinking into three-inch-thick carpet. Pumas and Tevas, rugby shirt and cotton button-down, blue jeans and khaki shorts, and starched white boxers and daisy-printed cotton all lay in a pile on the floor.

Twenty-four hours with Rob had lit Gracie's body on fire. Without inhibition and with smiling eyes, she rediscovered Rob's body while he rediscovered hers. She breathed in his scent, drank in his taste, shivered at his featherlight touch, immersed herself in the moment until her knees gave way and she tumbled back onto the sumptuous bed with Rob above her.

Sometime after one in the morning, they fell asleep, intertwined, spent, at peace.

ONE MOMENT GRACIE was sleeping, the next she was awake with her eyes open, unaware of why, but knowing that going to sleep again wasn't anywhere in the near future.

She looked over at the clock beside the bed. Three minutes to four.

Rob was breathing deeply in sleep two feet away from her. She looked over but could see only his silhouette in the dark.

I love him, she thought, staring up at the ceiling. Her heart beat harder inside her chest.

The old, familiar thoughts flooded back.

No, you don't! You're infatuated. You don't even really know him.

I'm in love with him.

It's too soon.

Too soon! It's been ten years since What's-his-name, the Prick, left.

Jilted me, you mean? Left me at the altar.

It's been ten friggin' years! Get over it already!

It could never work. Rob and I aren't anything alike. We go together about as well as . . . as . . . orange juice and toothpaste. He's city. I'm mountains. He's big money. Big. Money. I'm . . . not. He's beautiful, glamorous people and mansions and movie premieres. I'm regular homely folks and cabins and . . . solitude. Yeah, solitude. I need my peace. I need my quiet. It could never work.

You do this every time. Rob's the best thing that has ever happened to you, that is ever going to happen to you. It ain't gonna get no better!

Tears formed and slid down the sides of her face. She covered her face with her hands and sobbed in silence, trying not to shake the bed and wake Rob up.

Shit. Shit! It'll never work!

She pushed back the covers, and carefully, slowly so as not to wake Rob, she left the bed.

BY THE TIME the Ranger crossed the county line in Ontario, the San Bernardino Freeway was heavy with early-morning commuters. Gracie checked her cell and home phones for messages. Serene had never returned her call. Nor had Ralph. But Detective Krueger of the Sheriff's Office had left messages on both phones, providing his cell phone number and asking her to please call him back at any time, day or night. She called the number, but the call went straight to voice mail. She left the detective a message and hung up. Another call to the animal hospital told her that Minnie was continuing to improve, but they would like to keep her at least another day.

The entire trip back, Gracie rode an emotional seesaw on a roller coaster. By being with Rob, she felt that somehow she had betrayed Ralph, her best friend, who said he loved her and wanted to marry her. But Rob's mouth still burned hers. Ralph's blue-gray eyes filled with love seared her heart. Rob's golden smile. Ralph's strong arms. Up down up down. Elation. Guilt. Warmth. Betrayal. Peace. Indifference.

The Ranger headed off the highway onto the approach to the long meandering climb up the mountain to Timber Creek, to camp and the darkness there. Such a short time before, Gracie felt she loved her job, loved the camp, and wanted to stay there forever. Now with the thought of returning to camp, apprehension and dread pushed everything else aside and settled onto her shoulders like a physical weight.

CHAPTER

34

MADISON yanked the string on the overhead light, filling the little basement office with a feeble yellow light. She stood next to Gracie's desk, ponytail swinging back and forth, right foot tapping molto allegro. "Why were you sitting here in the dark?"

The slamming of the front door upstairs and footsteps on the basement stairs had forewarned Gracie, giving her time to lift her head from the desk and rub her eyes into some semblance of wakefulness. Leaving the living fantasy that was Rob, less than three hours of sleep, and the long grinding drive back from L.A. had rendered her positively cranky. She stifled the sudden urge to muss up all that perfect hair and makeup and ask Madison what she had cooking with Jay. "Hello, Madison," was what she said instead.

"Abe's on the low course with a very important client," Madison said. "*Very* important."

Very, very important.

The foot didn't stop. "The haul cord for the central belay is missing."

"Well, that's not good, is it?" Gracie said.

If one didn't hang on tightly enough to the haul cord—a length of parachute cord used to hang and remove the climbing rope—the weight of the rope itself could pull the cord out of one's hands, the device on the cable above and back down to the ground. The cable for the central belay was in the center of the trapezoid of elements fifty feet off the ground.

"Who's going to hang it?" Madison asked. "I can't find Eddie anywhere."

No surprise there.

"This is . . . this is just . . . unacceptable." The increase in pitch and volume of Madison's voice signaled rising panic. "Our client is . . . high dollar and . . . and . . ."

"Very important," Gracie finished for her.

It didn't matter how important the client was. The central belay was used for rescues. The haul cord had to be rehung, a daunting task Gracie had performed only once before. It looked as if today was her lucky day. She sighed and pushed herself to her feet. "I'll grab my gear."

Madison's Very Cherry lips pursed. "What do you mean? *You're* going to rehang it?"

It was Gracie's turn to purse her lips.

"YOU WANT A ride down to the course?" Gracie asked as she pulled open the door of the Ranger and climbed inside.

Madison stood in the parking lot, clearly conflicted as to whether riding in a questionable-looking pickup truck was preferable to walking the three-quarters of a mile back down to the high ropes course.

Decision made, she pulled the passenger's door open and climbed in.

Gracie had read about it in books but had never actually seen anyone get into a truck that way—butt on the seat first, then legs pulled in together as if she had been given personal instruction by Miss Manners herself. Quite a feat since the seat was more than three feet off the ground. But Madison managed it.

As the two women rode down the little hill and over the creek, Gracie considered the possibility that the woman sitting next to her along with her husband and Jay Wilson were defrauding the church that owned the camp and if the envelopes she had mailed before driving down to L.A. had already arrived at their corresponding destinations.

The Ranger bumped past the Serrano parking lot and down the Main Road hill.

Madison glanced at the blaze orange Search and Rescue parka with its identifying patches hanging behind the driver's seat. Her head snapped forward to peer at Gracie. "You belong to Search and Rescue?"

"Yup."

"Oh. I didn't know that. Oh. I'd love to do that. Search and Rescue. Those uniforms are so cool!" She thought for a moment, lips pursed again, then said, "Except I don't think I could deal with dead bodies. Don't you have to do that? Deal with dead bodies?"

Gracie stared straight ahead. "Sometimes."

"That part I don't like. Oh. I just don't think I could do that."

Gracie parked the Ranger on the flat area overlooking the high ropes course. She grabbed her ropes gear pack from the back and followed Madison down the amphitheater steps to the floor of the course.

"Do . . . do you need me to belay you?" A perceptible whine belied Madison's offer.

"I'll use lobster claws." Gracie bent to retrieve one end of the fallen haul cords and lifted a huge ball of nylon spaghetti from the ground. "You could work on this, though, while I gear up." Madison took the snarl between her forefinger and thumb as if she were receiving a tangle of worms rather than haul cord.

How in the world can you work on a ropes course without getting your hands dirty? Gracie wondered as she stepped into the leg loops of her climbing harness. *Getting dirty's half the fun.*

She cinched her waistband tight and doubled the end back through the buckle. She checked the harness loops, making sure all the paraphernalia was hanging in its proper place: carabiners—steel and aluminum, locking and nonlocking— a daisy chain of tubular nylon webbing, mini-pulleys, accessory cord. To the waistband, she clipped another carabiner attached in turn to lobster claws—a V of nylon webbing straps with carabiners on both ends.

She clipped on her helmet and tugged on worn-soft leather gloves, then taking the now-untangled haul cord from Madison, tied both ends onto a harness loop.

With the cord trailing behind, she climbed up the narrow, metal caving ladder that served as the access to the central belay, clipping and reclipping the lobster claws to successive rungs along the way.

At the first cable thirty feet up, Gracie stopped for a moment, leaning against the tree trunk to catch her breath. Then, using steel staples embedded in the tree trunk as hand- and footholds, she climbed the remaining twenty feet until she stood with her feet on the central belay cable.

She looked down at Madison watching her from fifty feet

below, reminded herself that looking down was a bad idea, and looked out to where the haul cord pulley dangled from the middle of the cable.

She took in a deep breath and blew it out slowly to still the butterflies in her stomach. Crouching down, she detached the little pulley from her harness loop, attached it to the cable, and fastened it to her harness with a carabiner and a short length of the webbing. "Ready, Freddy," she said, then stalled a little longer by squeeze-checking all of her carabiners again to make sure each one was locked.

Her hands trembled, heart thudded in her chest. "This is stupid. Ridiculous. Harebrained." To fortify her courage, she reminded herself of the breaking strength of each piece of equipment. With the built-in ten-to-one safety ratio, her system was strong enough to hold both Sergeant Gardner and Mr. Lucas with the scrawny Mrs. Lucas thrown in. "Bomb-proof," she said, then added, "I'm too old for this shit."

She took another deep breath. Leaning forward, she held on to the cable and let herself tip over so she hung upside down, allowing the webbing attached to her harness to take her body weight.

So this is how a two-toed sloth feels. Or is it three-toed? Concentrate!

Hand over hand, she pulled herself along the cable until she reached the haul cord pulley. Working with her hands over her head, she detached the haul cord from her harness and fed one end through the pulley.

"For goodness' sake, don't let it go again," Madison called up from below.

No shit, Sherlock. "I won't," Gracie called back. She tied a carabiner to the end of the cord and lowered it down to Madison.

"Got it!" Madison called from below.

The cable moved and Gracie jerked downward. "What the hell?" She dropped her legs and grabbed at the cable with both hands. "What's happening?"

"The cable's—"

The cable moved again.

Gracie jerked downward again.

Then she was sliding. Dizzying. The cable zipped through the pulley, burning her hands through her gloves, the ground rushing toward her.

Madison screamed.

Gracie plummeted to the ground.

CHAPTER

35

PAIN exploded in Gracie's ankle.

She lay sprawled on her side on the mulch in the middle of the ropes course, unable to move, unable to keep moans of agony from escaping with every intake of breath.

Madison appeared over her, screaming at the top of her lungs.

"Madison!" Gracie growled through tightly clenched teeth. "Be quiet!"

Immediate silence.

"Take my truck," Gracie said, gasping. "Camp kitchen best. Call Ralph Hunter. Number in. My cell. Day pack."

"The cable," Madison mumbled, her hands clamped over her mouth. "It just came off the tree."

"Madison. Call Ralph. From the kitchen. Number's on. My cell."

Madison stumbled up the hill to Gracie's pack lying at the base of the tree.

"Side pocket," Gracie yelled, and followed it up with, "Bring ice!"

MADISON REAPPEARED ON the ropes course after what seemed a geologic age, during which time Gracie medically assessed each of her limbs for injury, testing them in turn, moving, flexing, extending until she was reasonably confident that no bones other than one in her ankle were broken.

But her back, neck, and shoulders had seized up in agonizing spasm, like a giant hand clenching her muscles into its fist. She had managed to de-pretzel her body, turning herself ninety degrees so her injured ankle was higher than her head. Only after did she lie still, trying to manage the pain by sucking air in through her nose and out through her mouth and counting, "In two three four, out two three four, in two three four."

Through eyes open barely a slit, Gracie looked at the sandwich bag of ice Madison was holding. "Left ankle," she grunted. "Outside. Please."

Madison dropped the bag of ice on the ankle. Gracie yelled and Madison screamed again.

Gracie panted like a dog with the pain, an arm over her eyes. "Put the ice right on the break. Hold it there. Please. I won't yell again."

When no further ice pick of pain stabbed her ankle, Gracie opened her eyes a slit and looked around. The other woman was nowhere to be seen. "Madison?"

She reached uphill, grunting with the effort, grasped the bag of ice with her fingers, and set it on the break, then lay back, arm over her eyes again, groaning through her teeth, through the initial immobilizing agony, until the ice gradually did its work and anesthetized the pain.

Gracie lay alone in misery, unmoving except for taking in deep, regular breaths, wondering what the hell had just happened and how the hell had she fallen, for what seemed another infinity until, in a billowing of dust, Ralph's white pickup roared right up onto the high course and stopped five feet from where she lay on the wood chips.

He jumped down from the truck and in one long stride was kneeling beside her.

"Ralphie," Gracie said, gasping.

"What the hell did you do now, Gracie girl?" His voice was quiet, gentle, his old voice, the voice of the man who still loved her.

Where the pain hadn't, Ralph's presence moved Gracie to tears. They blurred her vision and rolled down the sides of her face into her hair. "Had. Get your attention. Somehow."

"I'm here now."

She gave Ralph a cursory medical assessment of her own condition. "Mostly the left ankle. Broken. Take me down the hill? Loma Linda?"

"Of course." He left her side for a moment, then reappeared to say in a low voice, "Oxy."

In spite of the gauze that was her brain, Gracie managed to compute the information. Oxycodone. Left over from his wife's battle with cancer. Potent painkiller. Closely controlled narcotic. Illegal for him to dispense to her.

Cradling her head with his hand, Ralph placed the pill in her mouth, then tipped up his water bottle so she could swallow it.

Madison reappeared from somewhere, salon-tanned legs inches away from Gracie's face. "Excuse me, sir," she said.

Ignoring her, Ralph placed an inflatable splint around the lower half of Gracie's leg.

Before Gracie could protest, he lifted her completely off

the ground and carried her down to his truck. She knew how much Ralph carrying her was costing him. "I can walk," she grunted. "Your knee."

"Be the patient and be quiet for a change," he said.

With much excruciating maneuvering, Gracie ended up sitting sideways on the bench seat behind Ralph, her back against the window, injured leg stretched out and padded in place with a rolled-up sleeping bag and a tent.

Ralph climbed into the driver's seat.

Madison appeared beside the truck. "Excuse me. What am I going to do about the central belay? The cable's in the middle of the course. I have clients coming in."

"Sorry. Can't help you," Ralph said, and pulled the door closed. He gunned the accelerator and fishtailed the truck back onto the road, spraying a rooster tail of dust, duff, and dirt flying out behind the truck.

Even with the splint and the painkillers, the hour-and-a-quarter-long drive down the mountain to the Level 1 trauma center at Loma Linda was an exercise in agony. Every bump sent a shock wave of pain up Gracie's leg.

"Knew you couldn't stay mad at me," she mumbled. "Knew you'd f'give me."

"And why's that?" came Ralph's steady voice from the front seat.

"Cuz."

"Cuz isn't an answer." She heard the smile in his voice.

"Cuz you're m'best friend 'n' best friends f'give 'chother."

A little windup alarm clock on a table next to the bed read three minutes after nine. Sunshine filtering through blue gingham curtains at the window on Gracie's right told her it was nine in the morning, not nine at night.

Oxycodone, this time legally obtained by prescription, had knocked her flat. She had been kept in the hospital overnight "for observation," then released too early the following morning. For forty-eight hours, she did nothing but sleep in the double bed in Ralph's guest room, injured foot propped up on a tower of pillows, rousing herself only enough to gulp down more painkillers from the water glass that was, miraculously, always full, and refusing Ralph's offers to help her use the bathroom.

She remembered the ER doc telling her that her ankle had been broken in two places, but they were clean breaks, no surgery required, and that she must have amazingly strong bones not to have broken anything else.

A half dosage of oxy taken earlier that morning had burnished the rough edges of her pain to tolerable. But where before, coherent thought had been impossible, now, at least, she could think.

She stared up at the ceiling.

What the *hell* had happened on the ropes course? How the *hell* had she fallen?

Hyperaware of the potentially catastrophic consequences of equipment failure, she was meticulous about maintaining her personal gear, inspecting each rope, each carabiner, each accessory cord, with anal-retentive regularity and thoroughness, often retiring it before its expiration date even if it showed no sign of wear and tear. The ropes course itself had gone through its annual inspection the month before. Every component—trees, cables, bolts, clamps, staples—had been scrutinized by an outside company.

Gracie had been lucky. Very lucky. She could easily have broken her neck or back, or been killed. What glaring error had she made that had almost cost her her life?

She simply couldn't remember.

She closed her eyes again and slept.

Hours later, in the semidarkness of late afternoon in an east-facing room, Gracie shoved back the covers and slowly pushed herself up into a sitting position on the bed, her body so stiff and sore, she wouldn't have been surprised if her joints had actually creaked with the movement.

"Ralph?" she called.

No answer.

"Ralphie, you here?"

Silence. She was alone in the cabin.

She turned on the lamp on the table next to the bed. A note card propped against the lamp base told her in Ralph's blocky handwriting to help herself to anything in the refrigerator. He was on a job site down the hill and wouldn't be home until seven or eight that night. *Call me when you're up. I don't want to call in case you're sleeping.* A stylized *R* was scrawled at the bottom. Impersonal. Revealing nothing.

"I'm so sorry I hurt you," Gracie whispered.

Her eyes traveled the length of her body.

She was wearing a faded Detroit Tigers T-shirt and a pair of Ralph's red plaid pajama bottoms cut off above the knees. The toes on her left foot stuck out the end of a Pepto Bismol–pink cast.

Friggin' hell. Who picked out that color?

Deep purple bruises and scabbed-over abrasions covered her arms and legs. Wood slivers from the mulch were embedded in the skin on her knees and elbows and the palms of her hands. While the spasms in her back and neck had released their vise grip, the muscles were still tender to the touch.

She had been bruised and scratched and cut before. She'd had torn tendons and pulled muscles. Her body always, marvelously, miraculously, healed itself. Again she puzzled over what she had done this time that had almost ended her life.

She sighed with frustration. Her mind was a complete blank.

Pushing to the forefront of her attention, however, was her stomach churning with hunger—a sure sign that she was feeling better.

Using a pair of wooden crutches she found lying on the floor next to the bed, she hopped first to the bathroom, pointedly avoiding a heart attack by not looking at herself in the mirror. From there she made her way into the kitchen where she found her day pack on a chair, and a stack of emergency room papers and doctor's orders and a mound of letters and magazines on the table. Ralph had retrieved her mail from the post office substation. "Thank goodness for small towns," Gracie said, adding, "Ralphie, you're too good to me."

The coffeemaker already held water and fresh coffee, so all Gracie had to do was press the On button.

She hopped over to the table, sat down, and propped her foot up on an adjoining chair. As coffee spit into the carafe, she looked around the spotless kitchen.

Yellow gingham curtains on the window above the sink and on the back door, cabinets and cupboards painted white, wallpaper with white picket fences and red barns and horses and yellow daisies in green fields. Ruffled yellow place mats piled neatly in the center of the Formica table. Homey, comfortable, all bespeaking of Eleanor, Ralph's wife who had died several years before and whose presence could still be felt in every inch of the house.

Various coats and jackets hung from pegs next to the back door. Ralph's hiking boots sat on a floor mat beneath. The only other thing in the room that was truly Ralph's was a hunting calendar from a local gun shop hanging next to the refrigerator.

Kinda like a shrine, Gracie thought.

Ralph had been devastated by his wife's death. Was changing nothing in the years since paying some kind of homage to her? Or was it simply that Ralph didn't care enough about homemaking to redecorate? Gracie realized with shame that, as well as she thought she knew her friend, she didn't know the answer.

The faint aroma of cigarettes permeated the kitchen. Eleanor had abhorred the habit, forcing Ralph to smoke in secret. After her death, he had taken up the habit again, though managing to keep it to only one or two with a beer or during times of stress.

The coffeemaker stopped sputtering. Gracie hopped over and poured herself a mug. She added a healthy dab of skim milk and stretched back to set the mug on the table.

Minnie! Her hand jerked, slopping coffee on the floor.

Gracie had forgotten all about the dog. She could be dead, for all she knew.

With panic constricting her throat, she lifted the receiver from the rotary telephone on the wall next to her head and dialed the number of the animal hospital from memory.

This takes forever!

The phone on the other end rang and was answered. Gracie asked for Dr. Peterson, sat down on the chair, and waited. The veterinarian came on the line, telling her that Minnie was recovering nicely, doing so well, in fact, that she was ready to come home. Explaining her own recent injury, Gracie arranged to pick the dog up the next morning.

Minnie, her dog, was going to be okay.

Reaching back to hang up the phone, Gracie smiled, marveling at how quickly and completely the little animal had captured her heart.

She took a sip of coffee and idly picked through her mail, sorting it into separate piles of junk, bills, and "really important," which remained empty. She stopped, a first-class letter from Camp Ponderosa in her hands. Tearing it open, she unfolded the letter inside.

Dear Employee,

Please allow this letter to serve as formal notice that, effective immediately, you are hereby terminated from your position as director of The Sky's the Limit and ropes course manager.

The signature at the bottom: Pastor Jay Wilson. Gracie's first thought was, *What? Jay can't fire me!* Technically she was an employee of Rob's foundation, which had hired her and paid her to run the summer program. Rob's people would have to fire her. The only thing Jay could really fire her from was her job managing the ropes course. And the church might have something to say about that.

Her next reaction was, *Thank GOD!* She would never have to go back to camp again. Never have to be immersed in that toxic quagmire again. Or deal with Eddie again. Or Jay. Or Elaine.

Her shoulders slumped.

Shit.

She would never walk the back acreage of camp again. Or see the lake. Or the kids. Or work The Sky's the Limit camp. Or the job she loved. Or the ropes course.

Then, as if someone had thrown a switch, Gracie saw the central belay haul cord lying on the ground at the high course. Inexplicably. Waiting to be rehung. She was able to recall everything in detail up to where, hanging upside down, she had pulled herself out onto the cable toward the haul cord pulley.

She couldn't remember actually falling and perhaps never would.

But what she could remember was Madison's disembodied voice saying as if from a distance, "The cable. It just came off the tree."

There was no way the clamp bolts holding the cable in place had loosened enough on their own for the cable to unwind from the coarse bark of the tree trunk.

Someone had sabotaged the cable.

Someone had tried to kill her.

BESIDES Gracie, there was only one person working at camp with the knowledge, the ability, and the access to loosen a cable on the ropes course, and that person was Eddie. The intent was clearly, if not to kill her, then to injure her severely enough to incapacitate her, remove her from the picture.

It had been monumentally stupid of her not to realize that if she tweaked the dragon's tail, she could expect to get burned.

The rescuer in her told her it had also been monumentally stupid of Eddie to assume that Gracie, and not some other staff member or facilitator, would be the one to shinny out and replace the haul cord. But then, Gracie didn't think anyone was going to accuse Eddie of being a Rhodes scholar anytime in the near future.

The tranquilizing effects of the oxycodone diluted what might have been bombastic outrage. Still Gracie indulged herself in a thirty-second fantasy of painfully rearranging all of Eddie's appendages.

After which she reminded herself that Eddie alone wasn't embroiled in whatever was going on at camp.

Jay was in up to his ears as well with the embezzlement and who knew what else.

The Brothers Wilson. In it together.

Another thought hit Gracie, causing her to sit up straight in the chair, staring straight ahead, considering.

She had made the automatic assumption that there was no one at camp but Eddie with the expertise and the ability and the access to loosen the ropes course cable. But there was. Someone with possibly as much to lose as Eddie or Jay if Gracie blew the whistle on everything that was going on at camp.

Abe and Madison Bonds. Co-owners of Adventures "R" Us.

Gracie just couldn't imagine one-half of the couple had acted without the other half knowing. Although she really didn't know them that well, she was sure Abe would never risk his own wife's life by weakening an element on the ropes course and not telling her. And vice versa.

The flaw in the argument for the couple's involvement, Gracie figured, was that she had no proof whatsoever that the couple was even involved in any illegal shenanigans with Jay. And as far as Gracie knew, no one, not even Jay, was aware she suspected anything in the first place.

Plus it was Madison herself who had said that the cable had been loosened. Surely, if she or her husband had done it, she wouldn't have said anything to draw attention to the fact.

Gracie frowned. At least she thought she remembered Madison saying the cable had just come off the tree. She had been in such a haze of pain at the time, she couldn't be certain she actually remembered Madison's words or was dreaming them.

For the umpteenth time, Gracie wondered about Jett's journal, what information it might contain, which questions it might answer.

Gracie reached over, opened her pack sitting on the chair next to her, and pulled out the satchel she had found on the side of the hill. She dumped the contents out on the table and sorted through it all again.

Nothing.

Where *else* on earth could Jett's journal be? Where else would her friend have kept something precious, something she had to keep safe, something she didn't want anybody to find?

It had to be at camp. There simply was no other possibility.

But, Gracie remembered, she was no longer a camp employee and no longer welcome on the property. Too late now to drive back up there and rummage around the kitchen office or Jett's trailer looking for the journal.

Except she needed to retrieve all her personal belongings from her office. All her books. Her gear. And her paycheck. Her truck, hopefully, was still parked above the high course. While she was there, maybe, at least, she could inspect the ropes course cable.

She looked at the little German cuckoo clock on the wall. Four forty-one.

Gracie knew she should wait patiently for Ralph to come home in two, maybe three, hours. He would drive her up to camp. That would resolve the problem of retrieving the Ranger and her belongings. But then she would have to explain the entire story and the thought of arguing with him about the things she had done and still wanted to do was more exhausting than just driving there herself. Plus by then it would be too dark to inspect the cable.

She hopped back to the spare bedroom where a duffel bag sat on the chair. Saying a silent blessing for Ralph's thoughtfulness and foresight, she pulled on another T-shirt, a pair of her own shorts, and a single hiking boot. She gulped down two generic over-the-counter painkillers and stuffed an oxycodone into the pocket of her shorts just in case. Back in the kitchen, she dumped out the remaining contents of her day pack onto a chair, put her arms through the straps, and grabbed up the crutches.

Outside on the driveway, Ralph's baby was parked—an ancient pumpkin and cream International Scout. Gracie peeked in the driver's-side window and smiled at the sight of the keys dangling from the ignition.

Ralph hated locks. In this neighborhood in this village, he could still get away with leaving his house and vehicles unlocked.

Gracie tossed the empty day pack onto the passenger's seat, climbed in, lifted her foot with its cumbersome cast inside, and closed the door.

She sagged in the seat. The Scout had a manual transmission. "How the hell am I gonna work the clutch?" She struggled to reach it with her right foot. "Who put it . . . ?" She turned sideways in the seat, lifted her left leg with its cast up, propping her knee against the door. She pushed in the clutch with her right foot, shifted into neutral, and started the engine. "Where there's a friggin' will, there's a friggin' way," she grumbled, and coasted backward down the steep, narrow driveway.

THE drive to camp from the north end of the valley normally would have taken only thirty minutes. It took Gracie more than an hour. With maximum "eeeps" and "acks" and "shits," she jerked, stalled, coasted, ground the gears, screeched the tires, and revved the Scout's engine down the winding streets from Ralph's cabin to the highway, west along the northern shore of Timber Lake, over the dam bridge at the far end, then east again along the winding southern shore. By the time she turned the little truck onto the road leading up to camp, she was exhausted, her nerves fried, muscles stretched, and her ankle was throbbing again.

She drove the five curving miles up to camp in second gear, the engine sounding like a jet winding up for takeoff, all the way praying, "Please don't let Eddie be headed down out of camp. Please don't let me meet him on the way."

But she didn't meet Eddie or Jay or anyone else on the way up the hill, and there was no one anywhere in sight

when the Scout rolled beneath the archway at the camp
entrance.

Having decided on the way that retrieving her paycheck
and personal belongings from her office was first on the
agenda in case she had to clear out in a hurry, she pondered
where to park. Eddie might investigate a strange vehicle
parked in front of the office and especially around back in
the maintenance yard. The Scout wouldn't arouse suspicion
if she parked in the Serrano parking lot among the other
guest vehicles, but then she would have to hobble the entire
distance from there to the office, a daunting prospect, especially with the creek at the bottom of the hill.

Gracie rolled the Scout past the Gatehouse and down the
hill, turning into the maintenance yard. She gunned the
engine one last time. The Scout jumped forward and died
out of sight behind a ten-foot-high boulder.

Gracie slung the day pack over one shoulder and, using
a single crutch, hopped across the maintenance yard,
through the deserted shop and into her office.

She pulled the string on the overhead light and looked
down at her desk.

No paycheck.

She thought back and remembered she had opened it in
the reception area just before Eddie had attacked her. She
would have to hop upstairs and look for it.

First things first. She sat down on the little folding chair
and propped her aching foot up on an equipment bin. She
began pulling books from the little bookcase and stuffing them
into the pack on the floor between her legs. With her hand
on the binder containing the ropes course log, she stopped.

Sandwiched between the binder and *Mountaineering:
The Freedom of the Hills*, pushed all the way back against the
cement wall, was a Bible.

Jett's Bible.

There was no mistaking it. Jett had sewn the frilly cover herself out of pink-checkered gingham with an eyelet lace border and matching ribbon page marker.

As soon as she saw it, Gracie couldn't believe she hadn't noticed it missing before. It had been Jett's most precious possession. She never went anywhere without it. There was no other way the Bible could have found its way to her bookshelf except that Jett herself had put it there so that Gracie and only Gracie would find it.

With reverence, she drew it from the shelf and opened the front cover. *Jett McKenna* was scrawled in blue ink in the top right corner.

Gracie sifted back through the pages, marveling at the countless notations written in red ink in the margins, entire passages highlighted in orange and hot pink and yellow. In no other place was it more startlingly clear than in what lay open in her hands how starved her friend had been for meaning in her life, for hope, for peace, for redemption.

Unexpected tears stung Gracie's eyes.

In the middle of the book of Romans was a yellow sticky note on which Jett had scribbled: Is. 48:22, I Sam. 2:9, Matt. 18:6, Matt. 23:27.

Gracie paged backward past Nahum, Lamentations, to the book of Isaiah, chapter 48, verse 22, which read, "There is no peace, saith the Lord, unto the wicked."

She flipped back and forth until she found the first book of Samuel, chapter 2, verse 9. "The wicked shall be silent in darkness."

Gracie's heart ached at the memory of Jett telling her in anguish that she was too wicked to be saved.

Matthew 18:6 read, "But whoso shall offend one of these little ones which believe in me, it were better for him that a millstone were hanged about his neck, and that he were drowned in the depth of the sea."

Later in Matthew, the final verse: "Woe unto you, scribes and Pharisees, hypocrites! for ye are like unto whited sepulchers, which indeed appear beautiful outward, but are within full of dead men's bones, and of all uncleanness."

Gracie sat back in the chair.

Was it possible that Jett wasn't talking about herself but about what had been happening at camp? About Eddie? Or maybe, finally, Jay's holy pedestal had crumbled beneath him.

As Gracie closed the back cover of the Bible, she spied a folded sheet of paper stuck in between the pages of the Concordance. She drew it out and unfolded it.

It was a Sheriff's Department Missing Person flyer.

Gina Ramirez smiled back at her.

GRACIE stared down at the Missing Person flyer in her hands. Did Gina Ramirez somehow fit into all of what had been going on at camp? Were Eddie and Jay connected in some way with the teenager's disappearance?

The presence of the flyer brought things to a whole new level. Gracie knew she was in way over her head and that it was way past time to sit down and have a good, long talk with Detective Krueger.

She replaced the flyer in the Concordance, closed the Bible, and placed it on top of the books already in her pack. She pulled the rest of the books from the shelf and laid them on top.

She swiveled around to face the desk, switched on the light of the gooseneck lamp, and pulled open the center drawer.

She looked down and smiled.

Jett, clever women that she was, had hidden her flash drive again where only Gracie would find it, in a place anathema to most men, in a place Eddie would never think of or want to look.

In the drawer, lying among the scattered pieces of strawberry bubblegum and pens and paper clips, was a tampon. Gracie picked it up, immediately feeling it was heavier and flatter than it should be. Examining it by lamplight, she saw one end of the paper wrapper had been carefully slit open, then resealed with a tiny piece of invisible tape. She tore the wrapper open and pulled out the tampon. A tiny flash drive had been wedged inside the cardboard applicator. "Bingo," she whispered, and pulled it out with two fingers.

A pill fell out and rolled across the top of the desk. Gracie picked it up and studied it under the light—a white tablet with a manufacturer name and numbers on one side.

Gracie stared at the pill and wondered what it was and why Jett had felt the need to hide it in Gracie's office.

Because Jett was in a hurry? Because she was about to be caught?

Gracie looked around the room.

The hair on Gracie's arms prickled and tiny fingers of apprehension ran a cold shiver up her back.

Had Jett called Gracie from her own telephone in her own little office? Had she been cornered in the little office with no escape? Had she been killed right here?

Get out of the room. Now!

Gracie stuffed the flash drive in her shirt pocket. The pill she secreted in a tiny pocket inside the waistband of her shorts. She pulled out the entire desk drawer and, tipping it at an angle, funneled the contents into the pack. She replaced the drawer. Standing up, she zipped the pack closed and humped it, now heavy with books, onto her back.

From the doorway, she took a last quick glance over her shoulder. "So long, ya lousy little office," she said with a sharp sense of sadness and regret and the realization of how attached she had already become to the small, windowless room.

Upstairs in the darkened front office, a prolonged search produced her paycheck propped up against the leg of one of the desks. Gracie retrieved it, folded it in half, and zipped it into an outer pocket of the pack.

Ankle throbbing, she leaned on her crutch in the middle of the office. The need to see whether the flash drive actually contained information linking Eddie and Jay to the disappearance of Gina Ramirez was overwhelming. And Jay's computer was right there down the hallway in his office.

Gracie hopped into the room and dumped her pack on the floor next to Jay's desk. She sat down in the chair and turned on the computer. As she waited for it to boot up, she reached over to draw the window curtains more closely together. With both hands, she lifted her injured foot and set it on the open bottom desk drawer. Then she inserted the flash drive into the port.

There was only one folder on the flash drive: *Camp*.

Gracie clicked on it.

Jett's diary began almost three years earlier. There was one folder for every month, one file for each entry—over six hundred files.

She opened several at random, finding they were mostly filled with the mendacity of everyday life at camp, some chronicling in vivid, painful detail Jett's sexual escapades, her anguished thoughts about redemption, her terror that her faith wasn't enough to save her from her sordid past.

Jett had described how in September of the previous year, Eddie had begun flirting with her, pursuing her in earnest over the course of several weeks, more and more insistent for a single kiss. The following January, lonely from a recent

breakup and bored with the long, colorless winter, Jett had
let him kiss her.

That kiss had been the opening of Pandora's box, leading
to more and more sexual intimacy until finally Jett had sex
with Eddie in the closet near the back door of the kitchen.

That little ol' closet has seen a lotta action, Gracie
thought as she closed the file and opened the next.

Immediately remorseful for having sex with the husband
of someone with whom she attended Bible study every day,
Jett vowed never to let it happen again. With a resolve bordering on obsessive, she rebuffed Eddie's further advances.

During the middle of all the drama with Eddie, Jett had
met Winston at the checkout line of the local Stater Bros.
grocery store. Gracie skipped over several files about Winston, resolving that maybe someday she would read that
bodice ripper.

Eddie's frustration at being spurned by Jett evolved into
anger and his constant teasing grew thorns. "Hey, Jett!" he
had called across the parking lot, holding a twelve-inch
sugar-pine cone in front of his crotch. "You want it. I got
it." His usual pranks of salt in the sugar bowls and switching
food labels developed a vicious edge. Within a single week,
Jett had found a dead squirrel on the seat of her car and a
rattlesnake in her office wastebasket. There wasn't a doubt
in Jett's mind that Eddie had left both greeting cards.

There wasn't a doubt in Gracie's either.

The grinding pain in Gracie's ankle insisted its way into
her concentration. Taking another oxycodone would only
turn her brain back into a jellyfish and right now she needed
all her mental firing pins in perfect working order. She lifted
her foot all the way up onto the desk, gritted her teeth, and
skipped way ahead in the files to the month before Jett's
death.

Apparently, several times, Jett had complained to Jay about Eddie's behavior. If Jay had ever spoken to his brother about any of it, there was no way of knowing, but it hadn't made any difference whatsoever in Eddie's actions.

So Jay had known about the harassment. *What else did he know about and do nothing to prevent or stop?* Gracie wondered. *His brother's thievery? Burying trash? Having sex with female co-workers including a seventeen-year-old?*

With Jay's prodding, Jett had been consumed with self-revilement for her sins, past and present. But what was the greater sin? Certainly, in Gracie's mind, proclaiming yourself to be a Christian, a preacher no less, and doing nothing in the face of unethical, if not criminal, behavior.

Gracie had never seen or heard Eddie quote Scripture or pray as if he had a private hotline to the Almighty. But Jay wore his religion on his sleeve, and in Gracie's book, those who placed themselves in positions of spiritual authority, who elevated themselves above others in the name of religion, were ultimately held to a higher standard of conduct.

She closed out a file and opened the next one. Jett had agonized over whether to quit her job. But decent-paying jobs for ex-hookers with records were hard to come by, especially in a resort town with a transient population and a plethora of pizza joints. Jett had decided to hang on, ride out the storm, and patiently accumulate ammunition against Eddie by keeping a meticulous chronicle of his actions.

That decision had cost Jett her life.

What staggered Gracie the most was that while Eddie was doing his worst, Jett had been praying for him, almost daily. "Come into Eddie's heart, Lord Jesus," she wrote. "Dear Baby Jesus, lift Eddie up and take him into Your loving arms." "Help Eddie see the true Light of the Savior." "Heal Eddie's heart."

Truly amazing, Gracie thought with a pang of sadness. If anyone deserved peace and redemption, it was Jett.

Jett's turning to Serene in confidence had proven disastrous. In a yelling match in the camp kitchen, with pots and even a knife thrown, Serene revealed that she, too, had been sleeping with Eddie the previous year but that he had dumped her without warning when Jett had finally given in and had sex with him.

Hell's bell, Gracie thought. If Serene reacted that vehemently and violently when she found out that Jett had had sex with Eddie, how was she going to react when she found out her own daughter had been having sex with him?

Gracie started at the sound of a vehicle rumbling up the gravel drive into camp. She poked the monitor off and leaned back out of sight of the window, gritting her teeth again as the movement jarred her ankle. She pulled the curtains open a crack and watched a car pass the Gatehouse, then bump on down the hill into camp.

With trembling hands, she leaned forward and turned the monitor back on, swiveling the screen so its light wouldn't be visible through the window. She skipped ahead again and opened a file dated the week before Jett's death.

"I found a pill on the floor of the lower men's washroom," Jett had written. "I think Eddie's dealing drugs at camp."

Gracie leaned back in the chair again, stunned.

The idea of Eddie dealing drugs at camp had never occurred to her. But it made perfect sense. Camp was remote. Isolated. There were always all kinds of strangers on and around the property. No one ever checked to see whether they were legitimate guests or not.

From the tiny pocket in her shorts, Gracie dug out the pill Jett had left her. On the computer, she minimized the journal, opened the Internet browser, and typed the name and number on the pill into the search bar.

Almost instantly she received the results: "Acetamino-phen and oxycodone 325 mg / 10 mg."

Oxycodone, in different form, but the very same prescription painkiller Gracie had been taking.

She frowned at the computer screen. There was no real evidence that Eddie had been selling the drug to anyone. In fact, there was no evidence whatsoever linking the pill to Eddie at all. It could have belonged to anyone who had stayed at camp.

But Jett hadn't believed that.

Gracie closed out the browser and reopened the journal. "I don't know exactly what I'm looking for," she read. "But I'm going to find out what Eddie's up to and fry his ass." With the tenacity of a bulldog, Jett had searched the main-tenance shop, every piece of equipment in the shop yard, Eddie's truck. She had even snuck into Eddie and Amanda's trailer when the family was down the hill.

What Jett wrote next sent ice water through Gracie's veins. "If Eddie ever finds out what I'm doing, I'm dead."

The words clanged inside Gracie's head. "If Eddie ever finds out . . . I'm dead. I'm dead."

Gracie clicked on the last file, dated the day before Jett had died, and read, "I told Eddie I was going to drive down to L.A. Tell the church everything he was doing."

Gracie's stomach wrenched. *Oh, God, Jett, why weren't you more careful?* Because the woman had lived her life at full throttle, that's why.

"He pushed me back over the hood of my car," Jett wrote. "Choked me. Screamed if I told anybody, he would make me fucking sorry."

Her words screamed off the page. "Couldn't move! Couldn't do ANYTHING!"

Gracie felt sick.

"He yelled don't fuck with me and don't fuck with my family. He said if I didn't keep my fucking mouth shut he would kill me. So scared, when he left, I puked my guts out."

Gracie clicked the file closed and sat with her head bowed, breathing in and out through her nose, trying to calm her roiling stomach.

She looked back up at the screen.

That had been the last file.

The last thing Jett had written was that Eddie had threatened to kill her.

It was high time she got the hell off the property.

Except she hadn't found anything whatsoever about Gina Ramirez, no explanation of her disappearance, no connection of the missing girl to Eddie or anyone else at camp.

Maybe there was no connection. Maybe Jett had simply stashed the flyer in the back of her Bible to keep it safe. Or maybe Gracie had missed a reference to the missing girl by skipping some of the more recent files on the flash drive.

She did a search in the entire folder for the words *Gina Ramirez*.

Nothing.

She counted back a week from the date Gina had gone missing and began opening the files in order.

Still nothing.

Gracie opened another file. Closed it. Opened another.

She stopped, staring at the screen.

There it was. Finally.

"I think I saw that girl that's missing," Jett had written. "At camp. Few days ago. Thought she was a camper. With two other girls down—"

The tinny piano playing "Für Elise" chimed from the side pocket of Gracie's shorts, making her jump.

"'Bout gave me a heart attack," she grumbled as she dug out her cell phone. The screen displayed an unfamiliar phone number. She pressed Answer. "Hello?" she said in a low voice.

On the other end of the line, she heard a garbled voice and what sounded like crying. Then "Please help me."

"Meaghan?"

An unintelligible jumble of words followed.

"Meaghan, if that's you, I can't understand you. The reception's bad. Where are you?"

More garbled words.

"Are you at home? Can you call me back? I'm at the office. Or I can call you."

A door in the basement slammed, sending a shock wave of adrenaline through Gracie's body.

Eddie.

It had to be.

She had forgotten all about looking out for him.

Gracie hung up her phone, grabbed the flash drive, poked off the monitor, and slid off the chair and beneath the desk, dragging the day pack in along with her. She crossed her broken foot over the other and pulled the wheeled chair in beneath the desk as far as she could.

Had she left anything in her office, any telltale sign that she was there now? She had removed all the books from the bookshelf, including Jett's Bible. She had dumped everything from the desk drawer into her pack. She had turned off all the lights before coming upstairs. What else could there be?

Her crutch.

Leaning against the wall just inside Jay's office door.

Panic bubbled up inside. Her breath came in quick, shallow gasps. *Stay calm. He doesn't know you're here. There's no reason for him to come upstairs.*

Six inches above her head, the office telephone rang, sounding as loud as a Klaxon horn. Another burst of adrenaline fizzed all the way down to her fingertips.

She counted off the rings. The answering machine picked up. The announcement played. The beep. Dial tone. No message.

There was no sound from below, no sign of where Eddie was or what he was up to. Gracie strained to hear. *What's he doing down there?*

The toilet in the downstairs bathroom flushed.

The tinny piano played from the phone in Gracie's hand. The same unfamiliar number. With shaking fingers, she pressed Decline.

Heavy boots clumped up the basement stairs.

CHAPTER

40

LIKE a turtle retreating into its shell, Gracie ducked in farther beneath the desk, pressing herself against the back wall, making herself smaller, more compact, invisible. She pulled the chair in even closer and held it there. With the screen an inch from her face, she turned down the volume on the phone. She hugged it to her chest, not remembering if it would play a little tune if she turned it all the way off, not daring to test it now.

With a heavy final step, Eddie reached the top of the stairs.

Silence.

Gracie waited, hardly daring, hardly able to take in a breath.

Where is he? What's he doing?

The office door brushed open, the merest whisper against carpet.

Eddie motionless in the doorway, listening.

Gracie could hear him breathing. She held her own breath.

The overhead light came on.

Polliwogs swam in front of Gracie's eyes. *I'm going to pass out.* She struggled to take in a silent breath. Her heart hammered in her ears.

An infinity passed.

Then Eddie switched off the light and walked back up the hallway. The door at the top of the stairs slammed. Boots clomped down the steps.

Gracie waited.

A full minute later, she recognized the sound of the engine of Eddie's truck roaring to life out in the maintenance yard.

Gracie pushed the chair out to give herself more room and drew in a full breath. Her vision cleared. For several minutes, she stayed where she was as much to let her heart rate slow as to give Eddie time to be far, far away.

Then she uncurled her body, pushed her pack out in front of her, crawled out from beneath the desk, and climbed to her feet. Stuffing her phone into a shorts pocket and zipping the flash drive into the outside pocket of her pack, she grabbed up the crutch on her way out the door and hobbled down the hall to the front reception area. She peered out through the curtains onto the maintenance yard below. No sign of Eddie's truck.

She descended the basement stairs, one step at a time, stopping for a moment at each one to avoid doing a forward header down to the bottom and feeling all the while like she was making more noise than Frankenstein monster.

Just inside the garage door of the shop, she peeked around the corner. Still no truck. No Eddie. She crossed the maintenance yard, climbed inside the Scout, and pulled the door closed.

She sat for a moment, conflicted as to her next move.

Eddie was at camp and she wanted nothing more than to get the hell out of there. But she needed to check on Meaghan. She couldn't just ignore that the teenager, possibly in some sort of real distress, had reached out to her.

Cursing the throbbing pain in her ankle, her aching body, Eddie and Jay, camp, and life in general, she started the Scout.

Gracie bumped and jerked out of the maintenance yard and across the little bridge. Opposite the Serrano parking lot, she turned left onto the road running parallel to the rec field and stalled the Scout in front of Jay and Elaine's double-wide mobile home.

The building was brown wood with dark brown trim and a front porch running along its length. A pair of white plastic chairs and a patio table sat out front. Baskets with faded red geraniums dangled from the overhang.

Using both crutches, Gracie hopped up the front steps, crossed the porch, and knocked on the screen door.

Almost immediately, Elaine swung the front door open as if she had been waiting for her, and glared out through the screen. "What are you doing here?" she demanded.

"Hi, Elaine," Gracie said, ignoring the woman's hostile tone. "Is Meaghan around?"

"She's in her room."

"Um, is . . . Could I talk to her for a moment?"

"Why on earth would I let you do that?"

"She . . ." *Oh, what the hell?* "She called me. I'm checking to make sure she's all right."

"Of course she's all right. Why wouldn't she be all right? And why would she be calling you when her mother is right here?"

Why indeed?

"And when you no longer work here."

Gracie didn't rise to the bait. "That's what I'm here to find out. I would just like to make sure she's all right. Then I'll leave."

Without taking her eyes off Gracie, Elaine shrieked, "Meaghan!" over her shoulder.

When there was no response, Elaine shot Gracie a "Don't you dare move" look and left the doorway.

Muffled voices filtered out from the depths of the mobile home: a question from what sounded like another woman, Elaine's harsh reply and fading calls for Meaghan.

Then a long, yowling scream.

CHAPTER

41

GRACIE yanked on the screen door.

Locked.

She bashed her crutch through the screen like a stick through water. Jamming a hand through the hole, she fumbled around with the lock on the inside, finally sliding the lever over and unlatching the door.

Even on crutches, she crossed the living room and was down the hallway in three seconds flat.

Elaine stood in the doorway of a room at the end of the hall, eyes wide in horror, face the color of chalk, hands gripping the doorframe.

Gracie looked into the room over her shoulder.

Meaghan lay on the floor of her bedroom, head toward the door, legs curled around the end of the twin bed, arms invisible beneath the white flounces of the dust ruffle. Blood had turned a large area of the light blue carpet to a purplish brown.

Meaghan slit her wrists.

Gracie ducked beneath Elaine's arm, straightened, and saw for the first time Amanda kneeling on the floor at the girl's feet, holding a bundled towel in her lap.

A baby.

Meaghan's baby.

"Holy shit," Gracie whispered. The girl hadn't tried to kill herself. She had given birth.

Gracie had heard of pregnancies remaining hidden to term, even of mothers not realizing they were pregnant until the baby was born. Still she was dumbfounded that she hadn't noticed or even guessed that Meaghan was pregnant.

But, at the moment, it was the girl's pallor and the abundance of blood saturating the carpet she found alarming.

Over her shoulder, Gracie said in a "Stay calm and do exactly what I tell you to do" voice, "Elaine, I need you to call 911. Get an ambulance here right away. Then warm up in the dryer as many clean bath towels as you can and bring them back here."

Hopping into the room and laying her crutch on the bed, she eased herself down so that she was sitting on the floor next to Meaghan's head, gently withdrew one arm from beneath the bed, and placed two fingers on the wrist. The pulse was weak and fast but steady; the skin, cool and clammy.

Gracie leaned over the girl and said in a soft voice, "Meaghan, honey. It's Gracie. Can you hear me?"

The girl's eyelids fluttered but didn't open. She muttered something that sounded like, "Going to hell."

A groan floated from the doorway.

Gracie looked back over her shoulder. Still in the doorway, Elaine was slumped against the frame as if, without its support, she would keel over. Jay, appearing from somewhere, looked in over his wife's shoulder, mouth hanging open, fleshy jowls sagging.

"Elaine, call 911!" Gracie said in a sharper tone. "We need an ambulance now. Jay, bring me some warm towels."

Neither parent moved.

"Go!" she barked. She sat back with her fingers on the girl's wrist again, counting the beats per second.

One hundred twenty.

Too fast.

She watched the girl's chest expand and contract, expand and contract. Fast and shallow.

The knot of anxiety in Gracie's stomach tightened even further. The girl was displaying all the symptoms consistent with shock.

A mound of warm towels appeared before her eyes. Gracie took them and handed one over to Amanda. The woman's face was pale, but her blue eyes were bright, alert.

As Gracie draped the remaining towels over Meaghan's body and legs, Amanda unwrapped the tiny baby, taking great care with the umbilical cord, still attached. She quickly enfolded the newborn again in the clean, warm towel.

With relief, Gracie noted that the baby looked healthy, its doll-sized arms and legs a grayish blue, but the skin of its tiny torso a healthy pink. The little cap of curling hair was black.

From the doorway, Jay said, "Oh, my sweet Jesus, what is that?"

"It's your own sweet daughter's baby," Gracie answered, concentrating on tucking the ends of the towels around Meaghan's body. "Your granddaughter."

"What? But . . . How . . . ?"

"What's the ETA of EMS?" Gracie asked.

When no answer was forthcoming, she looked back at the couple standing in the doorway. "Elaine, how long before the ambulance gets here?"

"A . . . Ambulance?" Elaine stuttered.

"Elaine!" Gracie yelled. "Call 911!"

Elaine blanched and disappeared from the doorway.

"Stupid fat cow," Jay muttered under his breath.

"Make sure she tells them Code 3," Gracie said.

"Tell them Code 3!" Jay yelled after his wife. Then he said, "My daughter's going to hell."

"Oh, please. Just shut up, Jay," Gracie said, patience nonexistent. "She's not going to hell. Not now. Not ever."

"Almighty Father," Jay prayed, "we just come to you in this time of great need, beseeching your forgiveness for the sins of this, Your child Meaghan."

"Shut up, Jay," Gracie said again, more loudly.

"We just ask Your Almighty forgiveness for her evil acts. That You would just—"

"Jay," Gracie snapped. "If you don't shut the hell up right now, I'm going to stand up and belt you with my crutch."

Silence.

"Amanda," she said then. "Let me have the baby, please." As she accepted the bundle into her arms, the other woman looked into her face and smiled. "It's a girl," she said. Her shining eyes held no judgment, no condemnation, only the joy of holding a baby, newly born. Gracie could have kissed her for it.

Gracie cradled the little bundle for a moment, looking with awe into the pinched red face, eyes squeezed shut, perfect tiny hands with their perfect tiny fingers and even tinier nails.

Lifting up Meaghan's shirt and bra, she placed the baby at the girl's bud of a breast.

There was a loud thunk from the hallway.

Gracie glanced over her shoulder.

Jay stood in the doorway, looking unconcernedly down on his wife who had fainted and lay in an undignified heap on the floor.

*   *   *

FROM THE FRONT yard of the double-wide, Gracie watched the ambulance lumber up the gravel drive, closely followed by the Wilsons' white Subaru with Jay, Elaine, and Amanda inside.

The sun had given up on the day, sinking low in the west, zebra-striping the rec field and Serrano parking lot with long blue shadows and rendering the sky as gray and soft as a mourning dove. Within the lodge itself, lights burned bright and warm, evidence of the impending ninth-grade talent show.

At the parking lot, the ambulance turned right, then picked up speed. Its emergency lights flashed on, throwing eerie bursts of red and white across the surrounding trees and boulders. The siren revved up to a full wail as it bumped off the pavement onto gravel and disappeared. The Subaru followed in its dusty wake.

"Miss?" The whispered word might have been a fleeting thought inside Gracie's head. Her eyes flew around the yard, finally alighting on a lone figure standing in the trees at the far edge of the yard.

Gracie squinted in the dim light. "Who is that? Emilio?"

The young man stepped out of the bushes and walked toward her, legs jerking and uncoordinated as if somehow his feet were operating independently from the rest of his body. As he drew closer, Gracie could see his eyes were wide with an agonized fear, his cheeks streaked with half-dried tears.

"Hi," she said.

"Is she . . . going to be all right? Meaghan? Will she be all right?"

Comprehension hit Gracie with the force of a flash flood. The baby was Emilio's.

Meaghan's sin, the sin for which she was certain she was

doomed for all eternity to burn in the fires of hell, was finding love, or at least physical closeness, in the arms of a
sweet, young Latino.

"I don't know," she said honestly. "She's very sick.
They've taken her to the hospital."

Emilio looked at the ground and nodded, surreptitiously
wiping away a tear with a finger.

"The baby is a girl," Gracie said.

The young man's head snapped up, the dark eyes searching hers.

"She's beautiful," she added with a smile. "I think she's
going to be just fine."

An unidentifiable emotion flicked across the Emilio's
face. "I love her," he said with a forthrightness and confidence that surprised Gracie.

"I can see that," she said.

Without another word, Emilio backed up, the soft eyes
never leaving Gracie's until he blended in with the gloom
of the trees and disappeared.

Gracie leaned on her crutches and shivered, unsure of
whether from the chill of early evening or the aftermath of
the scene that had just taken place. She needed to get the
hell out of camp, to leave it behind—all of it.

Except her Ranger was *still* down at the high course. The
mere thought of driving the Scout all the way back across
the valley to Ralph's cabin exhausted her.

And she *still* wanted to get a look at the central belay
cable. There was no way she was going to leave forever
without at least trying to figure out exactly what had happened when she had fallen.

As she eased herself into the driver's seat of the Scout
and lifted in her injured leg, she wondered where Eddie was
now. Surely if he was still on camp property somewhere, he

would have heard the wail of the ambulance siren and appeared to investigate.

Still, she wasn't going to take any chances. Leaving the headlights off, Gracie backed away from the double-wide. But instead of heading toward the lodge and Main Road, she headed in the opposite direction, turning right onto a secondary road serving as the boundary for the developed portion of camp. Rutted and rarely used, it paralleled Main Road, intersecting with Lake Road near the lower washrooms before continuing on to the little village of permanent platform tents.

Shaggy, untrimmed bushes scraped both sides of the Scout, sounding like eagle talons on a chalkboard. "Sorry, Ralphie," Gracie moaned. "I'll pay to repaint your truck, I promise!"

But those same bushes hid the Scout as it crawled forward in the near darkness, the only sound that of tires crunching dirt and an occasional pinecone.

The Scout coasted down the hill, past Eddie and Amanda's double-wide, no lights visible, no silver Dodge Ram in the driveway. Past Mojave Lodge, dark, unoccupied. Past Serene's single-wide, a lone dim light showing behind shades pulled low.

At the bottom of the hill, where the road intersected with Lake, Gracie braked to a stop. She looked behind her, then up the road, down, and back up again.

Off to the right, bug lights on the porch of the lower washrooms burned yellow through the trees. Otherwise, all was dark.

She rolled down her window and listened.

Except for the tinkling of running creek water, she heard nothing.

There was no sign of Eddie. Nor anyone else for that matter.

Gracie blew out of breath. *So far, so good.*

Concentrating hard on not popping the clutch and stalling the engine, she shifted into second gear and rolled the Scout around the corner, past the washrooms, the Main Road intersection, the lake. At the wide area above the high ropes course, she spied the Ranger sitting right where Madison had parked it the day she had fallen.

Thank God!

She parked the Scout next to her own truck, transferred her pack and crutches over to the passenger's side, and climbed into the driver's seat. The keys were still in it.

And no clutch.

It felt like coming home.

With a feeling of great ease and relief, Gracie drove the Ranger around and down to the high course.

Not caring if the tires chewed ruts in the ground, she gunned the engine and drove the Ranger up into the middle of the course, spitting out bark mulch behind. Turning it off and setting the parking brake, she grabbed an LED flashlight from the console and climbed down from the truck, pushing the door closed until the interior light blinked off.

She ran the beam of her flashlight up the trunk of one of the immense pines to where the central belay cable was wrapped neatly around the trunk, then out from there along the cable itself. Barely visible, fifty feet straight up, was the haul cord, fed through the sheer-reduction device, both ends wrapped around a cleat fastened to the trunk ten feet off the ground.

Gracie balanced on one foot, head tipped back and staring at the cable for so long that she wobbled and had to grab onto the outside truck mirror to keep from toppling over backward.

Everything on the course was as it should be. In a

mind-bending tip to reality, it was as if the haul cord had never come loose, as if the cable had never unwound from the tree trunk, as if she had never fallen.

But she had.

Whoever had loosened the cable—whether Eddie or Abe or someone else altogether—he had worked fast to return everything to its proper place.

With a final sweep of the flashlight around the mulch to confirm that neither her helmet nor her carabiners were still lying around somewhere, Gracie turned back toward the truck, grabbed the handle, and stopped.

What am I hearing?

She closed her eyes and concentrated on listening beyond the normal sounds of the night—the whispering of pine branches overhead, the drone of a mosquito somewhere near her left ear.

She felt it almost more than heard it, a low pounding so faint and indistinct, it was impossible to determine the exact direction or source.

With a mental "it's no longer my problem" shrug, she reached out for the door handle, stopping again as she heard something else, this time something easily identifiable—young voices. Someone was walking along the road leading past the ropes course.

Gracie didn't move, not wanting to startle whoever it was by announcing her presence as a disembodied voice out of the darkness.

She watched as two figures strolled into view, silhouetted against the lighter dirt road. From their high voices, she identified them as a boy and girl, most likely from Madison's ninth-grade group.

They certainly didn't seem to be involved in any organized evening game or activity, Gracie thought. No Capture the Flag. No Kick the Can. *What are they doing way out here at night with no supervision?* Again, she told herself, *Madison's group. Madison's problem.*

Directly below Gracie, the couple stopped and kissed. The girl giggled, said something unintelligible. The boy answered in a low voice. Then they continued their nighttime amble down the road, eventually blending into the darkness.

In the renewed quiet, Gracie heard the other sound again—still unidentifiable, a deep, rhythmic throbbing, like machinery being operated somewhere. But there was nothing industrial anywhere close to camp property. In fact, the closest buildings were vacation homes and rental cabins more than a mile away down the mountain.

With a final dismissive shake of her head, Gracie climbed inside the Ranger, started the engine, and backed down off the course. Still in stealth mode, headlights off, she drove back around and up the hill, emerging onto the road running between the swim beach and the wide, flat area where the Scout was parked. "Sorry, Ralphie," she muttered. "We'll come get it tomorrow."

The Ranger glided past the lake, as dark and still and smooth as black glass.

Yellow porch lights from the washrooms shimmered through the trees up ahead.

As the truck rolled to a stop at the Main Road intersection, the women's washroom door was shoved open, spilling out light and two figures, from all appearances, boys.

"What were they doing on the girls' side?" Gracie wondered aloud.

Talking loudly and laughing, the boys stumbled away from the building and onto the road. As Gracie watched, one of them tripped, falling hard onto his hands and knees. Then he lay down full length in the middle of the road, flung his arms out wide, and yelled, "Can't fucking walk!" His buddy, laughing and barely able to stand himself, grabbed his hand and hauled him to his feet.

Gracie's mouth fell open. "They're drunk!"

Ninth-graders wandering around camp, unsupervised, after dark, was bad enough. But drunk, especially with the attractive nuisances of canoes and the lake nearby, was a whole other dangerous, potentially lethal, matter, one Gracie couldn't simply shrug off or ignore.

The boys staggered up the road leading to the platform tents.

Letting up on the brake, Gracie let the truck roll forward and turned onto the road in the boys' wake.

With the Ranger at a crawl, using the lighter strip of sandy road as a guide in the darkness, pressing down on the accelerator only when needed to climb successive hills, Gracie followed the boys, glancing back over her shoulder every once in a while lest someone creep up behind her.

At the bottom of a long hill, she braked to a stop. Someone had stretched a heavy chain across the road, winding and padlocking the ends around massive ponderosa pine trunks.

"That doesn't belong there," Gracie said, frowning.

Trees, heavy brush, and jumbles of granite boulders on both sides of the road prevented her from simply driving around the chain and continuing up the road.

Tempted to turn around and drive home and be done with camp forever, Gracie peered up the hill. Just over the rise, she knew, the road dropped down several hundred feet and ran right through the middle of the village of platform tents.

You're almost there, she told herself and hauled on the steering wheel. The Ranger bounced off the road, crunched through a thick mat of fallen leaves and pine needles, and slid to a stop behind a large clump of manzanita.

As soon as Gracie hopped down from the truck, she heard what she hadn't been able to identify before, now easily recognizable as loud pop music, the cranked-up bass thudding like a heartbeat.

While most of the ninth-grade retreat group was happy and safe a half mile away at Serrano Lodge, a few, at least, had snuck away for a party of their own.

Gracie made her way up the hill—a long, slow slog, her uninjured foot and the tip of her crutch sinking deep into the soft sand with every step. Before her head topped the rise, she stopped, panting like a dog with the effort and wishing she had thought to grab her water bottle when she left the truck.

A flickering, golden light illuminated the branches of the trees up ahead.

No matter who it was partying at the tent village, there was no way she was going to simply waltz down the road right into the middle of the shindig.

She left the road at an angle and hobbled through the woods, circling around through fallen leaves and pine needles, over fallen logs and branches, barely able to see in the deep shadow of the night, one hand outstretched in front of her like a horror-flick zombie.

Finally, just outside the circle of light of the tent village clearing, she dropped down onto her stomach. Dragging her crutch along with her, she commando-crawled up behind the massive trunk of a fallen pine.

Raising herself up onto one elbow, she peered over the top of the log.

CHAPTER

42

THE sandy road leading in from Lake Road ran right through the middle of a collection of six large white canvas tents on permanent wooden platforms. Across from where Gracie lay behind the fallen tree, a campfire blazed in a deep pit encircled by log seats. A boom box blasted music from a tree stump.

On the opposite side of the campfire, a loose cluster of teenagers talked and laughed, some standing, some sitting on log seats, a couple dancing. One or two held cans of beer. Others plastic glasses of what Gracie presumed was alcohol of some kind. One of the drunk boys from the lower washrooms held a half-empty bottle of what looked like tequila in his hand. Another boy and girl, possibly the same ones who had walked past Gracie on the ropes course, leaned against a boulder, partially obscured, entwined in each other's arms and kissing passionately.

Three of the tents glowed from within with a faint amber light.

Only one adult was visible, standing off to one side, talking intently to two girls, beer in hand, smiling, totally at ease—Eddie.

Gotcha!

Finally, Gracie had caught him, dead to rights, doing something patently illegal, if not directly supplying alcohol to minors, then at least present at its consumption, granting tacit approval.

She dug her cell phone out of her shorts pocket, fiddled with it to disengage the flash, snapped surreptitious pictures of the entire scene, then stuffed it back into her pocket.

As she watched, the two girls talking to Eddie left him and, as if on a mission of some kind, walked down the road leading back toward the lower washrooms and the rest of camp.

Eddie looked up, glancing around.

Gracie ducked down behind the log, taking in slow, deep breaths to calm her heart suddenly beating its own loud bass in her ears. She waited a full thirty seconds, then slowly raised herself up again and, with a single eye, looked over the top of the log.

Eddie tossed a crumpled beer can into the campfire. He grabbed another beer from a cooler on the ground and sat down at one end of the log seats to watch two girls, dressed in shorts and camp T-shirts, dancing seductively with each other.

For a moment, Gracie glared at Eddie, reveling in the thought of that self-satisfied smirk disappearing from his pretty face when handcuffs were snapped around his wrists.

Her eyes left Eddie to move around the scene, taking in the teenagers again, the couple kissing, the campfire, coolers of beer and other alcohol sitting on the ground, until finally she focused her attention on the tents themselves.

What's happening inside?

Gracie raised herself up on hands and knees again and, under cover of the night, crawled around one end of the fallen log to the back of the tent closest to her. Pushing herself up onto one knee, she put an ear to the canvas and listened but could hear nothing above the music.

She pulled loose one of the fabric ties of the back entrance, separated the canvas with her fingers and peered inside.

What appeared to be a Coleman lantern on the floor at the far end of the tent threw out a halo of golden light, leaving the rest of the tent in deep shadow. Gracie could just make out the shapes of eight metal-frame beds and the head of someone sitting on the floor near the front entrance.

Slowly, quietly, she tugged loose two more of the door ties. Then, laying her crutch down on the ground outside, she wriggled in through the opening.

Just inside the tent, Gracie balked, wrinkling her nose against what smelled like a combination of burnt plastic and vinegar.

Whatever it is, she decided, *I don't like breathing it.*

On hands and knees again, she crawled across the wooden floor and up to the lantern, stopping only when she put her hand down on something soft.

She picked it up and held it up to the light. A cotton ball.

Glancing quickly around, she saw the floor was littered with more cotton balls, gum wrappers, spoons, lighters, straws, shoelaces, tiny glassine packets.

Crawling forward another couple of feet, Gracie looked down on the person sitting next to the front entrance. He—she?—hadn't moved or given any indication of awareness of her arrival.

Leaning up against the metal bedframe, head lolling back between the slats of the railing, mouth gaping as in death, was a girl—the same girl Gracie had seen in the Serrano girls' bathroom after Jett's memorial service, the leader of the trio, the girl with the cell phone, irritated because she didn't have enough reception to make a telephone call.

One long sleeve of her powder blue Camp Ponderosa T-shirt was shoved up above her elbow. A shoelace was tied around her upper arm. In the open palm of her hand resting on the wooden floor was a syringe.

Swallowing back the vomit that rose in her throat, Gracie sagged against the railing of the bed next to her and drew in a long, deep breath.

Jett's evil wasn't embezzlement. Nor a forty-one-year-old man having sex with a seventeen-year-old. Nor even that same man giving alcohol to minors. Jett's evil, the evil for which she had certainly been murdered, was that same man, sitting so casually outside, drinking beer, laughing and talking, as if without a care in the world, that same man supplying those same minors, ninth-graders, kids, with drugs.

Hard drugs.

Heroin.

Gracie blinked away the tears burning her eyes, leaned forward, and put two fingers on the girl's wrist.

Seconds passed.

Nothing.

Oh, God!

She held her breath. Shifted her fingers a fraction of an inch.

There! She felt it then—a pulse, faint and slow.

The girl was alive.

Barely.

There was nothing Gracie could do except call for help, get the girl to the hospital as quickly as possible. Even without a cast on her foot, she would never have been able to carry her out of the tent and back through the woods to her truck without Eddie or anyone else being alerted to her presence.

Gracie pulled out her cell phone again and squinted at the screen.

No service.

She tucked it back into her pocket.

Even though she knew the girl was unaware of her presence, she placed a gentle hand on her shoulder and whispered, "I'm coming back for you."

Then she backed out of the tent.

Masked by the night, Gracie retraced her steps back through the woods. Practically sprinting on the crutch, she hopped through fallen leaves, pinecones, and branches; around boulders; over tree trunks. Granite and bark sandpapered skin. Pine needles and sticks stabbed arms and legs. But any awareness of pain was obliterated by the all-encompassing need to gain cell phone reception and call for help.

If she was too slow . . .

If help came too late . . .

Gracie slid to a stop so abruptly she almost tipped forward and tumbled over the lip of a steep drop-off. At her feet, the ground fell sharply away in long, sandy embankment. Far below at the bottom, she could see a strip of bare dirt and a glimmer of yellow light shining through the leaves.

She was looking down on Lake Road and the lower washrooms.

Shit!

Somehow, as exhausted as she was, as overwhelmed with fear as she was that a young life possibly depended upon her gaining cell phone reception and calling for help, Gracie had missed the Ranger, bypassing it in the dark, traveling much farther than she had realized or even thought possible.

She hauled out her phone again. *Please, let there be*

service here. She squinted at the screen. One bar. She punched in 911, then Call.

Put the phone to her ear.

Nothing.

"Dammit!"

She retrieved Ralph's number from her contacts list. Texted: 10-33. Help. 911. CAMP. BRING EMS/LE. Emergency medical services/law enforcement.

She hit Send.

She stuffed the phone back in her pocket and sagged against her crutch. The pain in her ankle had ground its way through to her consciousness, but she couldn't stop yet. There was no guarantee Ralph would receive or see her text in time. She still needed to get to better reception or a landline and call the Sheriff's Office directly.

At the bottom of the hill, beyond the washrooms, was Serene's trailer, a landline, a telephone.

Gracie sat down onto the sand, dropped her feet over the edge of the drop-off, and pushed herself off.

She slid down the embankment on her rear end, feet held off the ground, dragging the crutch behind her as a brake, sticks, leaves, and sand pushing up her shorts and shirt.

Below, the women's washroom door opened. Illuminated by the exterior bug light, the two girls who had been talking to Eddie at the tent village, walked out and stepped off the porch.

Gracie fell backward onto the hillside. Throwing out the arm holding the crutch, she slid to a stop, sending a trickle of sand and leaves scudding all the way down to the road.

Heads together, intent, conferring quietly with each other, holding something in their hands, the girls walked back up the road leading to the platform tents.

They've just scored drugs.

Spurred by a surge of anger and growing suspicion, Gracie lifted her feet, pushed herself off again, and slid the rest of way to the bottom of the hill.

Hobbling across the road and onto the cement slab porch of the women's washroom, she threw open the door and hopped inside.

Leaning up against the back wall, cinching her blue backpack closed, wearing a black camp T-shirt, hot pink shorts, flip-flops, and a smug smile, was Jasmine.

CHAPTER

43

JASMINE looked up. At the sight of Gracie standing in the doorway, her eyes flew open, her mouth a small O.

Winded, sweat trickling down her temples, Gracie leaned on the crutch and struggled to catch her breath.

The two women stared at each other until, with a little shake of her head, Jasmine nudged herself off the wall and said, "I'm outta here."

She tried to elbow past, but Gracie grabbed her by the upper arm, fingers like pincers on the soft flesh.

"Ow!" Jasmine whined, trying to wrench free. "Let go! You're hurting me!"

Gracie's grip tightened. "What are you doing here, Jasmine?" With anger barely held in check, her voice sounded hoarse, foreign.

"Nothing."

Before Jasmine could react, Gracie lurched forward.

Using her own body weight and the unyielding wooden crutch, she shoved the smaller woman back against the wall.

"Ow!" Jasmine screamed. "Stop!"

Turning, Gracie fell back against the crutch, trapping the other woman behind. Then she yanked the backpack out of Jasmine's hand.

"Stop!" Jasmine screamed again, reaching around Gracie, grabbing for the pack. "That's mine!"

Gracie uncinched the top, turned the pack upside down and shook out the contents. Plastic bags with syringes, glassine envelopes of white powder, pills of all colors and shapes and sizes, spoons, lighters, and an enormous wad of money rubber-banded together cascaded onto the cement floor.

Jasmine pounded Gracie's back with her fists. "That's mine!"

Turning around again, Gracie easily grabbed ahold of her wrists, leaned in, and held her still. "How much is there?" she yelled, her face only inches from Jasmine's. "How much money have you made from ruining people's lives?"

Jasmine went suddenly slack, still. Her chin lifted. Face sneering, proud, she said, "More than nine thousand dollars. And that's only part of it. It's my ticket out of this hellhole." Hatred drew across her face like a curtain. "I *hate* it here," she spat. "It's worse than prison. I hate *them*!"

"Who do you hate?"

"They think they're, like, better'n me. And they're just shit! They're nothing!" Jasmine's eyes glittered with tears. "They make me want to puke my goddam guts out!"

"They who, Jasmine?"

"Those rich bitches that come up here! With their diamond earrings. And their JCrew. And their trips to Barbados. They just treat me like I'm trash!" Tears streamed down her cheeks. "I hate them! All of them! It's not fair! And it's not even their own money! It's their rich daddies' money!"

Gracie struggled to keep her voice even, steady. "So you and Eddie are in it together? That it? What? He buys the drugs? You sell them? Split the difference?"

"He asked me to help him," Jasmine said, triumphant. "*Me*. Nobody else."

"And you sell them. To kids. At camp."

"School, too. And it's so easy! I just tell 'em there's a party up here. Fuckin' rich Daddy's girls. Fuckin' Gi—" She stopped.

Comprehension hit Gracie with a physical blow. "Jasmine," she asked, "did you sell drugs to Gina Ramirez? Was she up here at camp?"

Silence stretched.

A fly buzzed at one corner of the window screen.

Gracie shook Jasmine's wrists. "Was she? Was Gina up here?"

Jasmine dropped her eyes. "It was an accident."

Gracie's mouth was so dry she couldn't swallow. "What happened? Did she die somehow? Overdose?"

A tiny nod. "Scared me at first."

"At first."

A thin shoulder shrugged. "It's, like, good for business."

"Good for . . . ?"

"Somebody dies means it's good shit. A good high. Brings in more customers."

Gracie closed her eyes, tipped her head back, shuddered in a deep breath, blew it out. Then she looked back down at Jasmine. "Okay." She tried to swallow again. "Okay. I have to get to a phone. Right away. You have one at home." She gestured to the floor with her head. "We're going to pick all of this up. Fast. Then you're coming with me."

Jasmine shook her head. "No, I'm not."

"Yes, you are."

"I like you, Gracie. You've always been really nice to me. But you better let me go or Eddie will hurt you."

"The way he hurt Jett?"

Jasmine's mouth fell open, then she clapped it shut. "He didn't . . . I don't know anything about that."

"Yes, you do." Gracie forced her voice back to quiet, to calm. "Did Eddie kill Jett?"

"No."

"Then what?" Gracie leaned forward. "Then what, Jasmine?"

"It was her own fault!" Jasmine yelled, spit landing on Gracie's face. "She found out!" Her face crumpled with tears. "I don't know how! I heard her call somebody. Tell 'em about the Jackpot."

Gracie's breath caught. "The jackpot."

"Yeah, you know. Jackpot. Avatar. Atom Bomb. God, there are so many of 'em. Chocolate Chip Cookies. I like that one."

"No," Gracie said. "I don't know."

Jasmine looked at her as if she were an imbecile. "You know! The drugs!" Her head fell back against the wall. "I didn't mean to."

"What didn't you mean to?"

"Kill her."

Gracie suddenly felt very tired. "How did you kill her?"

"Hit her with a hammer. From the shop. Not even that hard. I couldn't believe it. She just, like, fell right down and wouldn't get up again."

"Then what? Eddie put her in her own car? Drove her out to the Arctic Circle?"

Jasmine actually giggled. "God, he was so mad. He had

to walk all the way back to camp. It's really far. Over five miles."

Gracie stared at the young woman in front of her.

There it was. Finally. The truth.

"Okay, Jasmine." Gracie released her grip on her wrists and took ahold of the crutch. "We need to go." She looked up.

Jasmine was slowly shaking her head from side to side, eyes narrowed again, hard, emotionless. "No," she whispered.

"It's okay, Jasmine. It'll be okay."

"No. It won't." With a speed and strength that caught her by surprise, Jasmine kicked the broken ankle hard with the ball of her foot, pushed off the wall, and shoved Gracie backward.

Gracie yelped in pain and stumbled, almost falling. Jasmine ducked beneath the crutch, scrambled past her on all fours, and was out the door, screaming, "Eddie! Eddie!"

Gritting her teeth against the blinding pain, Gracie pushed herself upright and lurched outside.

But by the time she reached the edge of the porch, Jasmine had already disappeared over the first hill, her screams for Eddie fading.

There was no way to catch her.

Gracie hopped off the other side of the porch, across the leafy yard and up to Serene's single-wide. She fell up onto the little stoop and collapsed against the door. "Serene!" she called out. "It's Gracie! Call 911!"

With her ear against the door, she listened.

No answer.

She rapped on the door with her knuckles. "Serene! Call 911! We need an ambulance up here! And deputies! At the platform tents!"

Nothing.

Serene was there. A light burned inside. Her dented Camry was parked next to the trailer.

With desperation bordering on panic, Gracie pounded the door with her fist and screamed, "Serene! They're giving drugs to kids! Eddie, Serene! Eddie's giving drugs to kids! There's a girl maybe dying up there!"

Gracie waited until she thought her head would explode and then she put her mouth against the rust-flecked screen door and yelled, "Serene. Jasmine's up there!"

The door flew open. Serene stood in the doorway, eyes round with terror.

"She's not taking any," Gracie said. "At least . . . I don't think so. But she's in on it. I'm sorry. Eddie and Jasmine. In on it together. They've been . . . together. I need to use the phone."

The changing emotions showed as clearly on Serene's face as if a dial were being turned. Terror melted into doubt, then comprehension, then pain, and finally fury. The tiny woman shoved the screen door open, knocking Gracie aside. Serene leapt off the porch, ran across the yard, and up the road leading back to the tents.

Gracie fell into the single-wide, looked around, spotted a green Princess phone on the counter, stumbled over to it, grabbed it up, and punched in 911.

GRACIE SAT IN the sand at the side of the road, one leg beneath her, the leg with the cast stretched out in front. Her entire body trembled. Her ankle stabbed pain. The last remaining dregs of energy had ebbed away and she was unable to move, unable to think, unable to do anything, but wait for the help that was on the way and guide them back to the tents.

Detached as if she were watching a movie, she saw an enraged Serene drag her screaming daughter by her hair across the leafy yard and up into the single-wide.

Off in the distance, a man yelled, alarmed, angry. There was the sound of thudding feet. A straggle of teenagers stumbled past Gracie on their way up back to Serrano Lodge.

Somewhere up the hill beyond the washrooms, an engine roared to life.

Lights flashed through the trees.

She watched a silver Dodge Ram careen around the corner at the intersection, catching her in the full glare of its headlights.

In a giant plume of dust, the pickup slid to a stop next to her.

The driver's door opened and Eddie launched from the truck.

EDDIE furious. Afraid. Dangerous.

Gracie reached out for her crutch, tried to stand, tried to run.

But in two steps, Eddie had reached her. He picked up the crutch and flung it, spinning, out into the lake. Then he fell onto his knees beside her, yelled, "You bitch!" and punched her with his fist, a short jab in the jaw.

Stars exploded inside Gracie's head. She sagged back onto the sand.

She heard a familiar tearing sound. Couldn't place it.

Something was wrapped around her wrists.

Duct tape.

Eddie was tying her up with duct tape. She would never break free. Panic coursed through her body. Half-conscious, her brain screamed, "Get away!"

She kicked out with her one good foot and made contact with something soft. Eddie grunted. Grabbing her wrists, he lay across her legs, pinning her to the ground. Pain shot throughout her body.

Gracie fish-flopped her body, almost managing to buck Eddie off. "Goddamm it!" he yelled, and hit her again with his fist, a stunning blow to the side of her face.

Gracie's head whirled.

"You goddam bitch," he snarled into her ear, his breath stinking of beer. "You couldn't keep your fucking nose out of my business, could you?"

Gracie heard the tearing sound again and she felt him first bind her arms to her body, then her knees together.

Tape was slapped over her mouth.

She couldn't breathe. She snorted like a horse, trying to clear the dust clogging her nostrils.

Then Eddie grabbed her shirt at the shoulders and dragged her across the ground.

Grit and sticks and sand scraped away skin. Gracie tried to put her good foot under her so her boot dragged on the ground, not bare skin.

Sirens wailed in the distance.

"Goddammit," Eddie yelled again. He stumbled along the lake shore, dragging Gracie along with him.

Where's he taking me?

Heavy boots clumped on wood. Splinters pierced Gracie's legs.

The dock!

He was going to throw Gracie into the lake.

But instead of heaving her into the water, leaving her to flounder and slowly drown, Eddie knelt down on the dock and, with his hands under her armpits, shoved her body off the dock into the cold water.

Gracie barely had time to suck in a breath through her

nose before he grabbed handfuls of hair, pushed her head beneath the surface, and held it there.

Gracie wriggled and flailed but couldn't break free.

Her lungs were bursting.

She fought the impulse to take in a breath.

He was drowning her.

She was going to die.

The dock wobbled.

"What the . . . ?" Gracie heard Eddie's muffled voice above the surface of the water.

Then he let her go.

Gracie burst up out of the water and breathed in a lungful of air through her nose. And a single drop of water. She coughed behind the tape covering her mouth.

She dropped beneath the surface again. Kicked her way back to the top. Couldn't draw in enough air to expel the water. She coughed again, choking.

Arching her body, she thrust her hands upward, hit the dock with her knuckles, clutched the edge with her fingers. Slipped off. Reached up again. Grabbed. Held on.

Then, somewhere over Gracie's head, an explosion blasted the night wide open, an orange fireball in the darkness.

Above her on the dock, Eddie jerked violently, grunted, tipped sideways into the water, and fell right on top of Gracie.

She lost her grip on the dock. Eddie's body pushed her down again, his strangling limbs trapping her beneath the surface of the water.

Her body slackened. She drifted, sinking. *Like a mermaid*, she thought. *A walrus*. She almost giggled. *I'm drowning*, floated through her head. *This is what Minnie felt like.*

Minnie!

Gracie writhed in the water, fought free of Eddie, and shot back up to the surface. Her nose slammed into something hard. She tasted blood.

Then hands grabbed her shirt. She was hauled upward, held against the dock, head barely above the surface. As if from a distance, Serene's voice said, "I have you, Gracie. I won't let you go."

Gracie gripped the edge of the dock with her fingertips and held on. She drifted, weightless in the water.

Serene had her.

She wasn't going to die.

She heard a splash beside her. A gasping for breath. Coughing. A groan.

Eddie.

Gracie's eyes fluttered open.

Serene renewed her grip on Gracie, shifted her weight, and stretched out a bare leg, pale in the darkness. She placed her foot against Eddie's head and pushed down.

Eddie's arms flailed. Hands grabbed for the dock. "I'm hurt," he choked, the words garbled. "Drowning."

Serene said nothing but kept her foot where it was.

Gracie heard car doors slam. Men's voices rumbled.

"Help!" Serene screamed, withdrawing her foot from Eddie's head and tightening her grip on Gracie's shirt. "Help us!"

Flashlight beams crisscrossed the rippling water.

"There!" someone yelled.

Feet pounded the dock, shaking it.

"In the water," another voice said. "Get him."

"Here!" Serene screamed. "I need help here."

More feet running on the dock, rocking it.

Serene lost her hold.

Gracie sank below the surface.

Then hands grabbed her hair, her shirt, the waistband of her shorts, and she was hauled of the water and up onto the dock.

"Gracie!" Ralph's gravelly voice. "Holy mother of God."

The duct tape was ripped away from Gracie's mouth. She gulped in a huge, sweet lungful of air.

A knife blade sliced through the tape on her arms, her wrists, her knees.

Something scratchy was wrapped around her shoulders, and she was lifted up and carried up the dock.

GRACIE lifted the fifty-pound bowling ball that was her head from the back of the couch in Ralph's living room. She shifted to a more comfortable position, trying not to disturb Minnie who lay next to her on a towel, head and a paw resting on her thigh, a large white square of gauze taped to her side.

The midafternoon sun streamed through white ruffled curtains, warming the back of Gracie's head and neck and showing a light film of dust on the wooden coffee table on which her leg, with its new pristine white cast, was propped up on a pillow.

Across from her, in a straight-backed chair pulled from the kitchen, a detective from the California Bureau of Investigation, whose business card was safely tucked in the back pocket of her shorts and whose name had flown out of her head as soon as she heard it, sat perfectly still, chin on knuckles, elbows on knees, staring at his notes arranged in neat piles on the coffee table on which also sat a small voice-activated tape recorder.

The detective's dark brown hair had been brushed straight back from a square, heavily lined forehead. Tired basset-hound eyes, crooked nose, thin, dry lips. He wore a cream-colored oxford shirt, slightly rumpled as if it had been pulled on right out of the dryer, a navy-and-red-striped tie, navy blue pants. A gray wool sport coat was draped over the back of his chair.

Out of Gracie's line of sight unless she turned her head in his direction, Ralph sat looking uncomfortable and incongruous in the only other seat in the room—a wooden rocking chair with blue ruffled cushions.

In the momentary pause in the questioning, Gracie looked down at her hands, spreading her fingers wide, wincing as the scabs on every knuckle stretched and cracked. Red, raw bands outlined with the remnants of duct tape glue encircled her wrists and knees. The area around her mouth still stung, and one horrifying glance into the mirror that morning had displayed a neat bright-red oblong bruise. White gauze bandages covered one knee where gravel had abraded off a silver-dollar-sized patch of skin and the back of her upper arm where a small stick had gouged a two-inch-long furrow. Dark red scratches crosshatched her arms and legs. Every inch of her body hurt, especially her ankle. She felt shivery, nauseated and weary to the marrow.

Gracie laid her head back on the couch and looked up. But instead of seeing the tongue-and-groove pine ceiling, snapshot memories swirled inside her head, a slideshow of the aftermath of being pulled from the lake the night before.

The scratchy wool blanket thrown around her shoulders. Ralph's strong arms lifting her, carrying her up the dock. Looking back over his shoulder, seeing deputies dragging

Eddie's limp form from the water. Sheriff's Department units and ambulances parked haphazardly along the shoreline of the lake. Emergency lights a dizzying, shifting kaleidoscope of red, blue, white, and yellow.

With a feeling of detachment, Gracie had floated down onto the cool, crisp white sheets of the ambulance gurney and was covered up to her chin. With her eyes closed, she mumbled answers to questions thrown at her, growling that on any given day she didn't know what day of the week it was, how the hell was she going to know what day it was now, after which the questions stopped.

She heard rather than felt a blood pressure cuff tighten around her upper arm, the gurney belts being buckled, then Ralph's voice asking her from a long way away about the text she had sent him.

Gracie resurfaced from the fog enough to croak in a voice unrecognizable as her own, "Drugs. Kids . . . with drugs. Heroin. Girl. In the tents. Serene knows where."

Then the gurney was jostled into the back of the ambulance. The doors closed.

She remembered nothing more until the ambulance was backing into the ER bay of the hospital.

Drifting back to the present, Gracie lifted her head from the couch. She looked around the living room, country kitsch in keeping with the rest of the house, filled to the point of clutter with needlepointed quilts and pillows and bric-a-brac, an entire wall of shelves devoted to nothing but elaborately decorated teacups and saucers.

She looked over at Ralph and caught his eye. He winked at her. She smiled back, wincing at the sudden pain in her jaw.

She looked at the detective, unmoving, still staring at his notes. *Travis!* popped into her head. *That's his name. Detective Something Travis.*

So far, the CBI detective had been exceedingly polite, deliberate, and thorough, asking questions without accusation, emotion or judgment, revealing nothing to her about what had transpired after she had been transported from the camp.

She had answered every question as honestly and completely as she was able, struggling at times to remember exactly what had happened.

She had described seeing Eddie Wilson at the platform tents and taking pictures of him on her cell phone which, she suddenly remembered, had been in her shorts pocket when she went into the lake and was probably ruined. Hopefully, she told him, the photos had been sent automatically to her e-mail so she could still retrieve them.

She described finding a girl sitting on the floor of one of the tents, most likely under the influence of drugs, the syringe still in her hand. When she had asked in a quivering voice whether the girl had survived, whether she was still alive, Travis had looked at her, assessing, weighing, then nodded, saying, "Yes. She's alive."

Gracie related in detail down to the buzzing fly the scene in the women's washroom, her conversation with Jasmine Bishop, the drugs and paraphernalia and enormous wad of cash, her admission of dealing drugs to students and campers with Eddie as her supplier. She described how Jasmine had admitted to hitting Jett McKenna in the head with a hammer, her description of how Jett had just fallen down and wouldn't get up again. And how Eddie Wilson had helped the girl load the body into the Jett's own station wagon and sent it over the side on the Arctic Circle.

"I have a pill," Gracie said. "Oxycodone, I think. Jett found it and left it for me. Before she was killed. Before she was murdered."

"Do you have this pill?"

"I put it in the key pocket of my shorts. But I was in the lake. I don't know what happened to them, my shorts."

"They cut them off you in the ER," Ralph said.

"They did? Crap! I loved those shorts." She turned to Travis and repeated, "They cut them off me in the ER. Sorry." She thought for a moment, then said, "Jett left a journal. Of everything happening at camp. It goes back to last year. Earlier."

A long silence. "You have this journal?"

Gracie frowned, trying to think back through the mishmash that was currently her brain. "It's on a flash drive. In my day pack. In my truck. Still parked at camp, I think." Her eyes flew to Ralph's. "Your Scout. It's at . . . I . . ."

Ralph's eyes were kind, warm. "I know."

When Detective Travis asked Gracie if she had any knowledge that might lead her to believe Serene Bishop was aware of her daughter's activities, she answered without hesitating. "No. No way did Serene know what Jasmine was doing." She shook her head to underline her statement. "There's no doubt in my mind. She had no idea." It was on the tip of her tongue to add that Serene would have killed Eddie if she had known what he was doing with her daughter but decided that probably wouldn't do Serene any good and kept her mouth shut.

"When you—" Travis began.

"Now Jay," Gracie blurted, "Jay Wilson, Eddie's slime-bucket brother. He knew what was going on. Well, I'm pretty sure. He manages the camp. You should talk with him. And while you're at it, ask him about the cash he's been siphoning off from the camp and putting into his own damn pocket. Hypocritical . . . slimy . . . wallowing . . ." She stopped and frowned, unable to remember exactly where she was headed with that particular rant.

Again, Travis said nothing, revealed nothing, only scribbled a note on his lined pad of paper.

"I called 911 from Serene's," Gracie said. "Then I sat down and waited. I must have been really tired because . . ." She shook her head. "I forgot all about Eddie. He threw my crutch out into the lake. Sonofabitch. And he hit me. Couple of times, I think." Her voice cracked.

Ralph rose from the rocker and sat down on the couch next to her, taking her hand between his own.

Gracie stared down at his leathery, suntanned hands, and said, "He was really mad. He dragged me down to the dock." Unconsciously, she rubbed the splinters still embedded in her skin on her knee. "He lifted me into the water." She concentrated on the healing cut on Ralph's thumb. "He put his hands here, beneath my armpits. I remember because it pinched and really hurt. He pushed my head beneath the water. Held it there."

Ralph's hand tightened.

She couldn't stop her lower jaw from trembling. "I thought I was going to die."

There was a rustle and a faint click. "Ms. Kinkaid," Travis said, his voice unexpectedly gentle. "Would you like to take a break?"

"No." She let go of Ralph's hand and wiped her eyes dry with her fingers. "Thanks. I'm okay." She blew out a long breath, took a shaky sip of a glass of water on the table, and cleared her throat. "Let's keep going."

Travis leaned over and turned the little tape recorder back on.

Gracie described how she hadn't actually seen Eddie being shot. She was busy trying not to swallow the entire lake. After Eddie went into the water, Serene was there, pulling her back up to the surface and hanging on to her until law enforcement arrived. She mentioned nothing about Serene placing her foot on Eddie's head, about her pushing him back into the water and holding him there.

"Mr., uh, Detective Travis?"

"Yes?"

"Can you . . . will you tell me about Eddie . . . about Mr. Wilson? How badly was he hurt?" *Pretty damn badly, I hope I hope I hope.*

The detective straightened his tie in an unconscious gesture. He studied Gracie's face, calculating again, measuring. Then he said, "The bullet wound was through-and-through, a straight hit to the groin—"

Gracie barked a laugh.

"Taking out a testicle," Travis continued, "the end of his penis, and a chunk of inner thigh."

Next to her, Ralph shifted on the couch.

Woo-hoo! Nice shot, Serene! With no small amount of difficulty, Gracie kept herself from smiling. It would be a long time, if ever, until Eddie had sex again, much less with someone young enough to be his daughter. If, that was, he ever got out of prison. "Has he been charged with anything yet?"

"No charges have been filed."

"Not yet."

Travis gave a single nod. "Not yet."

Gracie looked down at Minnie lying next to her and put a gentle hand on her head. The tail thumped the couch. She slid her fingers through the long silky fur, drawing courage from the dog, from her innocence, from her unfailing love. "I think . . ." She stopped, clearing her throat of the sudden frog crouching there. "Jasmine said Gina Ramirez, the girl who went missing about two weeks ago, was brought up there . . . to camp. She overdosed. Jasmine said Gina dying was good for her business."

The living room was silent.

"I don't know what they did with her body."

The little German clock cuckooed the half hour from the kitchen.

"There's a kind of field," Gracie continued. "Of bare dirt. Up the hill, between Mojave Lodge and the lower washrooms." She looked up and met Travis's unreadable eyes. "Someone might want to dig through it. See what they can find." She took in a deep breath and blew it out slowly. "See if Eddie buried anything else there besides the camp's trash."

CHAPTER
46

GRACIE opened her eyes and squinted against the glare of the midmorning sun.

Beside her, Ralph concentrated on maneuvering the heavy F-150 pick-up down the winding road from his cabin, one hand gripping the steering wheel, opposite elbow resting on the open window ledge.

Minnie lay on the seat between them, her head on Gracie's lap.

The pickup slowed at the stop sign at the bottom of the hill, then turned left onto the two-lane highway running along the northern shore of Timber Lake.

Gracie looked over at Ralph. The blue-gray eyes crinkled back at her, then refocused on the road ahead.

She leaned her head back against the headrest and looked out the window.

While she had learned the gratifying information about Eddie and his physical condition, Detective Travis understandably hadn't been forthcoming with much other information because the investigation was still ongoing.

What was going to happen with Jasmine? And Serene? And the kids at camp? And, as a result, Madison and Abe? And Meaghan? And the baby? And Jay?

As if reading her thoughts, Ralph reached over and laid his warm, dry hand on top of hers. "I made a few calls," he said. "Learned some things.

In his careful, deliberate way, Ralph explained that fingerprints on the rifle retrieved from the bottom of the lake were smudged and inconclusive. Tests for gunshot residue on Serene had also been inconclusive.

Every ninth-grader, every adult chaperone, and every program staff member had been questioned by law enforcement that night. Some of the students had been transported to the hospital for evaluation.

In what was an enormous black eye for the church that owned the camp, the rest of the school retreat had been canceled with some parents driving all the way up to camp from L.A. to pick up their children, some, naturally, making noises about lawsuits.

"I couldn't find anything out about the girl involved," Ralph began.

"Jasmine?"

"Because, even though she's almost eighteen, she's still a minor."

"I'll call Serene," Gracie said. "See how she's doing. Find out what happened. Do you think they'll put her into some kind of juvenile detention center?"

"Probably. Dealing drugs—heroin—to kids is damned serious. They may decide to try her as an adult."

"Poor Serene. Jasmine is her whole life." Gracie closed her eyes and shook her head slowly. "God, what a mess."

"They found Jay Wilson at his home in Cathedral City," Ralph said. "Lying on the floor of his garage."

Gracie's eyes snapped open again. She looked over at Ralph. "Oh, shit! Dead?"

Ralph shook his head. "He tried hard to be dead. He hanged himself with a length of garden hose from the automatic garage door system."

"Tried?"

"He weighed too much. Pulled the entire system out of the ceiling. Broke his elbow when he landed."

Giggles bubbled up like champagne inside Gracie's chest. "Oh, *God*. That's *rich*! He tried to take the cowardly way out and blew even that." Knowing she was sounding a wee bit hysterical, she stifled her laughter. "What a spineless . . . Trying to leave his wife to deal with everything alone is low, even for him. What about Meaghan, their daughter? She had a baby. A little girl."

Ralph sighed. "I'm afraid she didn't make it."

Gracie blinked at him. "The baby died?"

Ralph's eyes were somber, gentle. "The baby's fine. The mother, the girl, Meaghan. She didn't make it. The death announcement was in the paper."

The news hit Gracie in a sudden painful intake of breath and a rush of tears. "That poor sweet girl," she whispered. "I'd *never* wish the death of a child on anyone, not even Jay and Elaine. Their suffering must be . . . I can't think of a word big enough."

Ralph rolled the truck off the highway and stopped in a wide gravel turnout overlooking the lake. "Gracie girl," he said in a low voice. "There's more."

"What more can there possibly be?"

"You'll hear about it soon enough. I'd rather you find it

out from me." He blew out a breath. "They found the remains of Gina Ramirez."

Gracie put her hands over her face, not wanting to hear, needing to hear. "Where was she?"

"Buried."

"At camp?"

"Up at the camp. Under five feet of trash."

Gracie choked back a sob. While they were searching, all that time, little Gina Ramirez had already been dead. Buried in the trash at camp.

Tears seeped out through Gracie's fingers and slid down the backs of her hands. "At least the family will have closure now. Do they know yet how she died?"

Ralph shook his head. "Autopsy results aren't in yet."

ON ARCTURUS, RALPH'S truck accelerated up the long, straightaway leading up to Gracie's cabin. It felt like centuries since she had last been there.

"Wait," Gracie said, putting out a hand. "Stop the truck."

The truck slammed to a halt.

Gracie stared out the window at the Lucas house.

Rolls of dirty and stained carpet, old toys, miniblinds, plumbing fixtures, and miscellaneous junk were piled high inside a large, metal Dumpster sitting in the middle of the yard. Fly-specked and dust-encrusted windows looked out from an empty house.

"They're gone?" she said. "They are. They're gone!"

"Big bust here two, three days ago," Ralph said. "Acting on an anonymous tip. After all these years, they finally got 'em. Found a huge drug stash beneath a mound of trash in the backyard. Oxycodone, fentanyl, crack, heroin. Everything under the sun along with the kitchen sink. Literally. There's some speculation that it was where your man, Eddie, was getting his supply."

"Wow," was all Gracie could say. "Wow."

GRACIE LAY SPRAWLED full length on the lumpy living room couch, a pillow beneath her head, another propping up her injured ankle. Minnie lay on the couch at her feet, her head also on the pillow.

From the kitchen came the sounds of Ralph puttering around. The whistle of the teakettle, the refrigerator door opening and closing, the crinkling of a bread bag, plates being lifted down from the cupboard.

Nice sounds. Comforting sounds. Sounds of a home. It felt right to have Ralph there. It felt peaceful and good.

Maybe I should just say yes, Gracie thought. *How could I ask for a better man?*

"There are messages on the machine," Ralph called from the other room.

"Play 'em, will you? I can hear them from in here."

"Grace Louise," her mother's voice pleaded from the answering machine. "Why haven't you called me? I need you. I need to talk to you. Please, please call me. MoMo is very ill. I need you here. I need you, Gracie."

Shit. Morris. Her stepfather. Her abuser. The man whose toupee she shot off with a shotgun after he had broken her mother's arm. "What the hell do I care if he's—"

"Gracie! What the effing hell?" Rob's voice reverberated throughout the cabin and sent a shock wave through Gracie's body. "You leave my bed without a word and I don't hear from you for effing days?" In a calmer voice, he said, "Gracie, love. Ring me, will you, please? So I at least know you're okay?"

Silence from the kitchen.

Gracie closed her eyes and waited.

A moment later, a ham-and-cheese sandwich on a paper plate and a steaming cup of hot chocolate appeared on the sea chest two feet from her head. Gracie looked up into a face set in stone. "Ralphie?"

He walked out of the room, returning seconds later to prop Gracie's crutch up against the couch. "Ralphie?"

"I need to go." His voice was neutral, wooden. "I need to check on my men."

Gracie struggled to sit up. "Wait. Don't go."

But he was already gone.

GRACIE sat on the living room couch in her own little cabin, injured foot propped up on the sea chest, fingers intertwined with the soft fur of Minnie's back.

Woman and dog, healing together.

The shade of the west-facing picture window had been drawn low against the hot afternoon sun, leaving the room dark, cool, and quiet with the sun peeking through at the edges.

As shining strips of sunlight crept across the wooden plank floor, Gracie sifted through the rubble that was her life.

She had called Ralph, hoping to fumble through some sort of an explanation for what had happened with Rob, which she herself didn't really understand, to try and sort through everything together with her best friend.

But he hadn't answered the phone or returned her calls. Again.

She had called Rob's cell, to apologize, to talk, to explain, to find out where she stood with him, where he stood with her, to sort through everything together. Her call went straight to voice mail. His service imparted no information whatsoever about its high-profile client, suggesting she was welcome to leave a message. After a moment's hesitation, she had hung up without leaving her name.

Let things calm down a little, Gracie thought. *Let a little time pass.* "I just want everything to be quiet for a while," she said aloud. "And still. And drama-free."

At the sound of her voice, Minnie lifted her head and looked at her with bright brown eyes.

Gracie stroked the silky head. "It's just you and me, little girl."

The tail thumped the couch.

"I love you, Minnie," she said, smiling down at the dog. "Drat it."

With her head resting on the back of the couch, she thought about the insular, patriarchal mini-empire Jay Wilson had established at the camp, the culture of no accountability, participating in and overlooking abuses and crimes. She thought about his promotion of the subjugation and control of women, including his own daughter. About his preying on the fears and vulnerabilities of others and the exploitation of the Almighty for his own personal gain. The spreading of his belief in an unforgiving, vindictive God, his narcissistic narrow-mindedness and intolerance, and how it had all led to the spiritual torment and death of Jett McKenna and the death of his own daughter.

She thought about Gina Ramirez, about her grieving family in unimaginable pain.

She thought about Jett and the young woman who had killed her and why.

She thought about mothers and daughters. About Jett's mother, whereabouts unknown, who still might not even know that her daughter was dead. About Gina Ramirez's mother, living with the hell of a child dead from an accidental overdose of drugs. About Serene, whose daughter was being charged with multiple crimes as an adult. About Elaine, whose only daughter was dead. About Meaghan's new baby girl and the fact that she would never know her mother.

She thought about her own family, from whom she had distanced herself, seeing them only occasionally, only reluctantly over the past ten years.

And about her own mother, Evelyn.

About hurt and failure and human frailty and weakness.

"I need you, Gracie." Her mother's words reverberated inside her head.

For the first time ever, Evelyn had called her Gracie. Since her childhood, her mother had resolutely refused to call her by the name she preferred, insisting instead on calling her Grace Louise, a name she hated.

"I need you, Gracie."

Gracie couldn't have cared less that Morris was ill.

But, with thoughts of irreversible events and catastrophic outcomes fresh in her mind, she picked up the portable phone from the sea chest and dialed her mother's number, listened to the ringing on the other end, a voice answering.

"Hi, Mom," she said. "It's Grace Louise."

Born and raised in Michigan, M. L. Rowland lived and worked in several states, including Hawaii and New York, before settling in the mountains of Southern California. There she served for almost a dozen years as a very active member of a very active Search and Rescue (SAR) team, participating in hundreds of SAR missions and trainings in all four seasons in mountain, desert and urban environments.

Rowland is an avid political activist, naturalist, and environmentalist. She's traveled extensively, including to all fifty states, Europe, Africa, the Caribbean, and the South Pacific. As often as possible, she hikes and explores the slot canyons of Utah.

Rowland lives with her husband, Mark, and their chocolate lab, Molly, at the foot of the Sangre de Cristo Mountains in south-central Colorado.